The Day After Never

Purgatory Road

Russell Blake

ISBN: 978-1533544117

Published by

Reprobatio Limited

Chapter 1

Marijuana smoke clouded the gloomy interior of the improvised saloon, and the pungent aroma blended with the acrid tang of stale perspiration, unwashed bodies, and rotgut home-brewed sour mash. Several women in ratty shifts leaned against the wall near a long plank propped atop four wooden barrels that served as the bar. Their faces were frozen in professional invitation, their eyes dead. Beside them, three heavily built gunmen with Browning shotguns lounged together, occasionally casting an eye over the forty or so customers, wary of trouble with the rough crowd. Filthy sawdust covered the floor of the tin-roofed structure in Mentone, one of a shabby scattering of buildings at a forgotten crossroads used as the home base for the group of miscreants known as the Raiders.

An emaciated dog, inured to the shouts and baying laughter from the rowdy throng, nosed around in a far corner where someone had recently vomited. Six Mohawked highwaymen sat at a circular wooden table in the rear of the room, their sweat-stained black leather vests and tattoos as menacing as a snake's rattle, bottles of cheap rum and whiskey at their elbows. A deck of frayed cards lay facedown in front of a graying man with a long, cadaverous face and spindly fingers that lent him the appearance of a praying mantis.

The dealer pushed a small pile of chips into the center pot with a smile as inviting as a mass grave. "Well, boys, put up or shut up. Day

1

of reckoning's at hand," he hissed, his voice barely audible over the bar's clamor.

Two of the players shook their heads and tossed in their cards, unwilling to push their luck any further. The remaining three met the dealer's raise and, once the betting was done, waited expectantly as he offered another grin, revealing pale gums marred with stubs of decaying teeth between earthworm lips.

"Full house, fellas. Just not your lucky night, I guess." He cackled, and the rest flung their hands into the pot with resigned groans.

"Seems like most hands you walk away with the chips," one of the larger Raiders growled. The man beside him elbowed his ribs as a caution and slid an amber bottle toward him.

The pair had been in the bar for the better part of five hours and were nearly through with their second bottle of rum. They, like the rest of the patrons, had checked their weapons at the door. The rules of the house were few, but those there were, were non-negotiable: no guns or knives inside, no fights allowed, and no credit extended. The security guards enforced compliance, and any violation meant expulsion with no appeal.

The large Raider took a pull on the bottle and winced at the burn of the cheap, harsh liquor. His meaty face was sunburned almost to the blistering point, his skin radiating heat, brow furrowed over reptilian eyes, greasy ebony Mohawk a spiked mane. The shaved sides of his head featured a collage of jailhouse art and crude gothic script, a grinning skull with a pirate's hat cocked at a rakish angle adorning the left temple, Nazi Schutzstaffel lightning bolts emblazoning the right. Pink scars, souvenirs of past fights, spanned his scalp, and a pair of green inked tears trailed below his left eye – mute testament to a lifetime of incarceration. The teardrops were a common emblem for many of the other Raiders, whose murderous and predatory habits had been hardened by a prison ethic that knew only hunter and prey.

He slammed the bottle down and considered his remaining chips, and then leaned into his smaller companion, whose sallow complexion and gaunt frame was the polar opposite: the little man's skin was as taut as parchment over sharp cheekbones and ropy muscles that undulated like snakes along bare tobacco-colored arms.

"Bastard's a cheat, Holt. I been watching him."

Holt glanced at the dealer with weasel eyes and shook his head. "Nah, Kurt, he ain't. Maybe we just been at the table too long, you know?"

"Gonna win it back."

The little Raider took a swig of the firewater and exhaled loudly. "Easy come, right?"

The dealer ignored the exchange, seemingly oblivious to anything but counting his chips. One of the players scraped his chair back and stood unsteadily. "I'm hitting it," he declared with a yawn.

"See you next time," the dealer said.

The playing resumed, and within half an hour Holt and Kurt were out of chips. Holt shrugged and rose. "Looks like that's it for tonight, man," he said.

Kurt's hand gripped his forearm with the force of a vise. "No. We're not done."

The dealer eyed them. "Don't see any chips."

"Shut your piehole. We'll get more," Kurt snarled.

The dealer's stare shifted to the smaller man, then back to Kurt. "Ain't going nowhere."

"Not with our loot, you aren't," the big Raider countered, and then lumbered over to a steel door.

Two of the guards moved in fast and blocked his way. Kurt glared at them. "I wanna see the man."

"Kind of late, don't you think?" one of the gunmen asked, his tone neutral.

"Place open for business, or isn't it?"

The pair exchanged a glance and the taller one shrugged. He knocked on the door, and twenty seconds later it opened and a fleshy Raider with a body like a sumo wrestler eyed Kurt with an impassive expression. "What?"

"I want more chips."

"You know how it works. What you got?"

"Couple of AR-15s. Another AK. Dozen mags."

The proprietor, a trader known among the Raiders as "the mayor," did a quick calculation. "Sounds like a couple hundred chips. Where's it at?"

"Your man outside is watching the horses. It's in my saddlebags."

The mayor's eyes moved to one of the guards. "Go with him and bring me the gear." He curled his lip at Kurt. "Chips will be waiting if it's all there."

The exchange took five minutes, and after inspecting the weapons and ammo, the mayor's door slammed shut with the finality of a gunshot. Kurt staggered back to the playing table with his trove of chips and sat heavily, piling them in front of him and then organizing them into stacks of twenty. When he was done, he pushed two into the center of the table and scowled.

"Maybe we should come back tomorrow," Holt suggested in a whisper.

Kurt waved him off. "No, Holt. We need to get our stuff back."

"All I'm saying is that after some sleep, maybe we'll do better."

The big Raider's nostrils flared. "You hard of hearing? I told you, we do this now."

The dealer appeared to just realize Kurt had returned. "Ready for another spanking?" he taunted.

"You want to keep what teeth you got left in that fool head of yours, best keep your trap shut and play cards."

The remaining two Raiders stayed in for a few hands and then took their chips and left.

An hour later the dealer yawned and considered Kurt and Holt, their chips now his. "Well, boys, been a pleasure, but it's getting late and I need my beauty rest," he said, scooping the tokens into a canvas sack and rising. "Maybe you'll have better luck next time."

Kurt threw back the remainder of his rum and tossed the bottle onto the scarred table. "You robbed us, plain and simple," he slurred, his voice dangerously soft.

"Nah, I done it fair and square. You shoulda quit while you was ahead. Nobody held no gun to your head," the dealer countered. His tone remained agreeable, but the warmth never reached his eyes. He turned to one of the guards behind him. "Time to settle up with the mayor."

"I won't forget this," Kurt threatened.

The guard regarded the two Raiders, his expression darkening, and his unblinking stare locked on Holt. "Best get your buddy out of here. Nobody wants no trouble – but you bring it, we'll finish it," he warned, fingering the safety of his Browning.

The dealer reached into his bag and tossed a few chips onto the table. "Come on, boys. No hard feelings. Have yourselves a bottle on me, and we'll see how things go some other night."

Kurt swiped the chips away and spun clumsily from the table. "Don't want no charity."

The dealer's eyebrows rose, and Holt stooped to retrieve the chips from the floor with a resigned look. When the big Raider was out of earshot, he leaned toward the dealer. "Sorry. Been a rough patch."

"We all been there," the dealer agreed.

Holt converted the chips into an unlabeled bottle of whiskey with a stained cork half stuffed into the top – one of the local concoctions that could kill you just as often as not. He wended his way to the exit and stepped out into the gloom. The accompanying wind carried with it the scent of desiccated rot from the latrine trench by the Raiders' camp area. Most only spent a few days at a time in the sad little hamlet to resupply and reshoe their horses, tend to any wounds, trade, gamble, and whore, and prepare for another few weeks on the road, where they would waylay any travelers they came across.

"Hey. Look what I found," Holt called to Kurt, who was stalking away, his movements uncertain in the spectral moonlight. "Come on, man. Wait up."

The pair found a welcoming spot beside an abandoned building – the remnants of a fifties-era gas station that had gone out of business decades before the collapse – and passed the bottle back and forth. An amorous owl hooted somewhere in the darkness, covered by the bellows of drunken laughter drifting from the bar. As the level of the bottle sank, more Raiders emptied out of the watering hole to stagger back to their tents with paid company in tow, leaving the two men to watch the night wind down.

"Damn mayor's in on it," Kurt grumbled. "It's a hustle. Whole thing. A con. Dealer, mayor, all of it."

Holt shook his head. "I don't think so…"

"They know we got to bring our stuff here – nobody else will trade with us. So they got us by the balls, and then they screw us every chance they get. Pay what they want for our booty, then cheat us out of our chips – and for what?" Kurt spit into the mud by his side and then burped loudly. "We take all the risk, and they walk off with the reward. I'm sick of it. Bet they're in there laughing it up at how stupid we are for doing it again and again."

Holt rubbed his face with a grimy hand. "Let's go sleep it off. I'm beat."

Kurt forced himself to his feet with a grunt and set off in the direction of the bar. Holt scrambled up and tailed him, leaving the empty bottle behind. When they got to where their horses were hitched beside a water trough, Kurt stood still for a moment as though in a trance, and then pulled his Kalashnikov AK-47 free from its saddle scabbard and pocketed two spare thirty-round magazines. Holt backed away and shook his head, his eyes wide. "No, dude, no…"

The big Raider's backhand slap caught Holt by surprise, and the little man's head jerked back from the force of it. His eyes welled as a trickle of blood ran from the corner of his mouth, and his fingers flew to his jaw. "Jesus–"

"Best keep your mouth shut," Kurt snarled.

Holt shook off the blow. "This ain't the way."

"You got a better idea? I'm not letting 'em steal a month's work."

Holt nervously eyed the building façade. "You're gonna get yourself killed."

"Not if I take them first."

"You got no chance."

"You gonna help me, or I do this alone?"

Holt shook his head. "No way. You're talking crazy. Just put down the gun, and let's clear out of here."

The big Raider moved surprisingly fast for his size and level of inebriation. The wood stock of the Kalashnikov caught Holt in the side of the head, dropping the smaller man like a sack of rocks. Kurt stood over him, breathing hard, but then blinked away the blurring vision from his bloodshot eyes and turned toward the saloon entrance.

Kurt pushed through the door and spotted the dealer sitting with the mayor at the card table. A half-full bottle sat between them, from behind which a curl of smoke from a pipe in a black plastic ashtray spiraled toward the ceiling. Both men looked up in surprise, and then Kurt's AK barked death at the lone guard holding up the back wall, who jerked like a marionette as slugs chewed through the ceramic plate of his plate carrier, his body armor insufficient to stop an entire full auto 7.62mm burst at point-blank range. The gunman slumped to the floor, and the dealer slowly stood, hands raised in front of him, shaking his head.

"Ain't got no gun, boy. Now just take it easy–" he began.

"Ain't your boy, bitch," Kurt growled, and squeezed the trigger as he moved toward the table. The assault rifle bucked in his hands, and the dealer's chest erupted with ruby blossoms as he pitched backward and slammed into the table, knocking the bottle over. He collapsed onto the wood slab and lay gasping for breath, staring at the roof in disbelief as his life pulsed from him in arterial spurts.

"I'm here for my gear," Kurt snarled at the mayor.

"I expect you are," the mayor said agreeably, and then the compact Glock 29 10mm pistol in his robe pocket blasted through the filthy fabric. The first round caught Kurt in the shoulder, the second slammed into his abdomen, and the third drilled through his skull above his left eye and painted the area behind him crimson.

The room echoed from the shots, and when the reverberations had died down, the mayor stepped forward with the gun freed from his robe, weapon trained on the dead gunman. The two remaining guards burst through a back door that led to the sleeping quarters, guns at the ready, and froze when they saw the carnage. The dealer groaned and stiffened on the table, and the mayor shook his head.

"Get them out of here. Throw the big one in the field out back as a warning, and bury Jed," he ordered, indicating the dealer with a nod. "And mop up the blood. I don't want a bunch of flies in here."

The men nodded wordlessly; bloodshed was nothing new. The mayor watched as they dragged the rogue Raider unceremoniously from the room by his feet, leaving a trail of coagulating sawdust. He stopped to collect the dead man's AK-47 as the Raider's body bounced over the threshold and into the street.

There was no point in wasting a decent weapon.

"If he's got a horse, it's mine now," the mayor called. "And if you see that little rat buddy of his hanging around, gun him down."

The taller of the bodyguards paused at the door. "Why?"

The mayor made his way to the bar and opened a bottle of rye. He took a swig, set it on the bar, and sighed before fixing the guard with a hard stare.

"Principle."

Chapter 2

Ruby and Lucas sat outside in their camp chairs, facing Sierra, who was watching Eve play near the horses. The ride back had consumed most of the morning, and the sun was high overhead as they discussed their next move. After considerable back and forth, Lucas had agreed to go in search of the USB and accompanying note, but as he thought through the logistics, the task seemed daunting. And there was still the matter of the kiss – the start of something or, at the very least, unfinished business he and Sierra would need to resolve.

"Is there anything you can tell me about the vest that would help identify it?" Lucas asked. "Distinguishing markings?"

"It was that tan camouflage color everyone seems to be wearing. I think…I think it had something on the front, like an emblem or something. I just don't remember what it was," Sierra said.

"You recall what color the emblem was?" Ruby asked.

"Black."

"How big?"

Sierra held up her fingers with a small space between thumb and index. "I don't know. Maybe an inch, inch and a half?"

Ruby leaned back in her chair and called to Eve. "Eve, can you come here for a second, please?"

The little girl ran through the tall grass, skipping occasionally, an expression of untroubled happiness on her face. When she arrived where the adults were seated, she grew serious. Ruby offered a smile and took her hand.

"We were talking about the man who was in charge of your trip from Lubbock, Eve. Your aunt says you have an amazing memory. Do you remember something on his vest? A design or picture?"

Eve nodded. "Yes. It was a bird."

Sierra snapped her fingers. "That's right. An eagle or a hawk. Stylized, like a military logo." She frowned. "I don't know why I was drawing a blank. I'm sorry."

"You've been through a lot, and you're still healing. Between the wounds, the infection, and the drugs, the mind can play tricks," Ruby said.

"And it wasn't a plate carrier?" Lucas asked.

Sierra frowned. "Not like yours, but it did have a front ceramic plate, so I guess it was. I'm sorry. I'm not really up on gear terminology."

Lucas had been asking for a more detailed description for some time, but it was obvious that Sierra's memory had been affected by her ordeal. He decided to quit while he was ahead, the emblem hopefully adequate to identify the vest. "Where was the hidden pocket?"

She tapped her sternum. "Inside, over the chest. It had Velcro that held it together so it looked like part of the inner seam."

Ruby smiled at Eve again. "You can go back and play if you want, Eve. Thank you, young lady."

"Welcome," Eve said, her voice small.

The child ran off. Sierra eyed Lucas. "So what are you going to do?" she asked.

Lucas watched Eve for a few moments and then stood. "I need to ride back to the gulch where Eve was hiding and see if there's anything I missed. Neither of the shooters I took out were wearing camo, so if the vest is there, it would be with the rest of the bodies."

"And if it's not?"

"Then I have to go to the canyon where Carl and his deputy ambushed the Raiders, and see how many they tagged, and whether any of them had the vest." Lucas paused. "If none of them were wearing it, the options get worse from there."

"What do you mean?" Sierra asked.

"The Raiders control a tiny town in Texas near the New Mexico border. Most traders avoid it because they know anything for sale wound up there from looting or robbery – or worse. But some don't care. I'll have to go and nose around, see if I can pick up the scent, assuming it was a Raider who grabbed the vest and not some opportunistic third party."

"What if it was?"

It was Lucas's turn to frown. "Then the technical term is we're screwed." He inclined his head toward Ruby. "But let's not jump to conclusions. I'm more worried about you three while I'm gone. If the cartel's still looking for you, they'll eventually show up at the bunker again, so you have to keep out of sight."

"We can do that," Ruby said.

"If something happens and you have to bug out, there's a place we can rendezvous that should be safe. About ten miles southwest of here. Blue Springs, over on the Black River."

Ruby nodded. "I know the spot. Been years, but gorgeous from what I remember."

"If you have to leave the cellar, wait for me there."

It took Lucas ten minutes to pack everything he owned in his saddlebags. Ruby hugged him when he was ready to go, as did Sierra, her body molding to his in a way he could get used to. Eve seemed unsure of how to bid him farewell, so he made it easier on her by kneeling down till he was at eye level and holding his arms out. She gave him a small, shy hug, and then he stood and reached into his saddlebag.

"Here. You're going to need some NV gear," he said, and handed Ruby the night vision monocle Duke had gifted him. "I've got my rifle scope. Operating the monocle's self-explanatory."

Ruby smiled. "I think I can figure it out."

"I'm sure you can."

Lucas turned to Sierra. "Promise me you won't do anything rash while I'm gone. The three of you need to stick together and cooperate if you're going to survive."

Sierra bristled at his tone, but her expression softened at the obvious concern in his words. She nodded in silent agreement and reached out to touch his hand. A small chill ran up Lucas's spine at a flash of the Eye of Providence tattoo on her arm. The swelling and redness of infection that had accompanied her chest wound had all but gone, from what he could see around the dressing. His gaze drifted to Eve and her matching tattoo, and he was filled with a cold foreboding that even the midday heat couldn't completely banish.

Tango, freshly fed and watered, followed the trail south toward the foothills where Lucas had discovered Sierra and Eve. Lucas knew he wouldn't be able to make it by nightfall and had already decided on where he would spend the evening, his knowledge of the area substantial from his repeated forays tracking feral mustangs.

As he rode, the big stallion's steady hoofbeats thudding with the regularity of a metronome, he thought about the obvious challenges facing him. While nothing was impossible, in reality he was going to have to cover a lot of ground in a hostile wasteland in the hopes of finding a needle in a haystack, all on behalf of a woman about whom he knew precious little and was conflicted about trusting – as well as how he felt about her. She was definitely attractive, with high cheekbones and a challenging stubbornness to her frank countenance that would have had him in hot water under other circumstances.

"Like you aren't in the soup now," he muttered.

Eve had also captivated him with her composure and the odd, almost adult maturity in her reactions that was as unusual as anything he'd seen. Then again, you could write what he knew about children on a grain of rice. Even so, he sensed there was something special about her, immunity to the virus notwithstanding.

High ribbons of clouds were streaking the cinnamon sky like colored smoke when he set up camp near a spit of sand that jutted into the bend of a creek. The lazy rush of shallow water over smooth stones burbled musically as he rigged his tripwires along the perimeter and tied a glittering chrome spoon to ten yards of monofilament fishing line. Before the sun had dropped behind the foothills, the hand line stiffened with a decent-sized trout, and Lucas finished his day with fresh fish roasted over a small fire while Tango refreshed himself from the brook.

When darkness fell, Lucas stamped out the remains of his fire and unfurled his bedroll onto the riparian slope, the glowing streak of a comet's flare-out providing celestial pyrotechnics as he lay down beneath the night sky. The few trees along the stream's course rustled in the breeze, and Lucas smiled to himself – it could have been worse, he reasoned. The reaction was barely formed when a wave of melancholy washed over him at the losses he'd suffered over the last week: his grandfather, Bear, his friends in Loving...

He shook off the morose thoughts. His philosophy of survival was to focus only on the present. The past was over and unchangeable, the future unknowable and not guaranteed to even arrive, which left him with the here and now.

And his pursuit of a pipe dream on behalf of an enigmatic beauty.

Lucas drifted to sleep with his hand on his M4, with visions of Sierra's eyes for company and the whisper of the stream's passage for his lullaby.

Several hours later he started awake, M4 clutched to his chest. Ten feet away, Tango stamped his front hooves again with a snort. The stallion had detected danger. Instantly awake, Lucas switched on the rifle's Exelis night vision scope and peered through it at a glowing green nightscape, taking his time to scan the surroundings, searching for movement or any hint of whatever had spooked the horse.

There.

Bushes rustling maybe sixty yards away, on the far side of the stream. Not the wind, which had died down at some point while he slept.

Lucas flipped the assault rifle's fire selector to three-round burst mode, and his index finger moved from the guard to the trigger. His pulse thudded in his ears and he willed himself calm, barely breathing, now fully awake, adrenaline flooding his system.

The bush stirred again, and a furry gray-brown form with glowing eyes stepped cautiously from behind it, its ears perked straight up as it sniffed the air. Lucas exhaled and switched the rifle's fire selector back to safe. The coyote drawn by the remnants of Lucas's feast was likely more fearful than dangerous.

"Relax, boy," he murmured to Tango, rising and walking to the stallion. He patted the horse's neck reassuringly, trying to calm him. "He's just hungry. My bad for not throwing the bones into the water."

Tango grew still, and Lucas took another look through the NV scope to confirm that there were no other nocturnal visitors. He watched as the coyote was joined by a second, smaller mate, and his heart ached for Bear. The poor creatures were trying to do the best they could, scavenging whatever they ran across, as was everyone these days.

Lucas lowered himself back onto the bedroll and passed the rest of the night in uneasy slumber, his dreams disturbed by the ghosts of the dead and an all-seeing eye from behind a wall of fire, disembodied and palpably evil, malevolence emanating from it like toxic steam as it glared triumphantly at a pile of corpses stacked like cordwood inside the Loving town hall.

Chapter 3

Houston, Texas

Magnus stalked from his headquarters to the massive parking lot that had once served tens of thousands of the faithful who'd worshipped in the church he'd commandeered. Framed on either side by gunmen and his inner circle of advisors, Magnus was scowling even more deeply than usual. His mahogany skin glistened in the torchlight as he neared a column of vehicles.

Four Humvees were parked near the entrance, flanked by heavily armed gunmen. Two troop carriers waited behind them, and a small tanker truck brought up the rear. Magnus inspected the trucks with satisfaction and grunted to Whitely, the head of his special projects group.

"The diesel's still usable?" Magnus demanded.

"Yes," Whitely said. "We've treated it with fuel stabilizer every year. We tested it recently, and it burns fine."

Magnus studied the tanker. "This is the last of it?"

"We have ten thousand gallons in an above-ground storage tank, and that's it. Most of it had degraded past the point of no return by the time we located any." Whitely hesitated. "You remember how it was. People were killing each other over a gallon of gas."

Magnus waved the comment away. "How long will it take them to reach Pecos? What is it, four hundred miles?"

"At least five hundred, but if the roads are clogged with debris and abandoned vehicles, they'll be lucky if they make a few hundred miles per day. So a couple days, assuming no complications."

Magnus nodded, accustomed to the long travel times – just part of the new world order where nothing worked.

"Still faster than horseback."

"Yes," Whitely agreed. They had discussed the options for supplying Garret with reinforcements and had concluded that it made sense to send some of their limited armor to Pecos to cut travel time by a fifth, as well as to provide a show of force. Operational vehicles were rare, most now junk due to scavengers and the elements. With no factories making parts or tires, every year there were fewer supplies to keep them running, assuming any fuel could be found.

The arrival of the trucks would underscore the Crew's supremacy to the cartel and quell any notions of rebellion the Locos might have when they heard the new conditions Magnus's envoy would bring.

Magnus looked over at a powerfully built man wearing a leather vest, whose head was shaved like his master's, the better to display the tattoos that covered it with occult symbols. The man approached and stopped in front of Magnus.

"Cano, are you ready?" Magnus asked.

"Yes. We have everything we need."

"Stay in contact via radio."

"Of course."

"You're clear on what to do once you've taken control of the town?"

Cano grinned, with wolf-like effect. "Crystal."

When Magnus hadn't heard anything more from Garret, he'd instructed Cano to kill him upon arrival. There could only be one price for failure, and that was death. Garret had been a good soldier, but Magnus lived in a universe where mercy was a weakness, and Garret had lost the woman, which was unforgivable. An example had to be made for the rest of the men. It was decided.

Magnus nodded. "Good. Your troops are prepared?"

"Of course. We'll crush any opposition. Not that anyone would be stupid enough to challenge us."

"Then go. The sooner you're there, the sooner we'll be able to recover from this disaster."

"I won't let you down."

"I hope not." Magnus looked him up and down, and then shifted his eyes to the column. "Once you're settled, send the vehicles back. We'll keep the men stationed in Pecos, but they'll use horses there."

"I will."

The engines started with a roar and the men climbed aboard, each gunman a hardened killer who'd proven his loyalty to the Crew countless times. Magnus watched as the heavy trucks rumbled away, the noise of motors jarring after the usual silence, and nodded again.

"You heading back to Dallas?" he asked Whitely.

"Yes. And then Lubbock. The work has to continue even in the girl's absence."

"I was under the impression you were at a standstill."

"Not completely. There are still tests that were in the queue to be performed, and their results correlated with what we've already collected."

"It's unfortunate she's the only immune one we've come across."

"We only need one."

Magnus led the way back into the church, his steps deliberate, his forehead wrinkled with concentration. His plan was so close to fruition he could taste it, his victory over circumstance almost complete, yet his moment of triumph had been stolen from him in the most unlikely way.

That could not stand.

He would prevail, would obliterate those who opposed him, as he had ever since taking over the region. That the woman and girl had escaped was a personal insult to him, and he would scorch the earth to find them and punish them, as well as those who had helped them flee.

There could be no other outcome. He would commit whatever resources it took to achieve it.

The very future of the world – his world – hung in the balance. There was nowhere far enough for them to hide from Magnus. He was a force of nature, and they had unleashed his fury, which would sweep across the land like a plague until he found them.

And then they would pay.

They would all pay, and beg for death before he was finished.

Chapter 4

Lucas pushed Tango harder during the cooler morning hours, anxious to make the gulch before noon. The big stallion was game and held to a trot much of the time until the terrain became too uneven. The sun was a blazing disk in the azure sky by the time Lucas crested the rise and spotted the track that led down into the gully. He adjusted the flat brim of his hat to better shade his eyes while Tango picked his way down the loose gravel trail. He gripped the M4 tightly as he scanned the area.

When he reached the sight of the massacre, at first glance nothing appeared disturbed since he'd last been there. He dismounted and made his way to the two Raiders he'd shot, whose bones had been picked clean by animals. He glanced at the pile of skeletons and stopped midstride.

The Raiders' guns, plate carriers, and magazines were gone. He remembered that he'd left them in his haste to spirit Eve to safety, but they were nowhere to be seen.

So someone *had* been there, though whether surviving Raiders or other scavengers, Lucas had no way of knowing.

His heart sank at the reminder of the long odds against success, but he continued on to where the dead lay, their bones bleached by the sun's rays. A quick survey of the skeletons confirmed that nothing of value remained – even their boots had been removed. Little went to waste in the wilderness for long.

He returned to Tango and mounted up. It was obvious that there was nothing left for him, and he was glad to be rid of the place, the atmosphere tainted as it was by recent death. Lucas directed Tango back up the trail, and once at the crest, the horse sprinted for the distant canyon, as though he could also sense the bad juju in the ravine.

Lucas arrived at the canyon mouth forty minutes later, and it didn't take long for him to piece together what had happened. The Raiders still lay where they'd fallen, only their guns and magazines missing, confirming to Lucas that at least some had survived. He walked the area slowly, the wind moaning as it funneled through the gap, and stopped when he came upon Carl's remains. His ruined flak jacket told the story of his demise.

"Poor bastard," Lucas whispered.

After combing over the other skeletons and finding nothing, he returned to the sheriff's bones and piled small rocks over his remains until they were covered. He removed his hat and murmured a prayer for the dead, and when he replaced it, his steel-gray eyes were hard.

Lucas did a count and saw that the sheriff and his deputy had succeeded in killing most of the Raiders. By his reckoning only two had survived, unless he'd missed a body. He did a final walk through the killing field to ensure he hadn't, and paused beside the outcropping from which Alan had fired, imagining the scene. For some reason Carl hadn't made it to safety – why didn't matter – but the deputy had managed to rid the earth of the lion's share of the miscreants. Many had died out in the open, but several of the dead marauders had taken up defensive positions behind cover of their own. The desiccated bones of four horses told Lucas they hadn't seen the ambush coming, and he wondered again at what had gone wrong for the sheriff that he'd been killed so far from Alan's hiding place.

Back at the canyon entrance, he spotted a patch of tan fabric shifting in the breeze about a hundred yards away. He rode toward the movement and recognized Alan's shirt and pants – or what remained of them. As they had with the other corpses, carrion birds and insects had cleaned the bones, but the condition of the dead man's clothing made it clear that he hadn't gone easily.

Lucas lowered himself from the saddle, crouched beside the remains to study the shredded garments, and shook his head, a frown twisting his features. The shattered ribcage, arm bones, and skull weren't difficult to interpret – he'd seen the same before. The dead man's boots were still lashed together, the Raiders too lazy to take them after loading themselves up with the guns and belongings of their fallen companions.

"They dragged you by your feet behind their horses, didn't they?" he muttered, closing his eyes and imagining the atrocity.

Overhead, a hawk wheeled lazily, riding an updraft in search of prey, the cycle of life grinding relentlessly forward even as Lucas mourned the loss of the young man. Deep down he understood that there was nothing he could have done to save Alan, but his guts still twisted at the sight of the deputy's broken body and the knowledge that his last moments on earth had been agonizing beyond imagination.

Lucas removed his collapsible camp shovel and dug a shallow grave while Tango stood by. When he'd placed the young man's remains into the ditch and covered them with shale and dirt, Lucas wiped the sweat from his brow with the back of his arm and spoke a few words, the prayer all too familiar of late. "May God have mercy on your soul," he ended, and then glanced at his watch. Time was wasting, and every minute he spent there any trail was going cold.

Lucas considered the dead Raiders but couldn't bring himself to expend the energy to bury them – the job would have taken most of the afternoon, and he didn't have it in his heart to forgive the scum. He was comfortable with that failing; Lucas would leave forgiveness to a higher power, because all he could think was that he intended to reward the surviving Raiders for their evil with payment in kind.

Just as he'd done to the cartel.

Although it gave him no happiness to recall the events in Pecos, he had to admit some satisfaction at having evened the score. And much as he didn't want to have to go into the belly of the beast in search of the surviving Raiders, he would do what he must and would show them the same mercy they'd extended to the deputy. While it might have been unenlightened, nowadays his approach was more Old Testament eye-for-an-eye than turning any cheeks.

The meek could inherit the earth; but in the meantime, he was going to bring the pain to those who reveled in their misdeeds.

"Come on, Tango. Got a long way to go, and nobody's getting any younger."

The horse eyed Lucas and waited for him to swing into the saddle. Once his boots found the stirrups, Lucas pulled the reins and pointed Tango east, toward Mentone, the shabby scattering of buildings at the devil's crossroad where any survivors would have gone to regroup.

Chapter 5

Lucas smelled Mentone long before he saw the glow of campfires on its periphery. Night had fallen an hour earlier, and he'd made his way cautiously after dark, using the rifle's NV scope to verify that he wasn't riding into an ambush as he neared the hamlet. The wind had shifted and was coming out of the east, carrying with it the smoke from burning wood and the stink of raw human waste. He knew from his encounters with the Raiders that bathing wasn't a big part of their culture, but even so the stench was overpowering as he reached the town limits.

He didn't have to search far to find Mentone's social center – a pair of torches framing the door of a long, low building and faint electric light seeping from its windows announced the spot even before shouts and ragged curses drifted to him from inside. A faded hand-painted sign hung crookedly over the entryway, featuring a crude depiction of a bottle and a woman's exaggerated curves, beneath which it proclaimed in red, "The Mayor's."

Lucas had heard of the place from Duke, but had successfully avoided traveling to Mentone until then. It had a reputation as a dung hole, even by postapocalyptic standards, which was saying a lot: barely six blocks of dirt roads and squalid dwellings, the Raiders having seized the town and turned it into their vision of hell soon after the flu had cleared the population for them.

Only the most unscrupulous traders set foot within its boundaries, although it was understood that those who came to dicker were safe from predation while there. A necessary safeguard, but one Lucas was skeptical of, and one he wasn't planning to put to the test if he could help it.

Seven horses were tied to a hitching post by a watering trough, and Lucas dismounted and nodded to an older Raider who was watching the animals from the shadows. His Mohawk was ratty and graying, a pale stump extruded from cutoff trousers above where his left knee would have been, and a sawed-off shotgun lay in his lap.

"Some rounds in it for you if you keep an eye out," Lucas said.

"Treat him like he's my own flesh and blood," the guard assured him.

"What's the story inside?"

"Leave your weapons in your saddlebags and keep your nose clean, things should be fine."

"They got food?"

"Guess some might call it that. Best to stick to the firewater, if you ask me."

"Fair enough."

Lucas had dined on some of his jerky on the ride and was used to long hours with an empty stomach, so the dearth of edibles didn't faze him. He had no intention of eating anything served in the saloon – rather, he'd wanted to see how honest the old man was.

He stowed his weapons and approached the doors. Inside, a guard with a fireplug physique gave him a cursory frisking as Lucas breathed through his mouth, the odor in the room nauseating. When the bouncer nodded him past, Lucas made for the bar and bought a bottle of rum, there being no beer or anything less than eighty proof available.

Lucas took a small pull on the liquid, almost gagged at the taste, and then set it down on the plank and glanced at the crowd in the gloom. Two overhead fluorescent lamps that had seen better days provided scant illumination, which was probably just as well – the six women there more resembled losing kickboxers than female companionship, and the men ran the gamut from filthy and rangy to worse than he'd seen in anyone still alive.

One of the whores looked him up and down and offered what Lucas supposed passed for a come-hither smile. He managed a small bemused smirk and looked away to where four Raiders were playing cards at the far end of the room. Lucas watched them for a hand and then felt a presence at his elbow. He turned slowly to find the prostitute at his side.

"Well, hello there, cowboy. Buy a lady a drink?" she asked. Lucas tried not to gape at her meth-rotted teeth and the grime crusted in her hairline, and forced a smile to his lips.

"Maybe in a few. Thinking about sitting in for a few hands."

"You can do that after. They'll be there all night."

"Sorry. Not in the mood right now."

She slid a chipped glass toward him. "Make a little deposit for later?" she asked, indicating the rum.

"Sure. Why not?" Lucas said, and splashed several inches into the cup.

"I'm Lacey."

"Pleased to meet you."

"Save enough chips to go for a ride, okay?" she said. Her eyes were hungry, the whites yellowed from jaundice that matched her sickly pallor, and her skin was pocked with sores and blackheads.

"Good advice," Lucas allowed, and went back to watching the players. Lacey tossed back the rum like it was water, brayed an abrasive laugh, and sashayed over to her companions, all of whom were equally attractive, from what Lucas could make out.

After ten minutes of sizing up the game, Lucas asked the bartender how to get chips. The man indicated a heavyset Raider at a small table in the corner with a bottle in front of him, and explained that "the mayor" was in charge of that, and to talk to him.

Lucas walked over to the man and introduced himself. "Want to get in the game."

"Sure. What you got?"

"Fifty rounds of .45, couple magazines of 5.56mm ball."

"Won't stay in long with that."

"Not planning on losing."

The mayor nodded. "Bring it in. But no guns."

"I heard."

When Lucas returned with the ammunition, the mayor examined the bullets and then counted out twenty chips. "There you go."

Lucas eyed the tokens. "That's it?"

The mayor pointed at a sign by the back door that listed the value of chips in both guns and ammunition. "Everyone's a winner here. You can trade 'em in on your way out, get your rounds back and then some if you know how to play."

"You own the place?"

The mayor answered with a complacent smile. "That's right."

"Only place to trade in town?"

The Raider nodded. "One-stop shop."

"You got anything besides guns and ammo?"

"Got everything you can imagine, and then some."

Lucas nodded. "Good to know."

"Whatever you want. Long as you got barter, sky's the limit."

Lucas took his chips and sat down at the table. Three of the men were obviously Raiders, and the fourth was a trader whose leathery skin and blackened nail beds spoke to weeks on the road.

"Gents. What's the ante and the game?" Lucas asked.

The men glared at him, and the one who was dealing eyed Lucas's paltry stash. "Couple chips to start. Five-card draw."

Lucas parted with half his chips to get a feel for the players' styles, those small tics or lack of them that indicated whether they were bluffing or not. Once he was confident he'd sized them up, he won small hands, keeping his bets modest, avoiding winning too much or losing to the extent that he ran dry of chips. As the evening progressed it became easier to win, the others getting drunk as time wore on, but nobody was talkative, and after an hour of play Lucas pushed back from the table, having learned nothing but that Raiders weren't conversationalists, and if anyone knew anything, they were keeping it to themselves.

He cashed in his chips and retrieved his ammunition and magazines, and with a few extra chips in hand, went in search of

Lacey, who hadn't been particularly lucky that night, either. After several generous dollops of rum, she grew increasingly talkative, and he invited her to one of the small two-top tables so he could pick her brain.

"Heard about a big to-do up north about a week ago," he tried, once half the bottle had disappeared down her throat.

"Yeah?"

Lucas nodded. "Big haul, but lot of Raiders killed."

She shrugged. "Occupational hazard."

"You hear anything about that?"

"About a week ago, you say?"

"That's right."

She drained her glass. "Might have."

He refilled her drink and took a pull on the rum straight from the bottle. "What did you hear?"

"Depends."

He placed three chips on the table. "Be mighty appreciative for any information."

Her eyes darted to the side for a beat. "Why?"

"Just because." He reached for the chips, but she shook her head.

"Couple of guys were in around that time. Talked about a big gun battle. Big score, too."

"You know them?"

She shrugged again. "I might."

"They here?"

Another head shake. "No. Cleared out a few days ago. Meaner than snakes, even by Raider standards."

"What did they look like?"

"One's short, black Mohawk. The other's skinny and tall, hair cut close to his head. Dark brown."

Lucas glanced around the room. "That could be half the guys in here."

"The short one had a tin star on his vest. Can't miss it."

Lucas's eyes gave nothing away. He pushed one of the chips across the table to her. "Know where they went?"

"They camp a couple of miles out of town when they're here."

"Which way?"

She regarded the chips. "Southwest. Probably the only ones there, if they're still around."

He slid the chips to her and stood. "You have a good night, Lacey."

"They'll gut you," she said softly.

He nodded. "Be a shame."

"You going to drink that?" she asked.

Lucas set the bottle down in front of her and looked away. "Not thirsty anymore."

She reached for it. "I'll watch it for you."

"Do that."

Chapter 6

The road west was paved, although like all the others, long since covered in a thick coating of dust. Tumbleweeds clogged the two-lane road in sections that had washed out, and abandoned vehicles rose from the earth like giant boulders in the starlit landscape, blocking the route. Lucas avoided the highway, preferring to stick to a trail that ran parallel. Hoofprints in the reddish dirt signaled that he was likely on the right track – other riders had passed that way recently, although he couldn't know whether hours or days before.

It wasn't lost on him that he was headed toward the highway that ran from Loving to Pecos, although he was a good five miles away. Still, the thought made him uncomfortable, given that it was a certainty the Loco cartel was on the warpath, turning over every stone to find them. While he hoped they would have given up after several days of failing to pick up their scent, he couldn't assume they'd thrown in the towel – especially in light of Sierra's revelations about the reason Magnus's group had enlisted their help. She was correct that the Crew would never give up in their hunt for Eve, which heightened his sense of futility at burning time looking for a vest that could well be in Mexico by now. But they were low on options, and given his slim odds of success, the vest was the best they had.

The husk of a ruined farmhouse materialized on the horizon, and Lucas thought he could make out the flicker of a campfire near it. He swung his M4 up and gazed through the night vision scope.

There. He was right. It was a fire.

When he was closer, he dismounted and walked Tango toward the ruins. At the edge of the property, he tied the horse to an old wooden fencepost and whispered in his ear, "Wait for me. I'll be back soon."

The fire was small and well-concealed, if he hadn't been looking for it. The structure shielded it from the east, which was where all but Raiders would be coming from, that being the artery to New Mexico. A lone horse, its ribs pronounced ridges along its thin flank, stood near what had once been the building's garage. As he approached the fire's glow, he could only see one figure, and after confirming his impression with the scope, he stepped into the open, rifle at the ready.

The figure looked up and reached for a shotgun leaning against the wall of the farmhouse. Lucas shook his head and called out, "Wouldn't do that if I was you." His tone softened. "Don't worry. I'm not going to hurt you."

He moved closer and saw that it was a woman, whippet thin, her arms covered with full-sleeve tattoos, her face emaciated, her greasy black hair cropped short. She regarded him with ill-concealed fear, her eyes darting to his gun and then back to the shotgun just out of reach. He easily read her intention and kept his M4 pointed at her. "Don't try anything stupid. I said I'm not going to hurt you."

"What do you want, mister?" she asked, her drawl pronounced.

"Just came from the mayor's. He said someone I'm looking for might be here."

"Yeah? Who's that?"

"Short guy wearing a badge."

"He ain't around."

He took cautious steps until he was within a few yards of her and could see that she was younger than he'd thought, maybe Sierra's age, but already worn down by a hardscrabble life.

"Where's he at?"

"How would I know? Ain't none of my business."

"What are you doing out here on your own?" Lucas asked.

"Just tryin' to get by, same as everyone. Don't like stayin' near town. Some of the guys get their booze on and go off, you know?" She eyed him and tried a smile. "But you're not like that, are you?"

"No, ma'am, I'm not."

"I can tell." She paused. "Name's Connie. I'm cooking rabbit. You ate yet?"

"Doesn't smell too bad," Lucas allowed.

"Guess if you was gonna shoot me, you woulda by now, huh?"

"Probably true." He glanced at the shotgun. "Stay clear of the scatter gun, and we'll get along fine."

"You can sit down, 'less you're afraid I'll bite or somethin'," she said.

"Don't mind if I do." Lucas decided to try the soft route with her, given there was no obvious threat.

"Why you lookin' for that guy?" she asked, reaching out and turning a rabbit that was crackling over the fire, skewered on a piece of rusted rebar.

"They said he might be able to help me find something."

"Yeah? What's that?"

"A vest. Some friends of mine lost one."

She made a face. "You're riding around in the dark lookin' for a vest? You crazy or something?"

"Or something." He looked around. "You're out here alone?"

"See anyone else?"

Lucas pointed to a pair of bedrolls. "More than one of those."

"I like to be comfortable." She smiled again. "Don't you?"

"I suppose."

"You scared the crap outta me, sneakin' up like that."

"Wasn't my intention."

She studied him. "You ain't from around here, are you?"

"Down El Paso way."

"Thought so. I'd a remembered if I'd seen you before." She edged a little closer. "You by yourself?"

"Just me."

She appraised him frankly and unfastened the top buttons of her shirt. "You lookin' for more than a vest?"

"It's not like that," he said, looking away.

"Just you and me here."

"I–"

The snick of a blade opening stopped him. He caught the gleam of steel in his peripheral vision and grabbed her wrist, stopping the hand that was snaking at him with a wicked-looking stiletto. Her smile instantly turned into a grimace of pained rage, and she swung the skewered rabbit at his head, hissing a curse as she fought to break free. Lucas avoided the blow and squeezed her wrist harder. She dropped the knife and squirmed, and he whipped the Kimber from his hip holster and pointed it at her head. He leaned toward the knife, .45 leveled on her, scooped it up, and tossed it into the darkness.

"This thing'll blow a hole in you the size of a grapefruit," he warned.

The struggle went out of her and she went limp. He slid away, gun steady in his hand, and pointed to the sleeping rolls. "Get up and bring me that rope."

She looked where he indicated and the smile returned. "Don't need to tie me up. 'Less you want to."

"Get the rope. Not going to ask again."

"Or what? You gonna shoot me?"

His tone was glacial. "Last time; then you learn the hard way."

"All right. Cool your jets."

He'd misjudged her, lulled by fatigue. She was high, probably on the home-made meth everyone was taking, dangerous as a pit viper and probably full-boat crazy. Had to be in order to keep the company she did, he figured. He wouldn't make the same mistake again.

"I see you grab anything but the rope and you're buzzard food," he warned.

"Just tryin' to defend myself."

It was as close to an apology as he was likely to get, even if an obvious lie. He nodded as though buying it. "No harm in that, but I'll still blow your head off if you make one false move."

"Forget what I said 'bout rememberin' you. You're just like all the rest."

"No, I'm not, or you'd already be dead."

He wasted no time and had her wrists and ankles bound within moments, tying her expertly, her struggling inadequate to do anything but delay the inevitable. When he was finished, he stood and considered her. "Waste of good rabbit."

"You can have it all, if that's what you're after. That and anything else you want."

He hastily searched her things and found nothing of value, other than a snub-nosed five-shot revolver with a taped handle and two disposable lighters. He did a quick inspection of the interior of the farmhouse and quickly returned.

"All right. Where's the guy I was asking about?" he demanded.

"Told you. Don't know."

"I don't believe you."

"Whatever."

He sat back down and retrieved the rabbit from the dust and set the rebar back across the rocks so it could continue cooking. "Know why you should care? Because when that iron gets hot enough, I'm going to go to work on you with it. Worst part about bad burns is they hurt for days. Blister, peel, get infected. Hell, I expect a lot of people die from them these days, with no medicine and all."

She shook her head. "I told you the truth."

Lucas smiled, and the effect was chilling. "Connie, assuming that's your real name, you have no idea what you're playing with here. But I'll offer fair warning. I intend to burn the skin off your face, then your nose and ears. Only way that's not going to happen is if you tell me where he is, no more stalling or lies. I have nothing against you, so no reason to hurt you unless I have to. But I will. You read me?"

Her eyes widened, and the look of panic told him that she understood.

"He…he may be over by the highway, near the spring. He's getting water."

"Is he alone?"

She shook her head. "No. A friend."

"This spring. You mean the one by Highway 285? The well?"

"That's it."

He eyed her skeptically. "Getting water? At night, with a buddy?"

She looked away. "That's what he said."

"They armed?"

"Course."

He debated what to do with her and decided to leave her tied up. "You lied to me, I'll be back."

"How am I supposed to get untied?"

Lucas studied her without expression. "You'll think of something." He removed the rabbit from the fire and tore a steaming chunk off the carcass before blowing on it to cool it. "No point in ruining the meal, is there?" he said, and then popped it in his mouth. "Mighty tasty. Enjoy it."

She watched him walk away, her shotgun only a few short yards from her, but about as much use as a life raft in her predicament. She waited until he was out of sight and then began rubbing the rope that bound her wrists against the hot rocks of the fire pit, determined to get loose before the madman came back for her, which she was sure he would, if he survived.

A big if, but she wasn't feeling lucky.

And there were other predators in the darkness for her to fear.

She swallowed the dry lump in her throat and sawed harder, praying to a God she didn't believe in that she was successful before he returned.

Chapter 7

Lucas watched through the NV scope from five hundred yards away in the darkness as the woman freed herself, gathered her things, and saddled up the emaciated horse. He didn't believe for a second she had told him the truth, but figured it was a near certainty that she would go in search of his quarry to warn him.

She set off to the south, confirming his suspicion, and continued at a gallop until she was barely a speck. He took off after her, Tango easily keeping up even after the long day's ride, covering the ground with fluid grace as Lucas hunched low over the saddle, rifle gripped tightly in his right hand.

Twenty minutes later, he slowed as he approached the highway in the distance. He could just make out her horse silhouetted in the moonlight, and pulled Tango up short. "Time for a rest. I'll handle it from here," he said as he dropped from the saddle and tied the horse to a tree.

He ran in a crouch toward Connie's horse, and as he neared, he could hear her screech of a voice from behind the carcass of a bus stalled by the side of the road – and the lower resonance of a man speaking in more hushed tones. Lucas didn't bother trying to hear their conversation, instead concentrating on narrowing the distance without being spotted and flanking them so he could see what he was dealing with.

Once he was only a hundred yards away, he peered through the night vision scope and saw the woman, arms akimbo, speaking to two Raiders, one of whom matched the description of his man.

As Lucas had suspected, the scumbags were lying in wait on the highway to rob and murder anyone stupid or desperate enough to be traveling at night by the main roads. He debated whether to take the woman and second man out right then and there, but the decision was made for him when the shorter Raider struck the woman with a slap he could hear. The men were in motion and the woman was running for her horse, and then she was riding back the way she'd come as the men mounted up, presumably to waylay him at the springs she'd misled Lucas about.

He could have shot the horses, but the smaller targets in motion were too difficult given the angle. His opportunity squandered, he returned to Tango and gave cautious chase. The Raiders rode hard on the highway, and Lucas followed silently through the scrub. He knew the springs she'd described, no more than a quarter mile off the road, and would wait for them to search the area and find nothing before moving on them.

When they arrived at the well, nothing more than a cinderblock utility building and a walled hole in the ground, they leapt down from their horses, guns in hand, and rushed the structure in as amateur a manner as Lucas could have imagined. He dropped from the saddle and crept toward the springs while they roamed the grounds, and closed in on them while they were busy inside.

When they emerged and were both clear of the doorway, Lucas called out from behind the cement rim of the well.

"Drop the guns or you're dead."

The small man's accomplice opened fire on full auto, and Lucas cut him down with a three-round burst. His target dove for the door, but Lucas's second burst caught his left leg, and he went down hard. Lucas fired another burst near the man's head and then yelled at him, "Throw the AK away and put your hands where I can see them, or the next round's between your eyes."

Lucas could practically smell the desperation as the Raider made his choice. His rifle rattled against the hard clay and he raised his right hand, his left clutching his wounded leg. Lucas rose and moved toward him, and when he reached the first Raider, toed his weapon away and knelt beside him to check his neck for a pulse.

Nothing.

The little Raider groaned in pain. Lucas straightened and approached him. He could make out the man's features, twisted with agony, but his eyes still possessed of cruelty and animal cunning.

"Hurts, huh?" Lucas observed, and spit to the side.

The man glared at him wordlessly.

Lucas eyed the man's injured leg, blood seeping between the Raider's fingers, and nodded. "Looks like it got you pretty good. Man could die from a wound like that."

"What do you want?"

Lucas's eyes narrowed and he shook his head. "That's not the one."

The Raider's expression changed to confusion. "What?"

"Your vest. Wrong one." Lucas paused. "Although the tin star's a nice touch. Where did you get it?"

"Found it," the thug said through clenched teeth.

"Huh."

"What do you want?" the man repeated, his voice strained.

"World peace. Understanding. The love of a good woman. But I'll settle for a straight answer. I'm looking for a vest."

"You shot us for a lousy plate carrier?"

"This is a special one. Sentimental value. A friend of mine's. He died west of here, in a gulch by the foothills. Bushwhacked by a bunch of you. Has an eagle on the breast."

The man's eyes widened in recognition, and then he quickly recovered, resuming his unreadable expression. But Lucas had caught the brief tell and nodded. "Seems like we have ourselves a winner."

"I didn't kill those dudes, man. I swear. I just found the stuff. They was already dead."

"Oh, I believe you. Based on your moves here, you'd have been dead if you had taken them on. That's not important. Where's the vest?"

"Why you so interested in it?"

"I collect them. Where is it?"

The Raider coughed. "I don't have it."

"Who does?"

The man shrugged with a wince. "I'm bleeding out here."

"Yup. Looks like you are. Where is it?"

"I lost it in a card game. Back in Mentone. Along with a bunch of other crap."

"To who?"

"Old guy. Dealer. But I heard he's dead."

"Tell me about him," Lucas said, his voice low.

"Partner or something with the guy who runs the bar. Call him the mayor."

"I know the place."

"Mayor's probably got it."

Lucas offered a humorless smile. "What does the badge say?"

"How would I know? Police. Something like that."

Lucas shook his head. "Nope. Says sheriff." He paused. "You the one dragged him over the rocks? Or your buddy there?"

"Don't know what you're talking about, man."

Lucas could see the lie in his smirk. "Friend of mine had a star just like that. Decent sort," he said, and looked down at his M4.

The Raider's hand reached for his boot and a small pistol appeared from an ankle holster.

Lucas's final two three-round bursts chewed the man's torso to hamburger, and the light went out of his eyes. Lucas knelt down and retrieved the Raider's gun – a piece of Chinese junk, .32 caliber, compact but deadly at close range. He pocketed it and quickly searched the thug, holding his breath at the man's odor, one of his rounds having punctured his abdomen and small intestine. He retrieved two curved magazines for the AK and slipped them into his flak vest, and then moved to the other Raider and repeated the process with much the same results – a few magazines, a lighter, and a battered Sig Sauer pistol that looked like it hadn't been cleaned in a lifetime.

Lucas hurried back to Tango and loaded the weapons into his

saddlebags. He knew his shots would have carried to the woman, who might circle around and try to ambush him. He doubted it, but he'd learned you could never assume anything but the worst.

He pointed Tango north and put three miles between himself and the well, and then made camp with no fire. He'd wait until morning to return to Mentone and continue following the thread to see where it led. Of course, the dealer could have traded the vest to someone before he was killed, or the mayor could have sold it, but Lucas had no better place to start and resigned himself to another trip to the hellhole once day had broken.

Would the woman say anything, warn them? Lucas didn't think so. She would assume the worst when her pals failed to show, but he didn't see her as being adventurous enough to ride to the well until it was light out, and he had put enough of a scare into her that she wouldn't go back to the farmhouse any time soon. No, she would find someplace to sleep, maybe go looking for her companions in the morning, and when she found them…it didn't matter. Lucas would have finished his business with the mayor by the time she could make it to town, if she dared – a lone woman without a vicious ferret like the little killer to defend her might decide that there were greener pastures than the open sewer that was Mentone.

He watered Tango and settled onto his bedroll, troubled by how easily snuffing out life had come to him since rescuing Sierra. After the collapse, he'd had to shoot three different men, all of them in self-defense, but he'd avoided most altercations – which was why he was still alive, he reasoned. None had been easy for him, and he'd struggled with his conscience many a night; the knowledge that he'd had no choice afforded slim comfort when their ghosts came to visit.

But now he'd butchered, what, over a hundred in a week or less? Had he become one of the monsters he so despised? Had the collapse finally taken its toll on his soul and robbed him of his humanity?

He closed his eyes and tried to dismiss the notion. That he had the thought at all was proof of a kind that he wasn't lost. Not yet. Animals like the Raiders didn't miss a beat and killed innocents so they could steal their possessions – or worse, to entertain themselves. Lucas wasn't that. Whatever he had become, he wasn't one of them.

A vision of Alan's and Carl's faces, riding into the night in search of Eve, putting themselves in harm's way to save a little girl they'd never met, filled his imagination, followed almost instantly by a memory of their abused remains. The men he'd gunned down tonight had done that. They had earned their reward, and Lucas had been nothing more than the messenger. Truth be told, he'd probably saved the lives of countless travelers who would have fallen prey to them, and he was quite sure that the Raiders hadn't suffered any crisis of conscience at their misdeeds.

Tango was munching on some scrub, the only sound his steady mastication and an occasional snort. Lucas sighed and willed the troubling doubts away. He was doing what he had to in order to prevail, nothing more. The world was a brutal place populated by more than its share of sadists and miscreants, and if his role in it all was to wipe the earth of a few of them, so much the better. He was under no illusions about human nature. His years in law enforcement had more than disabused him of any notion that evil wasn't an active and real force, and that every man didn't eventually have to either confront it and welcome it into his heart or banish it. Taking life was certainly evil, but when there was no choice, kill or be killed, it was...less so.

His breathing slowed, but with his churning thoughts, rest came hard, and he spent the remainder of the night in uneasy slumber. His dreams were violently vivid and jarring, a parade of departed companions. Tango looked over at him in alarm when he cried out softly several times in the night, rifle clutched to him like a lover, dead to the world but still reliving his battles in the unforgiving embrace of troubled sleep.

Chapter 8

Cano watched as his men moved a pickup truck from the center of the two-lane blacktop, where it had been abandoned at just enough of an angle to block the road. It sat on rusting rims, the tires having degraded to little more than dust from the desert sun, and it groaned like an angry walrus as one of the Humvees pushed it out of the way.

They'd made better time than he'd expected; the highway had been largely uncluttered by cars once they'd gotten fifty miles from Houston, and this was only the eighth such delay in their thirty-six-hour marathon. By his reckoning, they were no more than ten miles from Pecos, and he expected to be able to make out the city's lights at any moment.

Cano was part of Magnus's executive team, a troubleshooter who'd proved himself in prison as an enforcer and hit man, whose career had blossomed once he'd escaped with the rest of Magnus's group. His willingness to use excessive violence at the slightest provocation had made him a powerful force around Houston, and although Magnus had a higher opinion of Garret's resourcefulness, he clearly prized Cano's ability to get tough jobs done – including executing those who had failed him.

Being chartered with finding the woman was both an honor and a curse. He had no idea what situation he would find in Pecos, but he was confident that he could manhandle the Locos into providing enough support that he could pick up the woman's trail. He had no alternative, or there would be a replacement sent to take over his responsibility, and he could expect the same reward for disappointing his master that awaited the one-eyed freak at his hands. He didn't bemoan that – it was the law of the jungle, and so far, the harsh rules had been good for him.

Thirty-two years old and six foot six, Cano was shaped like a door, with bare arms protruding from his flak vest like tree trunks and covered with full-sleeve prison ink. Originally incarcerated at nineteen for the brutal murder of two youths with a hatchet, he'd shown no remorse for his misdeeds and had been diagnosed a psychopath by the system, about which he cared little, just as he didn't mind the prospect of life behind bars. One place was as good as any other to him, and he'd quickly climbed the prison pecking order with a series of vicious attacks that had added three more to his list of kills – not that the pair of youths had been his first. Part of his contempt for the legal apparatus was its inability to do its job, and there were four others that had preceded the ones he'd been busted for, all but one murdered with his bare hands. His first taste of blood had been when he'd beat another boy's head into the sidewalk one evening when he'd been in the wrong place at the wrong time. After smashing the kid's brains into jelly, Cano had gone home and eaten a sandwich in front of the television, alone. His meth-addicted mother was doubtless off somewhere earning her next fix, and his nameless father had departed ten seconds after the ejaculation that had created him.

Over the next days, the news coverage of the sensational slaying had amused him no end, but he'd never told a soul, only thinking about it occasionally, and when he did, without emotion.

"Come on. We don't have all night," he growled at the men when enough space had been made for the fuel truck to make it through. Cano signaled to his driver to push on, his customary impatience even more pronounced than usual due to lack of sleep and anxiousness to confront Garret.

Pecos rose from the plain like a glowing mirage, its lights bright in the night. The eastern approach had been blocked with a wall fashioned of debris and the carcasses of vehicles; a faded red arrow on a crudely painted sign pointed them to the southern gate.

The guard there looked up at the arriving motorized column like it was a formation of UFOs, and his mouth hung open at the apparition as he stood, his AK a laughable defense against the heavy equipment bristling with Crew members and guns. Cano signaled him over as the Humvee came to a stop, its diesel engine clattering from small impurities in the fuel.

"We're your reinforcements," Cano barked when the guard was within earshot.

"Reinforcements?" the man asked, his tone puzzled and not a little afraid.

"Get on the radio with whoever runs this operation. Tell him the Crew's arrived."

The Loco nodded and made the transmission, and several long moments later, Luis's voice crackled over the speaker, authorizing the guard to let the procession through. The man exhaled in relief at the instruction – it wasn't like he could have done anything to stop them from running him down.

He slid aside an iron gate, whose wheels squeaked a protest as it opened, and motioned the vehicles through, still shocked at the sight of a motorized transport – something he hadn't seen in years. The Humvee exhausts belched black smoke into the air and they rolled forward. Cano stood with his head in the wind on the passenger side like a conquering general, the bandana over his nose and mouth mottled with road dust.

They roared through the darkened streets as startled residents peered from windows and doorways at the unfamiliar sound of motors, and rolled up to the courthouse square, where Luis and two of his lieutenants waited. The vehicles eased to a stop, and Cano descended from the lead truck and approached Luis, pulling down the bandana as he strode.

"I'm Cano. Magnus sent us. We're here to help in the search for the woman and child."

"Welcome, Cano. I'm Luis. Head of the Locos," Luis said, offering his hand.

Cano shook it with a grip like a hydraulic press and looked back at his convoy. "My men and I have been on the road for too long. Where can we make camp?"

"There's a motel not far from here that we use."

"Good. Have one of your people show them to it."

Luis bit back the response that sprang to his lips at being ordered around in front of his men, and nodded. "Will do."

"Where's Garret?"

Luis's expression clouded. "He's dead. Killed with his men in the field."

Cano absorbed the information, his face unreadable. "When?"

"Couple days back."

Cano nodded. "What progress are you making on the search?"

"None. There's no trace of them." Luis didn't mention that it was because they'd given up looking.

The big Crew boss studied Luis for a long moment and then stepped closer. "I want your best men ready to ride tomorrow at first light. Mine need some sleep, but the top priority is finding the woman and child, and we're going to go over every square inch of territory until we do."

Luis's eyes darted to the vehicles and then back to Cano. "We're down to only thirty or so men. I need most of those to defend the town and keep everything in line."

"I'm in charge of that now," Cano said, with a wave of a tattooed hand the size of a ham.

"The deal we made with Garret was—"

Cano cut Luis off, his eyes black as coal. "Meaningless. The new deal, or rather, the only deal is that your men assimilate into the Crew and follow my orders. You decide not to, you better ride hard before I wake up, because you're either with us or against us." Cano let the words sink in. "There's no choice B."

Luis swallowed a dry knot in his throat. "We had discussed becoming Crew members. I don't think that will be a problem."

Cano sized Luis up, and one corner of his mouth curled slightly. "You're a smart man. No wonder you're running things, Luis."

"As long as I keep doing so once you're gone, we'll get along well."

"I want to stay in this shithole about five seconds longer than I absolutely have to. Then you can have it back."

Luis maintained his unreadable expression. Cano considered Luis's men for a moment and then continued. "We'll need horses. Figure enough for fifteen men. The rest will hold down the fort. Be ready to mount up at dawn." Cano turned to his driver and cupped his hands near his mouth. "Get ready to turn the convoy around and head back to Houston tomorrow." Cano pivoted back to Luis. "Now let's see this hotel."

Luis managed a fake smile and nod. "Of course." He barked an order to the man on his right, who made for the lead Humvee. Luis squared his shoulders and turned to Cano. "I'll be riding with you."

"Yes. You will. And find someone with tracking dogs."

Luis's steady stare faltered slightly. "I…I'll do my best."

"As long as that means you'll have them at dawn, we're good. Don't disappoint me right out of the gate, Luis."

The malevolence was clear in Cano's tone, and Luis nodded again, his mind working furiously to figure out where he was going to find dogs on short notice.

"See you in a few hours. I'll get to work," Luis said, and did his best not to storm off, forcing himself to breathe deeply as he willed away the rage clouding his vision at being ordered around like a prison bitch.

Chapter 9

Ruby brewed tea over a small wood fire outside the bunker. The morning sun was just beginning to warm the air twenty minutes after dawn's first light. She was conserving her supply of kerosene for the small camp stove in the root cellar; her natural tendency to hoard had served her well since the collapse. She looked around the clearing at the trees ringing it and wondered at their tenacity in what really amounted to a desert, and then smiled at the thought that they, like she, were survivors that had managed to flourish in spite of everything the world had thrown at them.

The root cellar door opened and Sierra stepped out, carrying her camp chair, her face lined from the folded blanket she'd used as a pillow. She sniffed and moved to where Ruby was sitting by the fire.

"Morning," Sierra said.

"Good morning. Want some tea?"

"I'd love some."

"Grab a couple of cups, and by the time you get back, it should have steeped enough."

Sierra was back in a minute, and Ruby poured a fragrant stream into their cups before dousing the fire with a jug of water. The two women sat contentedly, savoring the morning, and then Ruby sat forward.

"Eve get enough rest?"

Sierra nodded. "She's a good sleeper. Won't wake up until I shake the life half out of her."

"She's a remarkable child."

"In a lot of ways. She's been through a lot."

"They're resilient, aren't they?"

Sierra's expression darkened. "Not always."

An uncomfortable silence hung over them until Ruby broke it. "Do you have any kids of your own?"

Sierra nodded. "I did. A boy. He would have been almost seven by now."

"I…I'm sorry. The flu took so many."

"He actually survived that."

"Oh."

"When we got relocated to Lubbock, I couldn't take him. My cousin in Mississippi volunteered to care for him. Dallas was too dangerous, especially for a child all alone, and she lived in some sort of a prepper compound there with a bunch of like-minded folks. It seemed the safest place for him, but nothing ever turns out the way it should." Sierra paused. "His name was Tim."

"What happened?"

"I got word that the whole compound was wiped out by a rival gang. It was in the Crew's area, but right on the eastern edge. Apparently this gang went to war for territory, and my cousin and Tim – the whole town, in fact – were killed in the process. What did they used to call that? Collateral damage? That's what my son was."

The recitation was wooden, Sierra's tone tight, and when she took a long sip of her tea, her hand was shaking.

Ruby blinked away her reaction. "I'm sorry, Sierra. I didn't mean to stir up bad memories."

"It's not your fault. There are no guarantees, right?"

"Seems not."

Sierra sat wordlessly as a pair of doves took flight from the field and soared overhead. She watched the birds fly away and looked to the older woman, her eyes moist.

"What's the story on Lucas? How long have you known each other?" she asked.

"Oh, my, let's see. Until recently we hardly saw each other, but still, it has to be about three years. I was…uh, friends…with his grandfather, Hal. That's how I know him."

Sierra seemed surprised. "I thought you were closer."

"Well, I'm a loner, and he is too, so we mostly kept to ourselves until…until the cartel destroyed the town, and Lucas's ranch in the process." Ruby swirled the tea leaves in her cup. "No guarantees, as you say. Best to be grateful for the time you have and try to enjoy it while it lasts."

"Wise words." Sierra hesitated. "He's been alone as long as you've known him?"

Ruby nodded. "Yes."

"That seems…odd. I mean, he's a good man. Those are rare these days."

Ruby smiled sadly. "His grandfather was, too. Runs in the family." She set her cup on the ground beside her. "But you're right about it being rare, and not just now. Been that way for as long as I've been drawing breath."

"What did he do…before?"

Both women understood Sierra was referring to the collapse.

"He was a lawman. Texas Ranger."

Sierra nodded. "That explains a lot. He's so cool under pressure. I mean, at the hospital when he broke me out…I've never seen anything like it."

"You know the saying: One riot, one ranger. They have a reputation."

"Deserved, obviously." She frowned. "But then why wasn't he the sheriff back in Loving? Wouldn't he have been a natural?"

"Might have been, but he lived pretty far out of town. And I didn't get the impression he was all that interested in babysitting the folks there. His grandfather said he'd had a craw full from his time in El Paso."

"Did he say why?"

Ruby scowled. "I didn't ask."

"So he's always been single?" Sierra pressed.

"No. He was married. Lost his wife in the collapse," Ruby said, her tone clipped.

"No children?"

Ruby sat back and crossed her arms over her chest. "Sierra, no offense, but I don't discuss other people's business, you know? If you have questions for Lucas, you should ask them yourself. This kind of conversation makes me very uncomfortable."

"Oh. I'm sorry. I figured that after you and he drilled me about my background, turnabout was fair play…"

"All due respect, we weren't asking you to risk your life for us."

"I wasn't either."

Ruby stood. "Just being here puts us at risk, and we both know it. Now, if you'll excuse me, I'm going to find the ladies' room and freshen up. Glad I stored a mountain of toilet paper," she said with a fake smile.

"I can leave. You don't have to put yourself in danger on account of me."

"It's not on account of you, Sierra, charming as your company is. Eve deserves better than to be out in the wilds. You two wouldn't last long on your own, which is why Lucas is going the distance for you. So let's consider the matter closed and concentrate on more productive uses of our time, shall we?"

"I…I wasn't trying to pry. I'm just curious. I mean, we owe the man our lives, and he barely says two words in a day. I know nothing about him. That's all."

"I understand. Hopefully he'll be back soon, and you can have a long discussion with him, ask him all about himself. Until then, leave it be, Sierra. We have bigger fish to fry than gossiping."

Sierra offered a conciliatory smile. "Fair enough. And you do have a lot of toilet paper."

"It was one of the things I figured I'd run short of, sooner or later, so after the collapse I rounded up as much as I could find. That, kerosene, lighters, and ammo. Between my herbs and my stash, I was pretty well set." Ruby sighed. "But as you said, no guarantees. That was then."

"How did you learn about herbs?" Sierra asked, her tone less adversarial, clearly trying to make amends for the earlier tension.

"The Internet. It was a hobby of mine before the flu. I figured organic was always better than something made in a factory – especially medicines, where God knows what the drug companies were sticking in to cut corners. So I learned all about natural ways to achieve the same things. Mostly. Some you can't replace, but you'd be surprised how many you can."

"I miss vitamins."

"Don't really need them if you're healthy and you eat a decent diet." Ruby glanced at the trees and then at the root cellar door. "Now, I really need to get busy…"

"Oh, sorry, of course."

Ruby snagged a roll of plastic-wrapped paper from one of her sealable rubber tubs and made for the trees, mulling over Sierra's questions and wondering if she'd been too harsh with the younger woman. She hadn't meant to be, but she was out of her comfort zone and too old to pretend she wasn't.

That the woman hadn't figured out that she didn't stand a chance on her own was dangerous – almost delusional. The first thing you learned in a crisis was that, unless you had taken extraordinary steps like Ruby had, there was strength in numbers. She'd witnessed firsthand how the rules went out the window when survival was at stake, and if you appeared to be prosperous or well-equipped, it was only a matter of time before someone came for your stuff. If you were alone, unless you were in a mission-designed bunker like hers, eventually you'd be overpowered by the desperate. Even in a small town like Loving, where everyone had known each other, there had come a time when those who'd failed to plan ahead had turned on their neighbors, and the blustering men with the fanciest weapons and the newest camo gear had been the first to be attacked, their relative wealth a beacon for those on the edge.

Hal and Lucas had survived because they, like Ruby, kept a low profile, and Hal had a reputation as both capable and dangerous. Shortly after Lucas had shown up from El Paso in his loaded truck, a group of ten strangers had assaulted the ranch, and between Hal and Lucas, half of them had paid for the foolhardy effort with their lives. Word had quickly spread, and the ranch had remained untroubled after that; partly because neither man advertised how well prepared the place was for long-term survival, and partly because after the first wave of the desperate in the weeks after the collapse, those who hadn't figured out how to live off the land had perished, leaving only those who could. Loving was no different than most places she'd heard about, and after the first year it had settled into the delicate equilibrium that had been its peaceful existence – until it had been razed.

She shook off the feeling of unease her discussion with Sierra had brought about and sighed.

"No guarantees, indeed," she whispered, and made a mental note to better conceal the wire leading up the tree trunk to the solar panels, just in case.

Chapter 10

Lucas arrived in Mentone shortly after sunup and made straight for the mayor's place. He secured Tango and waved away a swarm of flies that assaulted him as he walked to the entrance. Stepping up onto the small porch, he knocked on the double doors. A voice called out from inside, and shortly afterward one of the guards swung the right one open and eyed Lucas groggily.

"Yeah?"

"You open for trading?"

"What's the hurry?"

"Got to hit the trail. You open or not?"

The mayor's voice boomed from the depths of the building. "What is it?"

"Give me a minute," the guard said, and shut the heavy wooden slab in Lucas's face.

Lucas waited patiently, and a few minutes later the door reopened and the mayor glowered at him. "This better be good."

"Need to get some supplies."

The Raider nodded. "Got pretty near anything you could want." He studied Lucas. "Provided you got enough to cover it."

"Don't worry about me," Lucas said.

The mayor eyed his M4A1s assault rifle. "Nice piece. Especially the flash suppressor. Don't see those every day. Where'd you get it?"

Lucas's eyes were unsmiling. "Santa."

"Worth a lot."

"Worth more to me."

"What are you looking for?"

"5.56 ammo. If you have any grenades, always a demand for those. Maybe a spare plate carrier or vest."

The mayor grunted. "Grenades? Planning on starting a war?"

"Dangerous world out there."

The mayor laughed and then was seized by a coughing fit, the sound gurgly and unhealthy, like swatting a wet blanket with a baseball bat. Lucas waited until it passed, and then the Raider nodded. "I knew I liked you last night. Might as well come on in. Let's see what I can find for you."

Lucas nodded and stepped inside. "My horse okay there?"

"Safe as the womb when you're in my place." The mayor eyed his M4 again. "What you got to trade?"

"Some pistols. Couple AKs. Some mags of 7.62 ball. And that ammo from last night."

The Raider grunted. "That's a good start."

"Let's look at what you have," Lucas said.

The mayor escorted him into the back of the bar under the watchful scrutiny of the guards. When they reached the door that led to the back office, the gunman there extended his hand. "Rifle stays with me."

"I'm not here to drink," Lucas observed.

"Rules."

Lucas looked to the mayor, who shrugged. "You'll get it back."

"I better."

"Pistol too," the gunman said.

Lucas unholstered the Kimber and set it on the table next to the meaty guard. The mayor eyed it without comment – merely a nod – and then led Lucas into the office and then through another door into a back room that would have been the envy of many SWAT teams. Assault rifles lined the walls, metal ammo cans rose in stacks from the baseboards, and a pile of camouflage clothing sat in the center of the room.

Lucas let out an appreciative low whistle, and the mayor grinned. "Kid in a candy store, huh?"

"Can't afford to stay in here too long," Lucas agreed. "Walk out broke."

"You want grenades, I got these," the Raider said, showing Lucas a crate with several dozen green M67 fragmentation grenades. "How many you in the market for?"

"Depends on the price."

The mayor named a figure in ammunition, and Lucas shook his head. "Too rich for my blood. I can maybe take...four."

"Pick your favorites."

Lucas did, and then his eye was attracted by an oversized weapon in a corner with a rotary magazine, like a shoulder-fired revolver on steroids. He walked over to it and paused, admiring the weapon.

"Is that what I think it is?"

"Yup. Milkor MGL 40mm grenade launcher. Holds six. Fires 'em as fast as you can pull the trigger, up to four hundred yards."

"How many rounds you have for it?"

The mayor's eyes narrowed. "Why? I thought you were on a budget?"

"Never hurts to ask, does it?"

"Got a dozen."

"How much you want?"

Lucas haggled for ten minutes, but in the end he agreed to a price that was probably double what the grenade launcher and projectiles were actually worth, provided that the mayor threw in a vest and the four hand grenades. The launcher would seriously increase his defensive capabilities from rifle distance, which could be the difference between life and death in an ugly pinch, he rationalized. Reluctant as he was to part with another gold maple leaf, he was willing to do so as a form of insurance. Armed with a dozen frag grenades, at that distance he could hold off a battalion and inflict serious damage almost out of range of many of the rifles in everyday use.

Lucas approached the vests almost as an afterthought and took his time sorting through them, studying the stitching and pockets for wear, evaluating the fastenings and workmanship. He concealed the increase in his breathing when he spotted the black stylized eagle and tried the vest on, fingers feeling for the tiny USB drive without appearing to.

He felt a small bump, almost imperceptible, and turned to the mayor. "This one will do."

"Not as nice as yours, but still, a good choice."

"Little blood on the front plate carrier compartment," Lucas noted.

"Slightly used. Prior owner didn't clean it." The mayor looked the vest over. "You can choose a different one if it's a problem."

"Nah. This will do."

"You got the coin?"

"Yes."

Lucas slipped one of the maple leafs from his pocket and handed it to the Raider, who looked it over with a practiced eye and then bit it and studied the marks before nodding. "Where are the AKs?"

"Saddlebags, along with the magazines and the pistols."

"Let's go get 'em."

They retraced their steps, and Lucas reclaimed his weapons. The guard's eyebrows rose when he saw the Milkor, but he said nothing. The mayor walked with Lucas out to where Tango was waiting patiently, and Lucas unpacked the rifles and magazines. The mayor made a face when he saw the condition of the guns.

"You use these to dig a ditch or something?"

"They could use a cleaning," Lucas agreed. "But they work."

"Sure you don't want to do a deal for your M4 or your Kimber?" the mayor tried again.

"Not interested. Sentimental value."

The Raider looked him up and down. "Didn't strike me as the type."

Lucas shrugged. "Never know."

The burly guard took the magazines and guns inside, and Lucas packed his new acquisitions into his saddlebags. When he was finished, he tipped his hat brim. "Pleasure doing business with you."

"Likewise. Enjoy the new toys."

"More than anyone on the receiving end."

"Want a bottle for the road?"

"Little early for me."

"Fair enough."

The mayor ambled back into the building as Lucas swung into the saddle and urged Tango onto the road out of town. The man watched him from the doorway, and when Lucas was near the camp area, twisted his head and called out, "Boyd, ride after him, but keep your distance. When he stops to rest, take him out and bring me his gear. And search him thoroughly – bastard's got more gold. I can smell it on him."

Boyd, the largest of the three men, nodded. "Might take all day."

"Once he's out of the city limits, he's fair game, far as I'm concerned."

Boyd, who had disarmed Lucas at the door, nodded. "Looks like he knows how to use that M4. Thing's clean."

"Take your Armalite. He'll never know what hit him."

Boyd grinned. The AR-50A1 .50-caliber rifle was notoriously deadly and had earned a reputation as a breathtakingly effective sniper rifle in the right hands. Boyd was ex-military and accurate with the gun up to a thousand yards for a human-sized stationary target, but would try for a kill shot at closer to five hundred – almost a third of a mile away, which was still an impressive distance absent modern conveniences like laser range finders and ballistic computers.

"Fish in a barrel," Boyd said, and the men laughed. Lucas would be safe until near the highway, and then the Raider would make short work of him.

"Give him a decent lead. No rush," the mayor instructed.

"Roger that," Boyd said, and went in search of his horse while his boss watched Lucas disappear into the scrub.

Chapter 11

The horizon swam from heat waves rising off the desert as Doug peered through the guard station telescope at an approaching group of riders still a half mile off. He caught sight of the pair in the lead and called behind him to the trading post building.

"Duke! We got us a potential situation."

Duke appeared in the doorway. "What is it?"

"Visitors. About fifteen riders. Look pretty hard."

"Crap. Bolt the gate." Duke yelled into the interior of the building, "Aaron, Slim, get your asses out here, and come hard. We got company!"

His men came at a run, armed to the teeth, and Duke ducked back inside to get his assault rifle and don his flak vest. After Lucas's warning about the cartel, he'd been on edge, but had decided to remain open – if he'd closed up shop, it would have simply delayed the inevitable, assuming the Locos were still looking for the woman.

They moved to the sandbagged guard stations on either side of the iron gate and waited as the riders neared, dust trailing behind them like beige smoke. When the group was no more than fifty yards away, the lead rider raised his hand, signaling his men to stop, and turned to a formidable-looking stranger on his right, his face covered in prison ink.

Luis called out to Duke, "Open up."

Duke shook his head. "Sorry. We're closed."

"You're open now," Cano yelled.

"Not how it works."

"Open the gate," Cano ordered.

"You boys must be hard a hearing. I said we're closed. Come back some other time."

"You're playing with fire," Luis warned.

"You come to my place and start threatening me, you're gonna find out right quick that you're not bulletproof. Friendly word of warning," Duke said.

"We're looking for someone," Cano snarled.

"Try a lonely hearts club."

Aaron couldn't help but snicker, and the big Crew boss caught it. He eyed Duke's men as though to melt them with the intensity of his glare.

"Let one of us come in and verify you're not hiding them," Luis tried.

"Why would I let you dictate terms to me? I'm curious. 'Cause I got enough rounds to mow you all down without breaking a sweat, if I want. What am I missing?" Duke asked.

"What you're missing is we have a good working relationship, Duke. We don't want a fight. We just need to cross your place off our list, and then we'll move on," Luis said.

"You think you've got the right to show up whenever you want and search my place? Have you lost your frigging mind?"

"I'm not telling you, Duke," Luis tried. "I'm asking."

"Funny way of going about it."

"Been a long ride."

"Might want to remember you're a long way from home out here," Duke warned.

"Let my man here come in and look around. Won't take too long."

Duke appeared to consider the request. "Gonna cost you."

"What do you want?"

After a minute of negotiation, Duke was ten magazines of ammunition richer, and Slim was opening the gate. Cano handed his rifle and pistol to Luis and rode forward, his body language relaxed, his posture easy. When he was at the gate, Duke stepped from behind the sandbags and walked toward him. "Keep a bead on him, Aaron. He so much as farts, drill him," Duke instructed.

Aaron nodded, his AR-15 pointed at the newcomer.

"Gonna have to search you, make sure you aren't carrying," Duke said.

"You saw me hand over my weapons."

"I have trust issues."

Cano stared off at a point a thousand miles past Duke's shoulder. "Get it over with."

"Off the horse."

Cano frowned but complied and put his hands in the air while Duke frisked him. When he was done, Duke stepped away. "Now why don't you tell me who you're looking for, and then I can tell you that they're not here, and we can go about our business? Little hot for all the theatrics, don't you think?"

"A woman. Wounded. Has a tattoo on her arm. Like this," Cano said, tapping the eye of Providence inked on his forehead. "You seen her?"

"Don't run that kinda place, pardner."

"Let me look around and make sure."

Duke shrugged. "Suit yourself. But make it quick. You're cutting into my nap time."

Cano looked like he was going to take a swing at Duke. "Got quite a mouth on you."

"You want to get this over with or butt heads?"

Cano eyed the buildings. "This is it?"

"You're looking at it."

Duke led the Crew boss through the structures, and within five minutes, they were back at the gate. Neither had spoken the entire time. When they reached Cano's horse, he turned to Duke.

"Broad daylight out. Why are you closed?"

"We heard about the town up north getting wiped out. Bad for business. Thought we might want to relocate." Duke eyed the gothic script ringing the man's skull. "You know anything about that?"

Cano looked away. "I'm not from around here."

"Yeah. I'd remember you." Duke paused. "What do you want this woman for, anyway?"

"That's between me and her."

"Reason I ask is, I talk to a lot of people. Nature of the biz."

"She stole something of mine. I want it back." Cano looked up at Duke's men. "I'm willing to pay for any information."

"Yeah? How much?" Duke asked.

"A lot."

"That's not getting me very excited."

"We just handed you three hundred rounds of ammo to walk through your dump for five minutes. Trust me when I say I'll pay as much as it takes."

"Dump?"

"Keep it in mind. I'm serious. Whatever it takes. You can name your price."

"I can dream pretty big."

"I'll bet."

"How do I get in touch with you if I hear anything?"

"I'm monitoring channel 12." Cano glanced at the building. "I see by your antenna you have a radio."

"Who do I ask for?"

"Cano. I'm staying in Pecos, but I've got a handheld."

"Good to know."

Cano's eyes narrowed. "You haven't seen her?"

"How many times do I have to say it?" Duke asked, annoyance in his voice.

Cano froze for only a moment and then mounted his horse. When he spoke, his words were a hiss. "I find out you lied to me, I won't be happy."

"I don't have a reputation for lying."

Cano's eyes settled on Duke. "Neither do I."

Duke watched as Cano joined the riders and reclaimed his weapons. Luis spun his horse and yelled something, and the men rode off, the ground shaking from the pounding of their hooves.

When they were out of sight, Duke set his AR-15 down and looked at the building.

"Seemed like a nice fella," he said. Aaron laughed nervously, as did Slim.

"Yeah. Kinda wound a little tight, though," Doug said.

"Women will do that to you," Duke agreed, and then yawned. "Keep an eye peeled in case they come back. I don't trust 'em as far as I can throw 'em."

"Will do." Aaron paused. "What do you want me to do if they do?"

"Shoot that Cano fella first. Should sort itself out from there."

"You serious?"

Duke glanced up at the sun and wiped sweat from his brow. "All out of funnies for the day. Take out Luis second. Probably won't have to do much shooting after that."

The men watched Duke trundle back to the building with his rifle, shrugging off his plate carrier as he walked. Slim and Doug exchanged a glance, and then Doug moved to the gate to close it as Slim collected his gear and followed the trader out of the afternoon heat.

Chapter 12

Lucas let Tango have his head and galloped as fast as the horse would carry him in the direction of the highway, this time well north of where he'd camped. The big stallion's hooves pounded the trail with the strident insistence of a jackhammer as Lucas tucked low, sure that the mayor would double-cross him as soon as he thought it practical. He'd seen it in the Raider's eyes. If he were a betting man, he would have gone all-in on the likelihood and was sure that there was already a party of assassins on his tail.

He crested a small hill and stopped at a cluster of bushes, where Tango would be out of sight to anyone following. Once out of the saddle, he raised his binoculars to his eyes and scanned the horizon. He didn't have long to wait – only one man, but he was good, far better than the usual sloppy Raider fare, sticking to the brush in order to avoid throwing any dust, sacrificing speed for stealth.

The man was riding fast, but his steed was no match for Tango, who was in peak shape and used to marathon rides of twelve hours a day. That was an advantage Lucas would use, and it bought him time to select a good spot to sandbag the man, well away from prying eyes.

Lucas rode for another hour and at a gravel area circled back around so he could come up behind him in much the same fashion he'd used to outwit the cartel trackers.

Once clear of the trail, he slowed to a walk and looked for a promising spot to lie in wait. Tango would appreciate the chance to catch his breath too.

He came to one of the numerous abandoned farms that dotted the hostile terrain and dismounted. There was sufficient cover to keep Tango out of sight, and he tied him in a shady spot and watered him before he slipped his long-range rifle – the Remington 700 – from its saddle scabbard and slid its sling over his shoulder.

Lucas paused at his saddlebags and dug in the right one for the vest. He withdrew it and felt along the inner seam for the pocket, and his fingers found it on the second try. Lucas pulled the Velcro apart, and a small dongle dropped at his feet. He fished around in the compartment and felt a thick square of folded paper, which he slid into the front pocket of his jeans, and then stooped to retrieve the USB drive.

There would be more than enough time to examine the note later. For now, he wanted to get up onto the building's flat roof, from where he would have a good vantage point and be able to pick off the rider with relative ease. He found a foothold in one of the exterior walls and pulled himself up. The sheetrock and siding crumbled in his hands, but the studs beneath supported him nonetheless.

Once on the roof, the sun was almost unbearable, but he ignored the swelter and moved forward in a crouch. At the lip he tested the roof for stability and, satisfied it would support him, lay down and prepared the rifle, chambering a round with the bolt action and then laying the weapon beside him and using the binoculars to spot the rider.

It took him several sweeps to locate the man, who was about a half mile off, apparently unaware of Lucas's ruse. Once Lucas had pinpointed him, he raised the rifle and looked through the scope, mentally gauging the amount of breeze so he could adjust for any drift. He was fortunate – there was almost no wind, he could see from the motionless scrub between them, which would increase his chances of a hit with the first shot.

Lucas looked again for the rider and swallowed hard when he couldn't find him. The man had been in a stretch with groves of spindly trees and fairly dense underbrush when Lucas had looked away and taken the measure of the environment; and now he was gone.

"Come on. Where are you?" he whispered under his breath. "You can't have just vanished. Follow the trail. You can do it."

Lucas continued sweeping the area with the scope, but he didn't make out any movement. Perhaps the gunman had stopped to check the tracks? Lucas had done his best to stick to soft dirt that would memorialize his passing, but perhaps he'd overestimated his pursuer's skills.

A flash of sunlight on glass stopped him cold, and his breath caught in his throat.

It had come from the brush.

He zeroed in on the spot and found himself staring at the bodyguard who had confiscated his weapons, squinting through a scope of his own – attached to a rifle pointed at the building.

Something had tipped him off. Too late for any surprise now; Lucas was obviously blown.

He did a hasty reckoning of likely trajectory – the man was maybe seven hundred yards away. Not an impossible shot for Lucas, but he'd have to be quick about dialing in the scope, whose default setting he always kept at five hundred. He rolled away from the lip so he wouldn't be in the open and quickly clicked the range dial to the appropriate setting. After checking it to ensure he'd gotten it right, he moved to a different spot and inched to the edge of the roof for another look.

It took him a moment to locate the shooter again, and this time when he peered through the lens, he could see that the man was using a bipod for the futuristic-looking rifle. Whether or not he'd spotted Lucas on the roof would be a moot point if Lucas had calculated his range correctly. Lucas slowed his breathing and exhaled softly as he squeezed the trigger with a delicate squeeze.

The recoil was significant enough to jar the scope from the target, and when Lucas steadied it again, he scanned the brush for any sign of the man. A chunk of the roof blew off two feet from Lucas's head and he rolled to the side, cursing. The report of the big-caliber rifle reached him a split second later, telling him what he already knew: his first shot had failed to find home, and the shooter had acquired him and was firing back.

Lucas clicked the scope adjustment one more setting and stopped again. He ejected the spent cartridge and chambered another, and quickly brought the rifle to bear on the gunman, a sense of quiet dread in his heart. He had four more bullets in the gun's internal magazine, but he'd already thrown one away, and judging by the shooter's equipment, he knew how to shoot – so Lucas had to make his rounds count.

The next shot Lucas was better prepared for the recoil, and he was able to keep the scope on the target. A spray of dust four feet short of the man told him he was still off, and he rolled away again and made the appropriate adjustment before loading another bullet.

An answering shot sent a piece of drain gutter flying no more than a foot from Lucas – far too close for comfort, the gunman now zeroing in on him with deadly accuracy. The next shot would be lethal if Lucas didn't perform this time, he understood, but in spite of the pressure his hands were steady as he leveled the rifle again and took his time. He saw the man working the bolt and put the crosshairs on his throat.

The gun bucked and Lucas was rewarded with a fountain of red from the Raider. This time Lucas worked the bolt while keeping the scope on the target, but there was no movement from the man. Lucas didn't hesitate, but emptied the gun at the shooter, wanting to ensure that he wasn't met by any nasty surprises later in the day.

He lay still, ears ringing from the gunshots, watching the area for signs of life, but saw nothing. Five minutes later he lowered himself from the roof and made his way back to Tango, his job done. Lucas knew what he'd seen: at worst he had wounded the man, and at best, flipped his switch. Lucas didn't care which – in neither case would the gunman be in any shape to continue following him, which was all he cared about.

Lucas reloaded the Remington and slid it back into its scabbard with a silent prayer of gratitude. The man's shots had warned Lucas that he wasn't invulnerable. His hand went to the bandage on his grazed arm and he reminded himself to change it again later – it would be bitterly ironic if he survived numerous gun battles but succumbed to infection from a flesh wound.

He checked the time and ran a quick calculation. At a moderate pace, Tango would be able to reach the root cellar within an hour or two of nightfall – close enough. There he could graze and drink his fill, and Lucas could get the rest he'd more than earned by achieving the impossible.

Which reminded him. He climbed into the saddle and rode away, feeling in his pocket for the note. Tango, in no mood to run anymore, settled into a fast walk as Lucas unfolded the paper and studied the neat script handwritten in ballpoint.

As Sierra had said, it was complete gibberish, a series of meaningless letters and numbers in no apparent order, six lines long, with little repetition that he could see.

"Great. Just great. Risked my neck for nothing," Lucas muttered and folded the note back up, brow wrinkled in thought. The jumble of code was a daunting problem – and one he couldn't shoot his way out of. His only hope was that Ruby might have some idea of how to go about decrypting the message, because at this point it might as well have been written in Swahili, so barring a miracle, they were dead in the water.

Chapter 13

Sierra craned her neck to see why Ruby had opened the root cellar door. It was pitch black inside, twilight having come and gone an hour before, and they had settled down for the night. Eve was snuffling nearby on her bedroll, and Sierra frowned in the darkness from the sleeping area at Ruby's silhouette framed in the doorway by faint moonlight.

"Do you hear that?" Ruby whispered.

"I'm trying to sleep."

"Listen."

Sierra sighed and forced herself to her feet. She joined the older woman at the threshold and cocked her head. After listening for several moments, she shrugged and made to return to her bedroll.

"Wolves," Sierra said.

Ruby shook her head. "I don't think so."

"I heard them before, when we were on the trail from Dallas. They howl like that at night."

Ruby turned and felt in her things for the night vision monocle, and then whispered to Sierra, "Stay here."

"Where are you going?" Sierra asked, her voice now concerned.

"Take a look around." She paused. "You might want to wake Eve up and get her ready to move."

"Wake her? Why?"

"Because I said so," Ruby snapped, shorter with the younger woman than she'd intended to be.

Ruby pushed up the steps and out into the field. Jax and Nugget were standing by the trees, and they raised their heads as she approached. She approached the animals and murmured reassurance to them, and then her ears perked up at the sound of another faint lowing from the north.

Ruby hurried through the field of tall grass to a rise of hill. She stood beside an outcropping of rock and scanned the area with the monocle. The landscape was basked in a green glow, and then her breath caught in her chest when she saw men in the distance, one of them with dogs straining at their leashes.

Bloodhounds.

Moving toward the root cellar from the bunker.

Following their scent.

The party was still at least three-quarters of a mile away and moving slowly, but Ruby didn't hesitate. She ran as fast as her legs would carry her back to the cellar and whispered through the doorway.

"The cartel is back. With dogs. We have to go. Grab your saddle and kit," she ordered, and then stopped at the sight of Sierra standing just inside the door. "Where's Eve? Did you wake her?"

Sierra shook her head. "I will now."

Ruby's mouth was a thin line. "You better get with the program, or you're going to get yourself killed. If I tell you to do something, you do it."

Sierra spun and moved to the sleeping quarters while Ruby gathered her bug-out bag and saddle. She carried them outside and then headed back for her nylon saddlebags. Sierra was leading a sleepy Eve from the back, who looked up at Ruby through puffy eyes.

"We have to go?" Eve asked.

"Yes, sweetheart. And we need to be very, very quiet," Ruby cautioned.

"Okay."

"You need help with your saddle?" Ruby asked Sierra, aware that her wounds were still healing.

"If you could. How far away are they?"

"Pretty damn close."

Ruby carried Sierra's saddle up the steps as the younger woman hoisted her bags, and within minutes they had Nugget and the mule ready to ride. Ruby helped Eve up onto Sierra's saddle and then climbed onto Jax, ears straining for any sound of pursuit. She could tell by the sound that the dogs were definitely nearer, and Ruby drove the mule forward while using the monocle to see. Nugget followed at a quick walk, and when they reached the limits of the property, Ruby paused to take a bearing with her compass.

"We head that way," she said, pointing southwest toward the mountains.

"I told you they'd never give up."

"They can't move very fast. They have to stay on foot for the dogs to follow the trail, so if we pick up the pace, we should be able to stay way ahead of them."

"But they'll find us eventually. They always do."

"Not necessarily. We can skirt the river and make our way to Blue Springs. Maybe the water will wash away the scent," Ruby said. "Or at least make it harder to follow."

"Is there someplace shallow we can cross, to switch it up?"

"We can keep an eye out," Ruby said, her tone doubtful.

"You think that will work?"

"I don't know that much about tracking dogs, but I've heard they're persistent."

Sierra's voice increased in pitch somewhat with anxiety. "Then what do we do?"

"We try everything we can, and pray."

"That doesn't sound very hopeful. Maybe we should ambush them or something?"

"There are more than a dozen men, and that's only the ones in the immediate vicinity. We wouldn't stand a chance."

"We can't run forever."

Ruby nodded. "True, but we can run for a long time. Remember that they have to go slow. We don't."

"How far to Blue Springs?"

Ruby looked at her oddly. "Ten miles. Didn't you hear Lucas and me discussing it?"

"Oh. That's right." Sierra paused. "Look, Ruby, I'm sorry about not waking Eve up. I didn't want to disrupt her sleep. She's been through so much…"

"I wouldn't ask you to do something if it wasn't important."

"I know. I…I'm not operating at a hundred percent. The meds, the wounds, the stress…I guess I'm just trying to say, maybe you should cut me some slack."

Ruby bit back her impatience and drew a deep breath. "Maybe you're right. But I wonder how much slack the Crew's going to cut you?" she said, and immediately regretted it. Her tone softened. "I know this has been rough. Let's concentrate on doing the best we can. That's over now. Let's keep moving forward."

"Sounds good to me."

Ruby dug her heels into Jax's ribs and the mule lumbered ahead, Ruby directing him with the reins in her left hand and monocle in her right. She hoped that the young woman wouldn't be a liability, but Sierra's stubbornness wasn't a virtue in a survival setting, and the next time she did what she felt best rather than following instructions, it could cost them dearly.

Ruby debated saying so, but decided not to antagonize the younger woman further, opting instead to concentrate her energy forging a path through the brush and finding their way to the river. She tried to remember what she'd read about dogs following a scent, but the specifics eluded her, beyond it being almost impossible to evade them once they were on your tail. She'd tried to sound optimistic about using the river to mask their passage, but at best it would slow the animals, not lose them.

Ruby eyed a slope and directed Jax along the faint outline of a game trail. After ten more minutes, she could make out the sound of rushing water and the air felt more humid, telling her that they weren't far from the river. Once they were at the water, the animals could drink, and she could test the depth to see whether they could get across. Her instinct told her that even if the dogs picked up their scent again on the far side, crossing back and forth would further stall their progress, and every hour they were searching for a thread to follow was another for Lucas to make it to the rendezvous and help them escape. If they were lucky, it could take days for the cartel to eventually make it to Blue Springs – that was the hope, at any rate.

She didn't want to consider what might happen if Lucas didn't return. Fifteen against two were impossible odds, even if everything went in their favor; and so far, nothing had. And with only a shotgun and Sierra's AR-15, their chances weren't good in a firefight.

Ruby banished the negative thoughts. It was fruitless to dwell on the situation. For now, they were ahead of the game, and for everyone's sake, Ruby had to see to it that they remained that way as long as possible.

She shifted in the saddle and urged Jax to greater speed, aware that even under the best of circumstances the mule was reluctant to move at more than a snail's pace. "Come on, boy. Just this once, please?" she whispered, and patted his neck.

The mule continued plodding forward with sedulous determination, unswayed by the urgency in his mistress's voice, picking his way along as though they had all the time in the world.

Chapter 14

Cano watched the trackers guide the dogs around the bunker ruins, trying to acclimate them so they could pick up a scent. They'd been there since dusk, but so far they'd had no success, and he was growing impatient.

The dogs had occurred to him because of another manhunt he'd led in Houston, when a group of scavengers had absconded east with one of Magnus's drug shipments they'd waylaid. Three days later they'd been skinned alive and crucified by the side of the road as a warning to any like-minded lowlifes, trailed by dogs when all else had failed.

Their quarry had been at the bunker, Cano knew, and even if it had been days ago, the scent might still be fresh enough to follow. The alternative was having to report to Magnus that he'd failed. Better to exhaust every possibility than that.

Cano felt like a death row prisoner as he listened to the trackers discuss what to do next. They'd failed to detect anything distinctive leading from the bunker, even provided with a blanket from the hospital where the woman had been kept hostage. The dogs had led them in circles, but had stopped at the decimated interior of the concrete shelter's depths, the trail dead from the explosion. He'd already been down to look over the devastation; the bowels of the shelter had been blasted out of recognition and provided no answers about the fate of the men who'd entered.

"What do you think?" Luis asked the handler in frustration. "Can you tell anything at all?" The man lived outside of Pecos on a heavily fortified farm that did business with the cartel, supplying it with vegetables and other foodstuffs in exchange for protection and stolen goods. His pair of bloodhounds had been used with successful results twice before when a rebel faction of the Locos had splintered off and tried to mount a competitive enterprise. He didn't look particularly happy at having been summoned at dawn and forced to ride north, dogs trotting beside him, but Luis wasn't interested in the hayseed's enthusiasm – just results.

"Well, we know she was here by the way they been acting, but problem is they ain't got anything more'n that." The man's West Texas drawl was thick as tar.

"Try having them nose around downstairs again. Maybe we're missing something."

"Worth a shot, I guess. Got nothin' else to go on."

Fifteen minutes later, Luis reappeared with the handler, a frown on his face. "We found a door, but we can't get it open. But it's probably how they made their way out. Dogs were scratching at it. Behind the pantry."

"What direction does it face?" Cano demanded.

Luis looked uncertain. "South, I think."

"Fine. If there's some kind of an escape tunnel, it would have an exit. We'll have the men spread out and walk the field. Call out if they spot anything suspicious," Cano said.

"Like what?"

"Like a door that says 'This way down.' How would I know?" Cano snapped.

Luis stalked off and spoke in hushed tones to his men, the Crew gunmen gathered with them, awaiting instructions. Soon they were creeping through the high grass, their few night vision-equipped squad leaders forging through the brush and the handler behind them, waiting.

Several minutes into it, a man called out from the right. "Got something here."

"What is it?"

"Big rock. Looks out of place." A pause. "It sounds hollow. I just knocked on it. Fake."

Cano and Luis hurried over to where a Crew gunman was waiting beside a boulder. The man rapped on it and grinned, revealing gold front teeth. Cano nodded, knelt, and attempted to lift the edge, but couldn't. "It must be locked in place from the inside. Probably a safety latch to keep anyone from knocking it over."

Luis's eyebrows rose. "You think they're still down there?"

The handler arrived with his dogs, and they began sniffing around the base and then moved south with noses to the ground. Cano looked out over the field. "No. Probably long gone. But we'll soon know where."

Two hours later they discovered the root cellar, and the dogs went crazy. Cano and Luis threw the doors open, guns leveled at the interior, but found it empty. Luis scowled as he entered and sniffed the air.

"Someone was here not too long ago. Can you tell?"

Cano followed him in and nodded. "Yes. Not long ago at all."

A cry from the field brought them back up to ground level. "What?" Luis called out.

"Got a bunch of horse droppings. Some of them pretty fresh."

Cano and Luis exchanged a dark look.

"How fresh?"

"No more'n a few hours."

Cano walked over to where the man was pointing and stooped to inspect the dung. When he straightened, an ugly expression twisted his heavily inked features.

"They were here. Maybe watching us," he growled under his breath.

"Could be wild horses," the Crew member said.

"No. It was them." Cano turned and eyed the handler. "Can the dogs follow the scent of this horse?"

"They can follow anything."

"Then get them to track it and let's see where it leads."

"Ain't gonna be quick in this grass."

"Just do it," Cano ordered.

"Sure thing, boss," the handler said, and brought the dogs forward. Soon the man was trailing the animals. Cano and Luis rode behind him on horseback, the rest of the gunmen following in a ragged column. Every now and then one of the dogs would pause, sniff the air and surrounding grass, and let out a low howl to ensure he had the handler's attention before pushing forward, tail wagging at his success.

The process was stop and go; the dogs would lose the scent and root around in a confused fashion before continuing with another howl. Cano glowered at the handler at a particularly loud ululation.

"Can't you keep them quiet? They're giving away our position," he snarled.

"Sorry, boss. That's just what they do. Got to take the good with the bad."

"Whole county knows we're out here by now."

Luis drew even with Cano's horse. "Won't matter. If you're right and this is one of their horses, we'll catch up to them sooner or later."

"Oh, I'm right. I can feel it in my bones."

Luis nodded wordlessly and allowed Cano to take the lead again, uninterested in challenging the Crew boss. It wasn't Luis's neck on the chopping block if he was wrong, and it was in his best interest to play along, even though he personally found it unlikely that the woman and her rescuers would have stuck around for days after blowing the bunker sky high. If it had been Luis, he would have already been across the border and riding hard, putting a hundred miles under his belt before stopping for breath. Then again, the woman was wounded, so perhaps her condition had required her party to remain stationary so she could recover.

Whatever the case, it wasn't his problem. Cano would receive all the credit if they were successful, and take the blame if they weren't. Luis's role was to cooperate and do as ordered, keeping his head down until this storm, like so many others, had passed.

Which he would do. He didn't believe for a second that some

unknown party had broken in and killed Paco. He'd known the head of the Locos since they'd been in jail together, and figured that he'd spouted off at the wrong time to Garret – he'd always had a big mouth, and it had probably been his undoing.

A mistake to learn from, Luis reasoned; one he didn't intend to duplicate with Cano, who made the deceased Garret seem like a huggable teddy bear.

Another howl pulled him back into the moment, and he smiled at the dog's plaintive song, taking silent satisfaction in Cano's discomfiture.

Chapter 15

Two hours after leaving the root cellar, Ruby and Sierra negotiated the Black River, which was surprisingly benign in places, the water barely moving and in some cases almost dried up entirely. They took advantage of the shallow conditions to cross back and forth, reasoning that if the dogs couldn't easily find the scent for a few hundred yards, it might take them many hours to find it again, especially as Jax and Nugget were wading in several feet of water.

The baying of the bloodhounds had receded until they could no longer hear them, and Sierra was visibly more at ease. The moon had risen into the night sky and cast a pallid luminescence across the landscape, rendering everything in shades of gray. The rushing water was nearly black beneath them, making it difficult to gauge depth. They followed the river for several miles before veering off to take a secondary dirt road that was barely negotiable after years of disuse. They zigzagged along until Ruby pointed at a stand of trees near the river and directed Jax toward the water again, her hopes of losing their pursuers now stronger than they had been earlier. On foot, it could take the trackers days to piece together their trail, buying Lucas time to make his way to them.

Once back at the river, they continued along the bank, and when it became obvious the bottom was rising toward the surface, Ruby coaxed Jax further into the wash. The mule wasn't enthusiastic about the exercise but splashed along resignedly, ears twitching, offering an occasional snort or grunt when it misstepped. She'd slipped the monocle into one of her saddlebags now that the moon was up, conserving its precious battery as long as possible.

"How are you holding up?" Ruby whispered as Sierra urged Nugget alongside her.

"Pretty good. You?"

"I'll be happy when I can get off Jax. Almost as happy as he'll be. He's not used to this much exertion. He's had a pretty cushy life lately." Ruby smiled at Eve, who was sitting silently, rocking with the horse's stride, eyes drooping from fatigue. "How about you, Eve?"

"Okay," she said in her small voice. "I don't hear them anymore."

"That's good. It means they're way behind us."

"Will we get to sleep soon?"

Ruby and Sierra exchanged a glance. "I hope so. But we still have a ways to go. You look tired," Ruby said.

"I am." Her forehead creased. "Is Lucas going to be able to find us?"

"That's the plan."

"When he does, he'll know what to do," Sierra said, her tone confident.

Eve nodded solemnly. "My bottom hurts."

"It's a lot of riding," Ruby agreed. "Mine does too." She paused. "Sierra, have you told us everything you know about Shangri-La?"

Sierra seemed taken aback. "Of course. I mean, it's pretty easy, since I don't know much in the first place. It's supposed to be safe and have power and is run the way things used to be. Civilized, in other words."

"And you believe that?"

"A lot of people risked their lives so Eve could make it there. They obviously thought it was important. So I'm giving them the benefit of the doubt." Sierra sighed. "We'll see when we get there, won't we? If it isn't all that, what have we really lost?"

"Assuming Lucas finds the vest."

The younger woman nodded, her face unreadable in the darkness.

Nugget's front hoof slipped off a treacherous submerged stone, and Eve's eyes widened as she pitched sideways. Sierra struggled to control the mare with the reins, and then the little girl's balance passed the tipping point and she fell off the horse, hitting the water with a loud splash. Eve cried out in alarm as Sierra fought with Nugget, the horse now panicked as the bottom dropped away unexpectedly and she suddenly found herself in chest-deep water.

"Eve!" Sierra cried.

The child's head disappeared from view; the current was not as gentle as they'd guessed in this stretch.

Ruby brought Jax up short and leapt from his back, flailing with her arms, trying to locate Eve. Jax stopped in his tracks, unwilling to go on, and she splashed toward Nugget, her footing unsure as the water pulled at her legs with considerable force.

"Do something!" Sierra screamed. "She can't swim!"

Ruby continued toward the horse, forcing herself to move faster. Eve's head popped from the surface ten yards downstream and she coughed water before going under again. Ruby gritted her teeth and abandoned trying to walk, instead diving forward as the river deepened and swimming with unsteady strokes.

"Eve!" Ruby managed as the little girl's face rose out of the river five feet from her, and she groped for her as Eve sputtered, gasping for breath. Ruby's fingers latched onto the child's shirt, and she pulled her nearer as she felt for footing. The bottom was suddenly shallower, explaining the rush of current as the river narrowed, creating a funnel effect.

Eve coughed water and Ruby clutched her to her chest, keeping her head above the surface as she struggled toward the bank. And then, just as quickly as things had come unwound, they were both in knee-deep water, Eve clearing her lungs and struggling for air.

Sierra dropped from Nugget and moved toward them, taking ginger steps as Ruby supported Eve. The little girl's hands were on her knees, her head bowed, hair hanging as she coughed.

"Are you all right?" Sierra asked as she neared.

Eve didn't say anything. Ruby nodded. "She'll be okay."

"I…I don't know how to swim myself, or I would have gone in after her."

"Don't sweat it. I got to her in time." Ruby eyed her. "Besides, probably not a great idea with your chest wound. It's healing nicely, but you want to avoid anything that could increase the chances of infection, and a dunking in this river probably isn't the best idea."

Eve gasped again and Ruby thumped her on her back. "Does it feel like you have water in your chest?"

Another hacking cough, more frothing spray, and then she took a big gulp of air and shook her head. "Don't think so."

"Let me listen," Sierra said, and leaned over to place her ear against Eve's back. After a few deep breaths, Sierra straightened. "Doesn't sound bad."

Ruby guided Eve to the bank, where she lay shaking, Sierra beside her. The older woman went after their mounts and led Jax and Nugget to them. Eve looked up at her apologetically. "I'm…sorry," she said.

"It wasn't your fault."

"You got all wet."

Ruby shrugged. "Nature's way of telling me I needed a bath. No harm done." Ruby brushed a lock of hair from her forehead. "You think you can ride now?"

Eve nodded.

"Okay, then. I'll help you back up once your aunt's in the saddle."

Sierra hoisted herself onto Nugget and used her good arm to take Eve from Ruby's arms. When Eve was seated, Ruby gave Jax a pat, and he flicked his tail. "All right, big boy, maybe we'll stick to dry land for a while. That work for you?" The mule greeted her question with stoic indifference, and she remounted the mule and directed him up the bank.

Ruby didn't complain, but her leg was throbbing from where she'd struck a stone during the rescue, and her back burned in protest from the unexpected exertion. She was reminded again that she wasn't a young woman any longer, but forced herself to shrug off the pain – she'd been through worse and was still standing, and if a few bruises and bumps were thrown her way, she'd take them in stride. After all, she had to be alive to feel pain, and most she knew no longer were. In that light, anything but death's hand on her shoulder was reason for optimism, she reasoned, and goaded Jax to greater speed. She was anxious to get away from the spot, unwilling to assume that their pursuers hadn't heard Sierra's yells.

The older woman was again struck by how composed Eve was. Even after her dunking, she hadn't cried and had recovered quickly without any drama.

"Thanks, Ruby. You saved her life," Sierra said quietly.

"Over and done with," Ruby said in a whisper. "Let's keep it down while we ride, okay? Don't want to attract any more attention than we already have."

"Of course. Sorry," Sierra said, and fell silent.

Ruby didn't respond, preferring to keep her own counsel rather than continue to engage. There was no point reprimanding Sierra for her cries and not much to be done about it other than to continue making their trail as difficult and convoluted to follow as possible, and pray that circumstances worked in their favor.

Ruby rocked side to side with the mule's stride, lost in thought as Nugget's hooves on the gentle slope of the gravel bank accompanied Jax's faster gait, the mule's short legs working like small pistons as they pressed into the desert night.

Chapter 16

Lucas paused on the trail that led toward the root cellar and tilted his head as he listened. An otherworldly baying drifted to him on the light breeze, and Tango stamped a restless hoof. Lucas's eyes narrowed at the sound and he dismounted. Another howl confirmed the need for caution, and he led the big horse to a grove of saplings and tied him to one. After giving Tango some water, Lucas set off at a jog, night vision scope activated on his M4, the rifle held at present arms.

When he arrived at the tree line, he stopped and surveyed the area by the root cellar through his NV scope. The horses and riders were easy to spot, as were the dogs – the source of the howls. He cursed under his breath as he watched, and slowly backed away when he was sure that the group hadn't taken the women captive; the obvious hunt for their trail confirmed that they'd somehow escaped.

He debated attacking the gunmen; the element of surprise was on his side and the newly acquired grenade launcher made a great leveler, but he discarded the option. It would be stupid given that he didn't know how large the total force was, and if he wasn't successful, it would leave the women at the mercy of the cartel without him to defend them.

The other possibility was to shoot the dogs, but he couldn't bring himself to do it. Besides, it was easier said than done, with a force of several dozen men firing at him and giving chase.

No, his best option – which he didn't kid himself was a great one – was to ride to the rendezvous.

Which meant that he was now in a race to reach them before the gunmen did. The only bright spot in the scenario was that he knew where the women had gone – a considerable advantage that meant he could easily beat their pursuers to the punch. It would mean more night riding, but given that he knew where most of the bad guys in the area now were, the risk seemed slight.

He made his way back to Tango and saddled up, and then guided the horse south, skirting the property and giving the search party a wide berth. Once out of earshot, he debated whether to take the most direct way to Blue Springs or a more circuitous route; he opted for the latter in case there were multiple teams of trackers working. He had no idea when the women had left, nor when the miscreants had shown up, and it was more than possible that this wasn't the first group to have worked the site.

Lucas recalled Sierra's warning that the Crew would never give up looking for them, and had to give her credit for calling that one correctly. He wouldn't have believed that their Loco cartel minions would have expended the effort to not only return to the bunker, where so many of them had met their end, but to locate and enlist tracking dogs – it wasn't as though you could shake a stick and find those.

He glanced at his watch. If he was careful, he could reach Blue Springs by sunup or shortly thereafter. He just hoped that Ruby had the presence of mind to wait for him and hadn't gotten spooked by the reappearance of the bad guys on her property. He didn't think so, but people did strange things under pressure.

There was only one way to find out.

"All right, buddy. Sorry to put you through this, but we're going to have to keep going," Lucas murmured to Tango. The horse had been on the trail all day and had to be nearing the end of his endurance. If Lucas didn't want to find himself walking, he'd have to give the stallion ample chances to rest on the route west – there were practical limits of what the animal could physically do, and Lucas was sensitive to the fact that he'd already put in a herculean effort.

Lucas allowed Tango to meander in the general direction of Blue Springs as he thought through their next step. They would need to find a safe place to go to ground – the springs would be a temporary solution, but they needed to put some serious distance between themselves and Pecos, and staying in the area of Loving was obviously a bad bet. But given the topography, there were few viable alternatives. West led into the mountains, which might be good for disappearing, but would be lousy for survival, especially when one of the region's storms hit. East was effectively desert for over a hundred miles, with unknown dangers and, worse, was headed back toward the Crew's territory. South lay the Locos and Raiders.

Which left north. The problem being that he didn't know much past Loving, having had no reason to explore and potentially expose himself to danger. He knew that further along the highway lay Carlsbad, which was another armed encampment like Loving had been, and then Artesia, and past it, the larger city of Roswell, but if the cartel had put out the word about Sierra and Eve, which Lucas figured they had, any of those places could result in them being betrayed in exchange for a reward.

That one would be offered was a given. It was what Lucas would have done under the circumstances, and with the stakes as high as they were, it was bound to be a big one.

Maybe they would do best to split up?

Certainly, that would be the smartest for Lucas's and Ruby's survival – they weren't the direct object of the manhunt. But Sierra and Eve would be dead meat. Just a matter of time.

No, he'd have to come up with a plan that would enable them to go to ground in a safe place and try to figure out what the note said. But no matter what, they couldn't stay in one place very long. Remaining stationary for even a short period was inviting detection.

The thought didn't bother Lucas much. He had nothing to go back to at the ranch, and Ruby had lost everything, so life on the road was no worse than waiting to fall prey to scavengers or the other marauders that roamed the badlands.

Lucas glanced up at the stars, and the sight of the heavens stretching to infinity calmed his racing thoughts. He'd figure something out. He always did. And now that Sierra and Eve were depending on him, he had no choice but to perform.

The white scar of a dirt road through the brush appeared on his right, and Lucas directed Tango along its shoulder for an hour before again opting for a game trail that led off into nothingness. The night air was still as the moon rose higher, and he found himself checking the luminous dial of his watch more than normal, keenly aware that he hadn't slept much and wasn't as sharp as he'd have liked. Once off the road, their progress slowed to a crawl, and when they reached the Black River, he took a breather and let the horse drink its fill and munch on the grass that carpeted the tree line.

A fox darted down the bank to Lucas's right, and he had to fight to get his heart rate back down. That was no good – he was getting spooked by stimuli that he'd have normally taken in stride. Deciding to occupy his time productively, he cleaned the Remington by the water's edge while Tango went about his business. His stomach rumbled, reminding him that he hadn't eaten dinner, and he removed the container of jerky from his saddlebag and chewed six ounces of it, remembering how his grandfather had taken such pride in the brick oven he'd constructed with ample space on either side for smoking.

Hal had prized skills like canning, gardening, and smoking food, as well as the ability to repair most mechanical items with whatever was at hand – a characteristic he had laughingly referred to as Mexican engineering – never intending it in a disparaging way, but rather admiring the ingenuity the neighbors to the south regularly employed to keep things operating even in the face of poverty and adversity it would have been impossible for most Americans to imagine, at least, before the collapse.

Now, with the population reduced to primitive conditions, pre-collapse Mexico would have seemed like a wonderland of riches, Lucas knew from his trips across the border. It was ironic to him that the rural peasants there had probably suffered less of a culture shock than his kind had. Hal had pointed out repeatedly that the world's poor made do with almost nothing, so the lack of running water or electricity or any but naturally grown medicine had changed little in their day-to-day lives. The man who had spent his entire life walking six miles to a river every morning since he'd been a boy to catch fish so the family could eat probably did the same thing now, the idea of a car or television or the Internet as alien to him as the notion of space travel. That man likely hadn't seen his existence impacted much from the collapse of modern society, whereas more developed nations had been devastated, and the ensuing chaos had opened the door for a descent into de facto civil war between competing factions of predators.

"They first raise up those the Gods would destroy," Lucas whispered to himself. There was some truth to that. The mighty had farther to fall, and America's almost total dependence on its government to provide everything the population needed had proved to be its Achilles' heel. Knowledge of the features of the latest iPhone or winning hacks to the newest video games had proved poor substitutes for rudimentary survival skills, and most had quickly perished, having evolved in just a few generations from a species that lived off the land to one of privileged consumption, many unable to do the simplest things for themselves.

And how they'd turned on one another when desperate! The most striking thing to Lucas in the weeks following the collapse had been how lacking most had been in a sense of community – an essential element of civilization that might have saved many turned out to be entirely lacking in the engineered isolation of modern life. Because most didn't know their neighbors and were unaccustomed to helping those in need, when things had broken down they'd had nothing to fall back on and had gone at each other like dogs. In the end, the every-man-for-himself ethos proved a deadly one for the majority.

Only those who had lived in small, isolated communities had developed the sense of kinship that all settlements on the fringes of civilization tended to have, which enabled them to pull together for protection and to create workable solutions to food, water, and basic care problems. Loving had been a good example, but one that had ultimately misjudged the ferocity that its enemies would bring to bear on destroying what had taken years to build.

The melancholy thought saddened him, and he finished with his rifle and reassembled it before clicking at Tango to signal it was time to ride. Dwelling on the unpleasant would accomplish nothing; what was done, was done. Now his future lay in finding a hidden sanctuary with an absurd moniker against odds so tall he didn't want to think about them.

"Nobody's holding a gun to your head," he muttered, and swung onto Tango in a single practiced move, sliding the M4 sling from his shoulder as he took the reins for more hours of travel, his only consolation that he'd long since stopped hearing the baying of the hounds.

Chapter 17

Blue Springs was little more than a hundred-yard-long by thirty-yard-wide lagoon fed by an underground spring in the foothills east of Carlsbad Caverns National Park. It met the Black River in a small white water rapids that Ruby could hear well before they arrived at the oasis. The pool was surrounded by oak trees, she knew, which meant the temperature would be cooler and humid.

The spot was a popular one with the local wildlife, and the women followed a clear game trail the final distance. Both Jax and Nugget seemed as relieved as their riders to reach the destination as a faint glow brightened the eastern sky.

Ruby located the footbridge over the rapids that marked the area where they'd agreed to rendezvous with Lucas, and they made camp on the sloping bank. Beige cliffs jutted from the water around them. Jax and Nugget strolled off to forage what they could, and Ruby spread her bedroll on the gentle incline as the sun rose over the crest.

Sierra helped Eve prepare her roll and then sat down heavily on her blanket. Ruby pushed some rocks together, gathered kindling, and started a fire using her lighter. When it was crackling, she removed a dented pot with a thick wire handle from her bag, filled it with river water, and then placed it into the fire using a branch. She watched the mesmerizing flames with Sierra and Eve, waiting while the water heated.

"You hungry?" Ruby asked.

"Yes," Eve said, nodding.

"Bet there are some fish in this river."

Sierra yawned and then managed a smile. "I take it you know how to fish."

"Not hard," Ruby said, going to her saddlebags and retrieving a length of monofilament neatly wound on a plastic spool, with a small spinning lure on one end. "All you have to do is be smarter than the fish. And more patient." She pointed to where a plant hung over the water. "I'd expect that would be a good spot. Bugs will drop off the leaves into the water, and the current will be mild from where the rocks above it are breaking the flow. If I was a fish, that's where I'd be."

Eve eyed the older woman. "Really?"

"Only one way to find out."

Half an hour later, they had two reasonably sized bass cleaned and broiling over the fire. When the fish were cooked through, the three ate greedily using their fingers and washed the meal down with some of Ruby's tea. Stomachs full, Sierra moved to her bedroll, accompanied by Eve, who looked ready to drop.

"Think it's safe to catch some sleep?" Sierra asked.

"I'm sure it is. They're miles away. With all the river crossings, I can't imagine them making it here anytime soon…if at all."

"How do you want to do this?"

"One of us needs to keep watch," Ruby said, patting her shotgun.

"You've had a rough night. I can take first shift."

"Are you sure?"

"Get a few hours of rest, and I'll wake you when I can't keep my eyes open any longer. Deal?"

Ruby felt the weight of every one of her years as she battled the fatigue that had been wearing at her since the adrenaline rush of the river rescue had burned from her system. She could barely think, she was so tired, which made her decision easier – the younger woman was more resilient.

"Deal. But wake me if you have even the slightest suspicion anyone's coming."

"I will."

Ruby took another look at Eve, who was already asleep, her face shaded by the trees, and smiled. Youth was wasted on the young. What she wouldn't have done for some of the little girl's calm assurance that everything would be fine, much less her stamina.

She lay down and closed her eyes to the rush of the frothing white rapids down the bank. Her back ached and her legs felt like she'd been beaten with a lead pipe. As she drifted off to sleep, her last thought was that they were really in deep weeds if Lucas hadn't been able to find the note or, worse, never showed up at the rendezvous point.

It seemed only moments later that Sierra was shaking her shoulder. Ruby jolted awake and found herself staring into the younger woman's frightened eyes.

"What is it?" Ruby asked.

"Someone's coming."

"Dogs?"

"No."

"How far?"

"I…not very."

Ruby leapt to her feet, shotgun in hand, just as four armed men with scraggly long hair and wild beards crossed the bridge, their weapons pointed straight at her. Eve rolled over, awakened by Sierra's warning, and sat up with a shocked expression at the sight of the gunmen. The one in the lead stopped twenty yards away.

"Drop your guns," he ordered.

Sierra looked to Ruby for guidance. The older woman shook her head. If they tried to shoot it out at that range, they stood no chance – and Eve would likely be killed in the fray.

"Who are you?" Ruby demanded, stalling for time to think.

"Drop 'em, or I shoot."

Ruby slowly lowered her shotgun and placed it on the ground. Sierra hesitated, but faced with certain death, tossed the AR-15 on the bank in front of her and raised her hands. The man stepped forward. "Keep 'em high. Skeet, search 'em."

A short man beside the leader moved forward and handed over

his rifle, and then continued to the women and did a thorough frisk. He held Sierra's 1911 pistol up, examined it, and then slipped it into his waistband. When he was done with the younger woman, he approached Ruby and did the same. Ruby suffered the indignity in frowning silence, not wanting to provoke anything worse than they were already facing.

Skeet moved to Eve and repeated the procedure. Once finished, he stepped back and regarded them. "That's everything," he said.

"What're you delicate blooms doin' out here in God's country?" the leader asked.

"Point A to point B," Ruby said. "What's it to you?"

The man ignored her and spoke to the gunman on his left, his attention still fixed on the women.

"All right. Lenny, throw Skeet some rope. Tie the two young ones up, and Rick, you get the horses."

"You can't!" Sierra protested.

"Who's gonna stop me?" The man spit. "Should be glad that's all I'm gonna do. Least for now."

"You have no right."

"Got more guns. That's all the right I need."

Ruby frowned. "What are you going to do with me?"

"Everyone's got a best-if-used-by date, lady. You're way past yours."

"Who are you?" she countered.

The man offered an evil grin. "Think of us as gypsies. We trade anything we come across. Sometimes stuff, sometimes animals, sometimes people." The man paused and looked her up and down. "Nobody's gonna give us anything for you. Not even Skeet there."

"I wouldn't be so sure about that. I'm an expert with herbs and medicine. Teeth. Horses. Anything that needs attention. That's more valuable than you may think."

The man's eyes narrowed. "Yeah? Prove it."

"In my saddlebags. You'll find a ton of herbs. You know many people that carry around large quantities of herbs who don't know how to use them?"

"Billy?" Skeet asked the leader.

"Go take a look," Billy snapped, his gun unwavering.

Skeet returned a minute later with Jax. "She ain't lyin'."

"So you're going to kidnap us?" Sierra demanded.

"Way you should think about it is more like I'm not gonna kill you," Billy corrected. He looked her up and down. "Come to think about it, you match someone the boys in Pecos put the word out about. Bet they'd pay through the nose to get you back."

"You bastards…"

Billy laughed. "Got some spirit. I like that. Make the trip go by faster." His tone grew serious. "Skeet's gonna tie you and the brat up nice and gentle, less'n you give him lip, in which case it'll go hard on you."

"You don't have to tie us up."

"Don't have to do anything. But I'll feel better once you're hobbled some." He looked around. "Just you three, huh? Damn fools."

"We haven't done anything to you," Ruby tried.

"World's done plenty. Just the way it is. Eat or be eaten. Today you're the food."

"It doesn't have to be that way."

"Lady, you're starting to get on my nerves, and I only been talkin' to you for two minutes. Maybe you should shut your trap before I think twice about takin' you on a ride with us."

"Where are we going?" Sierra asked.

"I'm thinkin' Pecos might be a good start."

"Please. Don't do this. They'll kill us," Sierra pleaded. "She's just a little girl."

"Lot of misery in this here world, candy pants. 'Sides, way you look, they won't kill you. Might wish you were dead by the end of it, but nobody's gonna let a fine piece like you go to waste."

Sierra looked away. "You're animals."

"Don't hate the playah, sweet thing. Hate the game. Ain't that the expression?"

Skeet and Billy laughed together at his mangling of the old maxim.

"Now hold still, or you're gonna get hurt," Skeet said, uncoiling the rope. "Be a shame to have to hurt you – bring a lower price with a broken nose."

When they were bound, Billy whistled, and another four men appeared from the trail, all of them filthy and feral looking. They approached Sierra and admired her with Billy, who was obviously the chief of the little band, and let their horses drink while Skeet and Lenny helped Sierra and Eve onto Nugget. Ruby got no assistance, but once she was on Jax, Skeet approached and tied her wrists. "Just in case, grandma," he sneered as he cinched the knot tight.

Ruby watched him wordlessly, trying to keep any antagonism out of her stance, wary of drawing their ire – something Sierra would be well advised to figure out before she got backhanded, or worse. Sierra, as though reading her mind, looked over at her, and Ruby gave her a blank stare, hoping she'd get the message. She appeared to, because she gave a small nod and then returned to eyeing the men with a neutral expression, her anger spent now that the reality of their capture had sunk in.

"Okay. Skeet, you ride caboose on 'em. Either one tries to ride off, shoot the brat," Billy said. He dug his heels into his horse's flank, urging him up the bank and onto the trail that continued south toward a connecting road that ultimately spilled onto the Pecos highway.

Chapter 18

Lucas stopped at the shallow stretch of the Black River that immediately preceded the spill from the spring and listened intently as Tango filled up on water in the cool shade. It had taken him longer than he'd hoped, but he'd heard nothing of the dogs on his journey, so he was sure they were still well behind him. He rolled his head to loosen his taut neck muscles and ran a hand over the heavy stubble on his face – a reminder to himself that he needed a shave. He thought of his straight razor that his grandfather had given him on his eighteenth birthday, a rite of passage memento that still caused a lump to form in his throat whenever he used it.

The old man had been crusty and hardheaded, but he'd also had the unique sort of deep compassion that only those in touch with the land displayed – a kind of holistic ease with his surroundings that allowed him to empathize at a greater level than city dwellers. He'd appreciated the circle of life from raising and butchering his own animals and had taught Lucas the same lessons. The bond Lucas had with Tango was a perfect example – the two were connected in a way that was difficult to describe, but as real as anything in his life. The big horse seemed to be able to read Lucas's mind in a way that shocked him sometimes, and part of the stallion's willingness to push himself beyond any reasonable limits of endurance was a testament to that connection.

"Okay. We're almost done. Only a little more to go," Lucas said, and then his attention was drawn to three buzzards circling to the north, high in a turquoise morning sky so bright it seemed artificial. "Bad night for something," he whispered, "or someone." He led Tango from the water with a gentle tug at the reins, anxious to reunite with Ruby and show her the note.

When he arrived at the bridge, he immediately sensed that something was off. The atmosphere was tense, as though the balance of the area had been knocked off kilter, and his hand moved to the stock of the M4 as he slid the sling from his shoulder. Gun in hand, he switched the fire selector switch to three-round burst mode and lowered himself from the saddle.

The fire pit stones were still encircled, and a lazy coil of smoke rose from the ashes in the center. The spines of two bass told him that the women arrived with sufficient time to catch the fish, cook, and eat. But the fire was dying, so they couldn't have gone far. He tried to imagine why they would have come to the springs as agreed and then suddenly left, and his imagination came up with nothing good.

The sentiment worsened when he saw the trail that led south. He knelt to study the tracks, his eyes flat beneath the brim of his hat. A lot of riders, but judging by the spacing of the distinctive prints of one horse with a mangled horseshoe, moving slowly.

Lucas didn't need any more data to fill in the blanks. There were plenty of vermin roaming the wastelands, and three females on their own would have been too tempting to resist. He'd heard no shooting, so they'd been taken by surprise, likely exhausted after an all-night ride. He didn't have to struggle to imagine just how tired, as his own muscles were sore from the trek – and he was accustomed to days in the saddle and had a better mount.

His gaze swept the clearing, searching for any other clues before he went after them. Unfortunately, the gravel riverbank left no footprints, so he was left with only the fire and the trail and his experience with the region's miscreants to connect the remainder of the dots.

There was no blood on the stones, which was a positive. And

whatever lead the group had on him would be trivial – the fire told him that much.

So it would be a matter of tracking whoever had grabbed them and dealing with them without the females getting hurt in the process. A tall order, given that he was only one man on a tired horse, who hadn't slept for thirty-six hours.

But if there was a way, he would find it. He hadn't traveled as far as he had only to lose his charges to some roving gang.

That it wasn't the cartel was obvious to him. There was no physical way they could have made it ahead of him since they had no idea where they were going. So at least it wasn't the Locos – not that any of the alternatives were much better. Raiders, scavengers, criminal gangs, the desperate and the sadistic…

You could never let your guard down. That was the lesson he'd learned over and over again: expect the worst, prepare for it, and if you feel safe, you're probably in danger of being killed.

"Sorry, Tango. I lied," Lucas said. Tango took another bite of grass and gave Lucas a long-suffering look, as though he'd already pieced together that any rest he'd gotten was short-lived. "Let's hit the road, buddy."

Lucas led the horse to the track and continued to walk beside him, reasoning that the poor beast had done more than his share over the last day and a half. It would do Lucas good to stretch his legs, as well as make it easier to note any discrepancies on the trail.

He'd ridden this one before on his jaunts into the foothills following herds of mustangs, and knew its twists and turns relatively well. Depending on how far ahead they were, he might be able to get past them and find an opportune area to lie in wait. There were several spots that could work, but first he needed to get a look at what he was dealing with.

The other complication was that the moment he started shooting, the cartel would be alerted and come at a gallop. Ten miles might have been a lot of distance stumbling around in the dark toward an unknown destination, but once they heard shots, they'd home in on the source like attack dogs, and then any meager advantage Lucas possessed would be finished – and it would be a bloodbath. Lucas wasn't anxious to invite that, and if it was possible to handle his current problem more tactfully, he would.

He checked the time and sighed. The sun had only been up for a couple of hours, and the day had already turned completely to crap.

Chapter 19

The scrub along the side of the trail turned from green to beige as it meandered further from the river, and the soil transitioned from hard-packed clay to loose dirt. Lucas had mounted Tango after walking for nearly half an hour and peered through his binoculars every few minutes in the hopes of seeing dust. That he hadn't told him that he had either badly misjudged the timing of the women's departure, or the group was moving at a walk and being careful not to leave any evidence of their passage.

The latter was the most likely, but also implied a more difficult target for him. He preferred reckless amateurs like the Raiders if he was going to have to do battle. Stealthy riders savvy enough to take precautions bode poorly for his chances of getting the drop on them – they'd be paranoid as their normal state, which would make his job more difficult.

Lucas rounded a bend and spied several doves rising over the brush no more than a quarter mile ahead of him. He stopped Tango and swept the area with his binoculars, and caught a faint beige tint to the sky just above the horizon – the telltale dust that a decent-sized party would be unable to completely avoid no matter how careful they were.

Half a mile away, he guessed. No more.

He recognized the area and eyed a rock monolith to his right that had been carved from the earth by millennia of flash floods. If they stuck to the path, they would pass through a dried riverbed framed by dense vegetation – perfect for his purposes. Lucas could see it in his mind's eye and nodded. Depending on the size of the party, it could be enough.

Keeping the attack surgical would be the challenge. He weighed the benefit of trying to get closer to assess the strength of the group and decided it was worth the risk. There was no point attempting to take on a force he couldn't overcome without jeopardizing the women.

Lucas urged Tango toward the landmark and cut to the east, sticking to brush in order to avoid stirring up any dust. It made for harder going for the stallion, but there was no choice if he wanted to avoid detection. His mind worked furiously as he rode, trying to figure out how to avoid drawing the cartel to their position once the shooting started, but he couldn't see any way around it. Which meant that the best he could do with an exhausted horse and the women in tow, assuming he was successful in freeing them, would be to choose the location of the confrontation.

When he had flanked the group, he cut back, sticking to the east so the sun would be at his back, knowing from years riding that the natural inclination was to avoid staring in the direction of its glare. He hoped that between the element of surprise and his orientation, he could avoid detection and size up his adversaries.

He lowered himself from the saddle and brought the spyglasses into play, and found the trail. A quick survey told him that they hadn't passed yet, so he'd been successful in the first part of his ambition.

Five minutes went by with the only sound the buzzing of a persistent fly around his face, and then he saw the first riders come around the bend. He counted heads and exhaled in relief when he spied eight. Sierra and Eve were near the end of the ragged procession, and Ruby and a gunman brought up the rear.

The men looked filthy and half starved; their clothing was little more than rags, their hats tattered and stained, their skin burnished the color of pecans by constant exposure to the elements, and every inch of them coated in trail dust and grime. Yet for their appearance, they rode in an orderly fashion and showed sufficient field know-how to keep a low profile. Their horses were as thin as they were, ribs jutting through their hides like washboards, but had the easy gait of animals who'd spent their existence on the road – unlike the domesticated creatures of the pre-collapse world, most horses still alive were working mounts expected to go until they dropped.

Three of the men wore plate carriers, but like their clothes, their gear looked worn and frayed. Still, Lucas would have to shoot around the body armor if he was to make each shot count.

The outline of a plan began to form. There were a few relics of utility buildings ahead on the trail where he could fire from cover as they neared, leaving them out in the open with no place to hide. The challenge would be to avoid hitting the women, which would require precision shots rather than bursts from the M4.

Eight riders, eight bullets, if he did this correctly. The Remington's superior range over the hardware the gunmen were toting would be his edge once the shooting started. The scope was still set at seven hundred yards, at which distance he would be deadly while they would be ineffective.

It could work.

He returned to Tango, removed the Remington, and dialed back the adjustments to what he reckoned was six hundred yards, which would be more than sufficient edge, given the AKs and ARs he'd seen. The trick would be to maintain a disciplined pace as the gunmen scrambled for nonexistent cover.

He would keep the M4 ready for when a few inevitably closed in. There was a limit to how long they'd take his fire and watch each other fall before desperation made them rush him, thinking he only had a single-shot weapon.

Lucas drove Tango through the brush until he reached the buildings, tied the horse out of sight in the shade of one, and set up in the other. He placed several magazines for the Remington by his side, along with six spares for the M4 for when it got sloppy.

He didn't have long to wait.

The first riders came into view, and Lucas held his fire until the final man was in his crosshairs. Because he was moving so slowly, that would be the easiest shot. Lucas took his time, watching the gentle sway from the horse's stride, and then caressed the trigger with even pressure.

The gun bucked against his shoulder and he watched a ruby blossom appear on the left side of the rider's chest. Lucas was already twisting the adjustment one notch to correct for the breeze that had caused the drift, and then worked the bolt and chambered another cartridge as the column disintegrated into a confusion of panicked horses and startled men.

His second shot drilled the rider next in line from the women, this time dead center of his chest, high in the sternum. He flew back off his horse as it bolted, and it dragged him by one leg as it ran for the hills. Lucas worked the bolt again with calm deliberation, his gaze through the scope unwavering. As he'd hoped, the remaining six gunmen were disorganized, two of them trying to ride into the nearly impenetrable brush in order to evade his shots, the other four dropping from their horses and opening fire at the building with ineffective fury.

Another of his rounds caught a rider in the back, and he fell. The gunman was one who was wearing a plate carrier, but Lucas had fired low, calculating that the body armor wouldn't reach his lower spine, given its fit. Lucas didn't dwell on the downed rider, but switched to the remaining man, who was struggling through clumps of prickly pear, his horse all but stopped by the natural barrier.

His attention was drawn momentarily to Ruby and Sierra; they'd wisely remained on their mounts, who'd turned tail and run in the opposite direction from the shooting. Every step took them further out of harm's way, and he returned his focus back to the rider.

A few slugs thudded into the cement wall to his right as Lucas pulled the trigger again. The shot missed, and Lucas swore and reloaded as more rounds found the building. So the ragtag scavengers had found the range even with their limited-accuracy weapons, which presaged a final rush, he was sure. He fired at the horseman, and this time was rewarded with an explosion of blood from the man's torso and a scream that split the air like the cry of a wounded calf. More rounds thudded into the building and one ricocheted off the wall behind him; it was only a lucky stray that had entered the window, but still potentially deadly if his good fortune ran dry.

He switched magazines and loaded another round, his ears ringing from the long gun's report. The surviving shooters were on the ground, presenting smaller targets but stationary ones, which made all the difference to Lucas. His next shot vaporized the top of the nearest man's skull, and the gunman slumped over his weapon.

That acted as the catalyst for the charge Lucas had been expecting. The men fired and screamed like it was a Civil War reenactment as they ran toward the building – a classically amateur suicide run that worked no better in present-day combat than it had in the old days. Lucas set the Remington aside and held his fire until the men were three hundred yards from him, their magazines emptied, creating a lull in the onslaught. They jettisoned the spent ones as Lucas peeked over the bottom of the window with his M4, and then he was firing three-round bursts, cutting the men down without mercy.

It was over in less than ten seconds, even those with flak vests terminally wounded or dead once their body armor failed. Lucas waited until he was sure nobody was in any shape for a final bite at the apple and stepped through the building entrance, M4 pointed at the downed men.

Lucas was halfway to them when a burst of automatic fire coughed from his right, and he dove for cover. One of the riders still had some fight in him – probably the one hit in the lower back, he thought grimly. The rounds missed Lucas by a fair margin, but still, the snap of incoming bullets shredding the air by his head was a sensation he'd never get used to. He waited for another salvo and, when it came, returned fire, burst after burst as he drove himself to his feet and ran for the dead shooters, intent on using their bodies for cover.

Another volley echoed through the brush as he threw himself amid the downed men and got a fix on the shooter's location. When more shots sounded, he narrowed in on the likely area and saturated it with five three-round bursts.

He swapped magazines, but there was no more shooting. After he was sure he was out of danger, Lucas rushed into the brush to confirm that he'd neutralized the last gunman, and looked down at the scavenger's bloodied form.

Lucas then spun and ran as hard as he could toward Nugget and Jax, who were clomping away, now at least four hundred yards down the trail.

"Ruby! Sierra! Stop!" he cried between gasps, his energy waning now that the battle was over. Ruby must have heard him because she reined the mule to a stop and looked back over her shoulder.

"Lucas!"

Sierra turned Nugget and they rode back to where he was bearing down on them. He slowed to a stop and waited as they approached, and only saw their bound wrists at the last moment. Lucas unsheathed his big Bowie knife and made short work of the rope and, when he had freed Ruby's hands, repeated the effort with Sierra and Eve. Once they were untied, Sierra helped Eve down and, after dismounting, hugged Lucas impulsively, as did Eve from behind. Lucas stepped away after a long moment and patted Eve's head for lack of a better response.

"Who were they?" he asked softly.

"Gypsies. Trail bums," Ruby said. "Looks like a bad day for them all around."

"Thank God you found us," Sierra said. "They were going to sell us to the cartel. There's a reward."

"That's not going to happen," Lucas said, looking away from Eve's piercing cobalt eyes.

"How did you find us?"

"Followed your trail."

"So you know they're searching for us–" Ruby said.

Lucas shushed her with a curt gesture and cocked his head.

"What is it?" Sierra asked.

"If I could find you, so can they," Lucas said quietly. "I heard dogs."

"I know. We outran them, though, and hid our trail. We'd hoped…"

He tried to keep the impatience from his response; he knew the women must be half panicked as well as exhausted. "Hope isn't a great defensive strategy. See if you can find your guns – I'm guessing they took them away. Once you do, Sierra, try to catch one of their horses – you can see one over in the brush, hanging around, grazing. Maybe Eve can ride it, or Ruby. But we don't have all day. We need to try to make some decent time, because they're on their way, no doubt about it."

"The shooting," Ruby said, nodding, realization clear in her expression.

"Right," Lucas said. "Let's move."

"What are we going to do?" Sierra asked.

"You're both okay?"

"Just beat," Ruby answered.

Lucas eyed the dead men and frowned. "Hopefully not too tired to shoot. We've got work to do."

"Shoot?" Sierra blurted.

"They aren't going to quit. You said so yourself. So it's either them or us. I prefer us."

Ruby looked him over. "You ride all night?"

"Been a rough few days."

"Did you find the USB?" Sierra asked.

"We'll talk about it later. Go find a horse. Ruby, gather up as many of the full magazines as you can, as well as the best-looking AKs." He paused. "You ever shot an AK?"

She looked away. "It's on my bucket list."

Lucas turned to the corpses.

"Then you're in luck."

Chapter 20

Cano stood at the bank of the Black River, glowering into the murky water while the bloodhounds tried to pick up the scent again. The night had crawled by with agonizing slowness; their quarry had zigged and zagged through the water in a vain attempt to throw the hounds off the scent – which told him they had heard the dogs and were alerted to their pursuit.

There was nothing to be done about the speed, but he was on edge, sleep-deprived and tense, his stomach a ball of burning acid. Luis was watering his horse beside him when the sound of distant gunshots echoed through the canyon. Luis glanced up as everyone froze, and then Cano was in motion.

"What's over that way?" he demanded.

The dog handler shrugged. "Blue Springs. Not much else till you get to the caves."

"Caves?" Cano repeated.

"Carlsbad. Famous. Ton of 'em."

Luis nodded. "I heard of them." He paused. "You think they might be headed there?"

"Which direction are the caves?" Cano asked.

"Due west. Past the spring."

More shooting sounded, and Cano strode to his horse. "Luis, stay with the dogs. I need ten good men to come with me."

"What are you thinking is going on?"

"I don't know, but I plan to find out."

"You think it's them?"

"Could be. But listen to that. Sounds like a pitched battle. Could be somebody else. Let's split up, and you keep working the dogs while I go ahead."

Luis nodded. "Makes sense."

"They've been trying to make it hard for us to follow them, and it's worked. This may even things up," Cano said.

"Told you nothin' throws the hounds off for good," the handler said.

"Yes, but it's too slow," Cano complained.

"Been at it all night. Even dogs get tired."

"Ten men," Cano repeated. "Five of mine, five of yours in each group."

Luis called out to the assembly and selected his best troops. They mounted up and followed Cano west along the river until they arrived at the spring. Cano swung down from the saddle and inspected the bank, and then nodded to himself as he approached the fire pit. He held his hand over the ashes, felt the rocks, and stood.

"Radio Luis. Tell him to get over here. They must have just left," he ordered. One of the cartel gunmen activated his two-way radio and spoke into it as Cano continued studying the perimeter. When he was done, Cano motioned to him. "See that?"

The man joined him and looked to where Cano was pointing. "Tracks."

"Want to bet the dogs go ape when they get a whiff of them?"

The gunfire had stopped a few minutes earlier. Cano paced impatiently as they waited for Luis's entourage to reach them. When they did, he led the handler to the track. The dogs howled and strained at their leashes, and the man nodded.

"That's them, all right."

"Let's go," Cano ordered, and returned to his horse and climbed into the saddle. They followed the handler, who was being nearly dragged at a trot down the trail, the dogs issuing joyful howls periodically to signal that they were on the scent. They covered a mile that way, and Cano called out to Luis impatiently, "I want to ride up ahead. Leave two men with the dogs and bring the rest. We know this is their trail – there's no need to go so slowly now."

Luis selected a pair of gunmen and relayed the instruction. Cano was already riding ahead, tailed by the remainder of the cartel force. Luis scowled at the sight of his men following anyone else, but bit back the natural resentment that rose in his throat.

"Eyes on the prize," he reminded himself quietly, and galloped after them. A full-scale war had erupted within shouting distance, and he was stumped as to what it meant. They'd been tracking only a couple of horses, according to the dog handler, but based on the gunfire, they were now dealing with a small army.

The question being who was shooting at whom, and why.

Luis frowned again. He wasn't big on horseback riding, preferring the town and its relative stability. He was tired, he ached, and now he was riding into a question mark – and the unknown could easily get you killed.

He didn't like it, but he was committed.

One thing he could definitely say, though, was that he hoped he never incurred the wrath of the Crew, because based on Garret's, and now Cano's, tenacity, their reputation for never letting go was well deserved.

A timely reminder to himself to stay on their good side at all costs.

Fifteen minutes later, Cano slowed and studied the two corpses by the side of the trail. Further along, four bodies lay in the dirt, already bloating from the heat, their faces covered with flies.

"What do you make of that?" Luis asked, drawing even with him.

"Could be they rendezvoused with this lot, and they got ambushed. That's what it looks like to me."

"How can you read that from six dead men?"

"You see any women here?"

"No."

"Then she's still alive. Simplest explanation is they were attacked by somebody, and either these were the attackers, or they died defending themselves." Cano paused. "Those are the only scenarios I can think of that make any sense. Did I miss anything?"

Luis had to give the man credit – his mind worked at lightning speed. "Sounds about right to me."

Cano nodded slowly as he eyed the dead. "Damn right it does."

Luis regarded his men and then turned to Cano. "Now what?"

The corners of Cano's mouth wrinkled with a lupine grin. "Now we finish the job."

"What about if there's more where these came from?" Luis asked, indicating the corpses.

"Then they'll have company in hell soon." He thought for a moment. "Get the handler and the men here. They're wasting time."

Luis nodded, his face a blank at being ordered around. Cano spurred his horse forward, eyes on the trail, the imprints of the departing horses as clear as a painted line stretching through the desert scrub.

Chapter 21

Lucas shifted behind the rocks where he had taken cover, binoculars glued to his eyes. Ruby and Sierra sat beside him; a little ways off, Eve was keeping the horses company beneath the shady spread of a tree. They were on the eastern ridge overlooking a canyon through which the trail passed, having ridden along the wash to lead their pursuers into the narrow passage, and then climbed a track at the far end before circling around the top.

He'd thought through the best location to take on a large force, and the only way he could see them prevailing was if they had the high ground and the gunmen were boxed in. The canyon was well suited to the purpose with its sheer walls; the sun would be in the gunmen's eyes as the blistering orb ascended in the sky. They would wait until the riders were almost directly beneath them and then open up on them, the Kalashnikov rifles they'd taken from the dead gypsies on full auto in the women's hands, Lucas's M4 on three-round burst.

Beside him lay the green canvas bag in which he'd placed his precious four hand grenades, next to which he had the Milkor launcher and the spare 40mm projectiles. He hoped he wouldn't have to use them – if things went according to plan, he wouldn't need the range. Then again, things often didn't, and it was better to be prepared for the worst than caught by surprise.

"Okay. When they enter the canyon, hold your fire until I give the signal," Lucas said. "Then just spray them with bullets. We want to hit them hard and fast before they can react. That's our best chance of walking away from this." He paused. "Ruby, you focus on the last ones. Sierra, you shoot at the front of the group. I'll take the middle."

The women nodded. "You really think this can work?" Sierra asked.

"We have no choice – we need to make it work." He looked to Ruby. "Are you clear on how to cock your rifle and eject the magazine?"

Ruby smiled. "I may be old, but I'm not an idiot."

"You'll want to get behind that cluster of boulders, Sierra," Lucas said, pointing to his left. "And Ruby, you take that one. It'll put you into perfect position. But under no circumstances shoot until I tell you to. You go off half-cocked, and we're screwed. Keep your fingers off the trigger until you want to shoot, and don't just fire indiscriminately. Give it a short squeeze, get used to the kick, and then empty the magazine once you can control your aim. Worst case, shoot low. The barrel will tend to rise."

"You think you can hit them with the grenades?" Sierra asked, eyeing the bag.

"Got a good throwing arm."

"How many men do you think there are?"

"I saw plenty, so I'm going to say twenty or so."

Sierra nodded. "I'm a little scared."

"That's normal. But a word of warning – it's all going to happen fast. So you have to stick to your plan, and don't panic. Once the shooting starts, don't freak out or you'll fumble your magazines or make stupid mistakes. Try to stay calm, and understand that your ability to be methodical is your big advantage. They're going to be caught in the open, surprised, bullets everywhere, on horseback. Use that advantage – don't throw it away. And don't close your eyes. That's a rookie mistake. A lot of people close them and just shoot, hoping for the best. Force yourself to stay focused."

She eyed him with a frown. "You sound so confident."

"Because I've been through my share of this in just the last week.

It gets easier every time. But I remember how I felt the first time, and it's scary."

"I was in the gulley, remember?"

"Then you know." He turned to Ruby. "You going to be okay?"

"I don't scare easy," she said, her lips a bloodless line.

One corner of his mouth twitched, and he nodded. "No, I'll bet you don't."

The sound of hooves from the north drew Lucas's attention back to the canyon, and he raised his binoculars. "Get into position," he said as he peered through them. "And remember – hold your fire. Put your spare magazines beside you so you'll be able to reach them easily."

They scrambled away and Ruby called over her shoulder, "Good luck."

"You too."

Lucas watched as the first riders appeared, all of them wearing plate carriers, but most with their weapons strapped on or in scabbards – a small piece of luck in a game where seconds would matter. He spotted two furry forms loping at the rear of the line, their leashes taut. Their handler was obviously tired even from a distance; his movements were slow and his stride hesitant. The party slowed as the trail became more uneven in the wash, and Lucas counted twenty-three men, a third of them covered with prison ink, identifying them as members of the Crew. Which didn't matter – they would die just the same as their Loco brethren. As long as they stayed grouped tightly as they negotiated the canyon, they'd be sitting ducks.

Lucas held his breath as the riders entered the funnel-shaped gulch, and estimated the time it would take for them to reach the spot directly below him. Thirty seconds, no more. He lowered the binoculars, felt for the grenades in the bag and removed them, and placed them by his side, ready to be thrown.

Something spooked the lead rider, a monster of a man who sat tall in the saddle, and he slowed further, eyes scanning the canyon walls before moving to the crest. Lucas looked over to where Sierra was crouched behind the boulders, her AK at the ready, and nodded to himself. He checked Ruby and saw that she already had her rifle pointed at the riders, and he waved at her. She glanced over, and he signaled for her to back away. She did, and he winced as the wood stock of her AK scraped against the rocks.

The column kept coming, the lead man with his weapon clutched at his side, as if some sixth sense was warning him of an impending attack. Lucas waited with a grenade in hand as the group made its way along the wash until they were near his optimal range, and then called out in a stage whisper to Ruby and Sierra with another wave.

The women moved into position, and Lucas pulled the pin on the grenade and lobbed it over the edge, and then followed it with another without waiting to see the effect of the first. Ruby began firing, and Sierra's rifle joined the older woman's moments later, and then Lucas's M4 chattered staccato bursts as he waited for the grenades to detonate.

Many of the women's first rounds went wild, but at the close range they were able to adjust their aim quickly, and some of the riders fell to the ground. Lucas targeted the lead rider and stitched three rounds at his chest, praying that the plate carrier would shatter and at least one would make it through and take him out. Only one struck the man, knocking him backward from the impact, and then the first grenade exploded no more than twenty feet in front of him, which threw him off his horse. Four of the men behind him were also knocked from their saddles, guns flying from their hands as shrapnel tore through them, and then the second grenade detonated in the midst of the procession, raining havoc among the gunmen and turning man and beast into hamburger.

Lucas's rifle barked again and again at the surviving gunmen, and within thirty seconds all but three riders and the dog handler were neutralized. Those at the back had turned and galloped for the canyon mouth, and in spite of Ruby's best efforts, had made it beyond easy range of the Kalashnikovs, riding for their lives. A few of the downed men tried to take cover behind fallen horses, but Lucas shot them without compunction as they moved– the costlier this little adventure proved for the Crew and the cartel, the less appetite they would have for any more of the same.

Ruby's third magazine emptied and she was slapping a fourth into place when Lucas screamed at her, "Enough!"

Ruby looked at him, eyes wild but her mouth a determined line, and stopped shooting. "What? They're getting away!" she protested.

"Doesn't matter."

"But the dogs…"

Lucas set the M4 aside and raised his Remington. "Don't sweat it."

He sighted on the handler, who was running for all he was worth, the dogs bounding ahead of him, and squeezed the trigger. His shot caught the man in the center of the back and knocked him forward like he'd been struck by an invisible fist. Lucas ejected the round and chambered another, but his next shot missed the last of the riders, and he sat back and shook his head.

"God…" Ruby said, and then leaned to the side and vomited up fish and tea.

Lucas took deep breaths, calming himself, and then peered over the rocks again at the carnage below. Nothing moved; the wash ran red with blood, the bodies of horses and men intertwined.

"What about the dogs, Lucas?" Sierra demanded, and he rubbed a hand along his jaw before responding.

"I got the handler. They won't be back."

"But they know…"

"The trail will be cold by the time anyone gets it into their head to try this again. They lost most of their men. I doubt they're going to mount another effort."

"What if you're wrong?"

He spit to the side. "Haven't been yet."

Sierra had no rejoinder and fell silent. Lucas pushed himself to his feet and gathered the remaining grenades, the Milkor, and the spare rounds, and shouldered his M4 sling before carrying his Remington to where Tango waited. Eve looked at him with trepidation, and he realized that his face must have been frozen in a frightening expression. He exhaled and tried a smile.

"Are we okay?" the little girl asked hesitantly.

"Yeah. All taken care of."

She visibly relaxed. Sierra joined him moments later and set her rifle down to hug Eve. Ruby made it to them half a minute later. Her complexion was as gray as her hair, and a cut on her cheek streamed crimson where a rock chip from a ricochet had sliced it open. She wiped away blood and stared at it absently, and then pressed her sleeve against the gash to blot it.

"I never want to do that again," she said.

Lucas nodded. "There was no other way." He considered the women and shrugged. "It's over."

Ruby nodded and waved away his concern, a vacant look in her eyes. "It's…it's horrible. How can these animals do this kind of thing every day?"

Lucas slid his Remington into its scabbard and patted Tango's flank. "They're not like you, Ruby."

Nobody commented on his use of the word *you* rather than *us*.

There was no need.

Chapter 22

After circling around on foot with a pair of branches to erase any evidence of their tracks, Lucas led the way east. He seriously doubted that the cartel would be able to find anyone willing or skilled enough to employ the dogs again, but there was no harm in taking precautions. Likewise, he had little fear that the few survivors would try to give chase – like all cowards and bullies, once their superior numbers had proved useless in winning the battle, the stragglers would continue on their way back home, tail between their legs.

Even if he was wrong, he knew the area better than they, and with only three riders remaining, he wasn't worried. The cartel gunmen would have to first find them and then work up the appetite to confront them – neither likely, given that the Locos were a city gang, unlike the Raiders, and were out of their element on the range.

He'd discarded the idea of riding down into the canyon to retrieve the dead men's weapons, preferring to put distance between himself and the site of the battle. They'd won a hard-fought lead, and wasting it on scavenging would be stupid. The women were anxious to be rid of the area too, and he couldn't disagree – the sight of all the dead strewn where they'd fallen was a gruesome reminder of the savagery that was now their everyday norm. He'd said a short prayer, commending their miserable souls to judgment, and they'd ridden away from the mountains.

"Where are we headed?" Ruby asked.

"There's a decent place to camp for the night about twelve miles away," Lucas said. "Figure four hours at this rate, maybe more, given the terrain."

"Is it safe?"

Lucas shrugged. "Safe as anyplace, I suppose."

"Shouldn't we try to get further away?" Sierra asked.

"Horses have about had it. Can only push them so far, and then they'll be of no use. They need rest." He paused. "So do we."

They reached the campsite in the late afternoon. It was sheltered by a high bluff and featured a creek below where they could rinse off and water the animals. There was plentiful vegetation around because of the moisture from the brook, and after Lucas removed the saddlebags from their backs, the horses, followed by Jax, picked their way to the water's edge while Lucas set up camp, taking care to deploy his tripwires so they'd have plenty of advance warning if anyone tried to sneak up on them.

They ate much of Lucas's remaining jerky and then settled in to sleep in the shade of a sprawling black willow tree as the sun continued its arc west. Lucas took the first watch, and they agreed that Ruby would take the second in three hours. He regarded the exhausted females with mixed feelings as they fell asleep – on the one hand, they were a responsibility he didn't want or need; but on the other, they represented hope for the future. Eve stirred as though reading his thoughts, and he smiled at the little girl's angelic face, haloed by her unruly dark locks, as she slumbered.

He removed the note from his pocket and studied it, but with no better results than before, the jumble of characters just as meaningless to him. That their fortunes lay in deciphering the note worried him, but he was too tired to give it more than a passing thought. More pressing was that they were out of provisions and running low on ammunition – either of which could cost them their lives. More survivors died from exposure, thirst, and starvation than at the hands of gunmen, and Lucas was acutely aware that those naturally occurring hazards were as deadly as anything man-made. Infection was the other fatal risk, he reminded himself, and he checked his arm wound, which thankfully seemed to be healing with no complications.

Time passed slowly, and he was relieved that a constant scanning of the horizon detected no dust. Their gambit had worked, and they were clear of their pursuers – although he understood it was a temporary reprieve. It was just a matter of time until another expedition was mounted, but by then they'd be long gone.

The question was to where.

For now, mundane realities like food were the most pressing, and he'd have to deal with those before thinking bigger – tomorrow, come morning, once they were all rested. For now, he needed to turn off his brain and get some rest as soon as his shift was over.

When the three hours was up, he shook Ruby awake. She sat up with a yawn and looked at Eve and Sierra.

"That was way too short," she grumbled, and Lucas nodded.

"I agree. But it is what it is." He hesitated. "You think we can depend on Sierra to keep watch when you're done?"

Ruby frowned. "She was guarding us when the gypsies grabbed us. Not saying it was her fault, but they were right on top of us before she sounded the alarm."

"You think she nodded off?"

"I don't want to say yes, but the truth is I don't know."

"Then I don't want to chance it."

"We can split duty with her, if you're worried. That way we'll both get at least some rest."

Lucas nodded and fished in his pocket for the note. He handed it to her with a grimace. "That's the encoded message. See if you can make anything out of it. I can't. I've tried, but it's all Greek to me."

Ruby squinted at it in the waning light. "Nothing jumps out at first blush. But I've got nothing better to do while on watch, so let me see if I can spot any patterns. It can't be that complicated if the guy with Sierra referred to it and was able to decode it in his head."

"That's what I figured."

Lucas unfurled his bedroll and lay down with his M4. "Wake me if you see anything. Even if you just think someone might be out there.

I'd rather have a false alarm than be surprised."

"I will."

Lucas unstrapped his watch and gave it to her. "Wake Sierra in three hours. You take the first half of her watch with her, and I'll take the second."

"It's going to be a long night like that."

"That's life."

Lucas had barely shut his eyes when he was awakened by Sierra's voice. She and Ruby were talking in the dark, and he pushed himself to a sitting position.

"Oh. Sorry, Lucas. I didn't mean to wake you up," Sierra said.

"You need to keep your voice down," he warned.

"I was," she insisted.

Lucas looked at Ruby, who was clutching the note in her left hand and the AK in her right. "Any luck?"

"I tried the likeliest combinations, but nothing." Her jaw clenched. "It's so frustrating. I mean, I could write a program to try thousands of different possibilities if I had a computer. Trying to do this manually could take forever."

With a sweep of his hand, he gestured to the surrounding area dimly lit by the vaporous glow of the moon from behind high clouds. "Don't see any Apples around here, Ruby. Try your best, but don't make yourself crazy with it."

"Good advice. Go back to sleep. I'll wake you when I'm tired. I got some sleep this morning, so I'm more rested than you."

"Not as young, either," Lucas said.

"Don't remind me." She smiled. "But we fossils require less sleep. About the only plus to it I can see. And don't worry. We'll keep quiet."

Lucas glanced at Eve beside him and nodded before lying back down. "Wake me when you're ready."

Ruby set the AK down and sighed. "Will do."

He drifted off to the sound of Ruby and Sierra discussing the note in hushed whispers, frustration evident in their subdued tones. The sound faded as he lost consciousness, and his final thought was that they would need a miracle to make sense out of the gibberish he'd gone to such lengths to obtain.

Chapter 23

Sweat coursed down Luis's face in spite of the cooling breeze from the west as the sun sank behind the mountains, his eyes on the crest above the canyon from which the shooting had erupted. He crept toward the scene of the massacre with cautious steps, leading his horse on foot. His two surviving men followed close behind, weapons at the ready, although they were all sure that the ambushers had long since absconded. They'd waited until dusk, unable to help any wounded in the barren wash, and were returning to load up on the force's weapons and ammunition – better to have those stores of wealth than to leave them for someone else, Luis had reasoned.

They'd managed to recover two of the downed men's horses that had bolted during the attack, and the last gunman had secured their reins to his saddle horn and was walking them along with his own. The rout over the last week had been devastating for their numbers – in just a matter of days, the cartel had gone from two hundred strong to no more than thirty-something – so every bit of gear would be precious in attracting new recruits.

Luis was stunned at how rapidly everything had fallen apart. He'd gone from the new leader of a still reasonable force to the head of a handful of survivors, which made the cartel's hold over Pecos tentative at best, and with it, their power base.

Luis sighed. There was no more cartel – the Locos existed only in their minds. Cano had made that clear enough. Now that their numbers were negligible, they would be absorbed into the Crew without discussion – leaving Luis to explain to his men why they had gone from rulers of the town to subordinates to anyone with Crew ink on their face. He didn't expect it to go down well with his men, but since the alternative was execution, they'd get used to it, he was sure.

Vultures flapped from the corpses when Luis and his men entered the gap, and orbited overhead as Luis moved to the first body, his nose wrinkling as he neared. The carrion birds had wasted no time, and much of the man's face was gone. Luis reached down and scooped up his AK and slid it into his saddlebag before looking over his shoulder. "Get the magazines and pistols," he instructed, and his men scrambled to obey his order. "It'll be dark soon, and I want to be out of here by the time the sun sets."

The men went to work, moving from body to body, picking the dead clean and packing their things in the saddlebags of the spare horses. Luis was going after an AKM lying on the shale when he heard a groan from behind him. He spun, his AK in hand, and searched for the source of the sound. It came again, and Luis abandoned the AKM in favor of approaching the survivor to put him out of his misery.

Luis froze when he saw Cano lying on his back. His plate carrier had been shredded by shrapnel, and the rocks behind his head were stained crimson. The grenade blast had left countless wounds on his legs and arms, and his face was crusted over with dried blood. Luis neared the man and knelt beside him to hold two fingers to his neck, and stopped when the Crew boss's massively muscled chest rose as he inhaled.

"He's alive!" Luis called to his men.

They rushed to join Luis and stood over Cano, mouths open in disbelief. The shorter of the pair shook his head. "He's not going to make it. Best to put a bullet in him and get it over with."

Luis frowned. "He's of value alive. None dead."

"Look at him. No way he survives."

"He's tough. He might."

"With wounds like that? It's a miracle he's still breathing."

"Get his plate carrier off."

The pair removed Cano's flak vest, and Luis studied his torso, which was largely intact where the ceramic plate had protected him from the shrapnel and the single round that had hit it over his right pec. Cano groaned again, and Luis nodded slowly.

"We need to get him back to Pecos."

The gunmen exchanged a glance, and the shorter one looked doubtfully at Cano. "Whatever you want, boss. But he's gonna be dead before we're halfway home."

"Maybe, but we need to try." Luis pointed to the corpses. "Finish with the weapons and then we'll deal with him."

The men obeyed, the sun working against them, the scraggly trees at the top of the crest casting long shadows as the light faded. If the man made it, he would owe Luis his life, which would guarantee that the Locos remained largely unmolested by the Crew or at least became an autonomous branch of the organization. At least, that was Luis's hope. Whether things worked out that way was a different story, but he had nothing better, so he'd play the cards he had.

Which right now, was a piece of hamburger who looked like he was moments from the grave.

Not a great hand; but still, better than being out of the game entirely.

And you never knew. Some folks were just too mean or stubborn to go gently. Cano appeared to be that kind. Luis had known others like him – inmates who'd been stabbed a dozen times yet just kept coming, intent on killing their attackers, and had lived to tell the story. They were the most feared in the yard, and Luis had no doubt that to ascend to a high position in the Crew, Cano had to have been cast from the same sort of clay.

So they'd spirit him back to Pecos, and if he died en route, leave his body for the scavengers.

For now, though, he was Luis's insurance policy – one that he didn't plan to squander.

Chapter 24

Lucas awoke to a spangling of sunlight against his face, the rays reflecting off the stream's surface like yellow fire. He rolled to the side and rubbed his eyes, then sat up. He'd swapped duty with Ruby and taken her slot in the wee hours of the morning, and now she was sitting with quiet calm, surveying the horizon through his binoculars.

She set the glasses down and glanced at Lucas. "Well, good morning."

"Morning." Lucas twisted to where Sierra and Eve were still asleep. "Any breakthroughs on the code?" he asked quietly.

"Afraid not. Although I did have a thought."

Lucas waited for her to voice it with raised eyebrows. "And?"

"We could really use some computer power."

"You said that yesterday. We don't have any."

"I know. But I was thinking that I know someone who does." She paused. "Or at least, who did the last time I spoke with him. It's been a while."

"Someone has a working computer?"

"Don't be so surprised. I had one in the bunker. All you need is electricity. It's not like every laptop in the world stopped working when the grid went down."

Lucas nodded. "Makes sense. Where is he?"

"Artesia. Or at least, he was."

"You don't sound too sure."

"He was complaining about his situation up there last time I talked to him. He might have moved on." Ruby hesitated. "I wish they hadn't destroyed your grandfather's radio. I could have called him."

"Got a lot of wishes," Lucas agreed, and then his eyes flitted to where Eve was shifting and yawning as she awakened. "My buddy Duke has a radio. I was thinking we should go by there to stock up anyway. Two birds with one stone if you can reach your friend."

"That would be great."

Lucas regarded her. "What's his story?"

"He's a computer geek. Programmer, nerd, the whole nine yards."

"Not a lot of calling for that these days."

"No, but he can fix just about anything. Solar, batteries, you name it."

"Seems like I remember the doc talking about a guy from up north like that – he could fix anything. But he said the fella was a nut job."

Ruby nodded. "He's definitely eccentric."

Lucas studied her face. "How well you know him?"

"So-so. We had mutual interests."

"You ever meet him in person?"

"Couple of times."

"You trust him?"

"Much as I trust anyone these days. More important, we're not going to figure out the note without some processing horsepower and some know-how. Right now I'm shooting in the dark. So is he better than nothing? Absolutely. Is it a lock? Nothing is."

"What's his name?"

"Bruce something…Combs, I think. But I'm sure about the Bruce."

Sierra coughed and sat up. Ruby stood and stretched. "How far are we from Duke's?" she asked.

"Maybe a couple hours' ride." He looked to Sierra. "Morning."

"Good morning. Did I overhear you saying we're leaving?"

"Yep. Either that or starve."

"Do we have time to clean up?"

"Sure. Just don't dawdle."

"Yes, sir," Sierra said with a half smile, and held out her hand to Eve. The little girl took it and they walked together to the stream. Lucas eyed them as they left and turned to Ruby.

"You get enough sleep?"

"More or less. You?"

"About the same." Lucas paused. "You really think this Bruce character can help with the note?"

"I have no idea. But I do know that I can't figure it out on my own, and he's the only one I know I can reach out to. I've tried some substitution cyphers, but to have a chance at making those work, it's trial and error. If you don't know what the actual characters to be substituted are, it's almost impossible to figure out – which is where a computer comes in. If you write the program correctly, it can try a million different variations in the time it takes to go to the bathroom. So unless we have unlimited time to decode the note, that's our best bet."

Lucas nodded. "Part of me thinks this may all be a wild-goose chase."

"Not like we have any other options, do we?"

"True." He smiled grimly. "What do you make of Eve?"

"Make of her? I like her. She's whip smart and very mature. And she likes horses. Why?"

Lucas debated telling her about the odd feeling he had about the child, but decided it would sound crazy to give voice to his thoughts – thoughts he hadn't fully processed. She was undoubtedly mature for her age, but that wasn't it. There was something more to her, something he was having a hard time defining.

Whether or not it was important was hard to say. He couldn't see how; but then again, you could fit under a microscope what he knew about children – especially females. He'd had a hard enough time figuring out the adult versions, much less the new models.

"Probably nothing. She's just…really calm, you know?"

"Could be post-traumatic stress, Lucas. Or delayed shock. What do we actually know about her?"

"Just what Sierra's told us."

"Exactly. We have no idea what she was subjected to while she was a captive. But I think we can assume the worst, judging by the stories." Ruby contemplated the rushing water of the stream for a moment before she spoke again. "Besides, even assuming that Sierra did tell us the whole story, think about what it must have been like. Whole town dead. You're all alone. Then the monsters come and take you prisoner. Next thing you know, you're in a strange place, being experimented on. I don't know about you, but it doesn't take a lot of imagination to see how that could scar a youngster. Remember before the collapse, the news stories of the child soldiers in Africa? Six-, seven-year-olds who had killed dozens of people? I remember seeing a special about them on TV. They had a similar detachment. Maybe that's just how you get by in an impossible situation – you pretend it isn't real, that it isn't happening to you, that it's not you doing the things you're being forced to do. If they…if there's more to it than what Sierra let on, you can see how that would be a natural reaction."

Lucas nodded. "That might be it. I hadn't thought about it that way."

"She's just a child, Lucas. She's been to hell and back. That's going to leave its mark."

"Quite a world we live in, isn't it?"

"We didn't choose it, Lucas."

"Nobody did." He stopped. "Except scum like the cartel. Or Magnus. This is their wildest dream come true."

Ruby rose. "Seems like the devil's turn at the wheel, doesn't it?"

"Can't say as I understand much, Ruby, but for the life of me, the thought of what those animals do to innocents like Eve…"

"All we can do is counter it with good, Lucas. And believe that eventually sanity will be restored. It doesn't stay dark forever."

"It does for people like Hal. He's gone. Nothing's going to bring him back."

"True, but a part of him lives on, Lucas. Like a chain. He passed on his good to you, and now you pass it on to others who need it."

She held his gaze. "Seems to me Eve needs it. And so does Sierra."

"You really believe it's that simple?"

She shrugged. "Sure. And no. Life's complicated, but in the end, far as I can tell, it's a sequence, like programming code. We're born, we think we're special and different, and as we get older, we recognize ourselves in others and see the commonalities. And it occurs to us that everyone who came before us also felt the same specialness, that same sense of being different and uniquely important. When you get to be my age, Lucas, you'll see that there's nothing but patterns everywhere for those whose eyes are open. Things are complicated on the surface, like each snowflake is intricately unique, but they're all snow. Age teaches you to recognize the snow and stop being so concerned with the differences." She offered a smile. "Try having a little faith in the species, Lucas. It's not all bad."

"Hard to believe you're saying that after yesterday."

"Everything happens for a reason." She sighed. "Think we can risk a small fire so I can make some tea? Probably be all in our stomachs for a good stretch."

He looked around. "Can't see where that'll cause too much harm."

"Then gather some wood and get it started, young man, while I freshen up."

With that, Ruby followed the path down the stream, leaving Lucas to ponder unsolvable mysteries while she cleaned off the road dust and prepared for another hellish day. Lucas looked over to where Tango was considering him with equine dignity. "You know everything, don't you? You're just watching me fumble around for fun. Don't think I don't know your game," Lucas said, and then smiled. Talking to his horse once a day seemed reasonable under the circumstances. "Just don't make a habit of it," he muttered, and then went in search of enough kindling to warm Ruby's charred pot. The pungent concoction she brewed would offer slim relief from the miles of misery they'd have to endure that day under the sun's relentless fury.

Chapter 25

Duke's compound was sealed shut, and Doug stood manning the guard post beside the gate with weary resolve. When they had approached within hailing distance, Lucas waved a greeting and called out, "Duke around?"

"Sure. Just the four of you?"

"That's right."

"Stand by. I'll open the gate."

The iron barrier slid aside and Lucas rode through the gap, followed by the women. Doug closed the panel behind them and yelled to the main building, "Duke! Got company."

"Who is it?" Duke's voice called from inside.

"Your buddy." Doug looked at Lucas. "The Ranger."

Duke poked his head from the doorway and eased himself down the stairs, clad only in shorts, revealing a hirsute midriff and shoulders that would have been the envy of any orangutan. "You back for more abuse?"

"Got some goods for you, you old pirate."

Duke eyed the women, and his stare stopped at Eve. "What are you in the market for?"

"Food. More ammo for my long gun and the M4."

"What're you bringing?"

"AKs. Random pistols."

"There might be a swap in there," Duke allowed, and considered

Sierra for a moment. "Look a damn sight better than the last time you were here."

She offered a smile. "Thanks."

"Horse treating you okay?"

"She's a good one," Sierra said, patting Nugget's flank.

"Practically gave her away." Duke looked over at the gypsy horse Ruby was now riding. "Where'd you find that barn-sore nag?"

"Had a run-in with some desperados. They felt bad about their misdeeds, so they gave us their guns and horse," Lucas said.

"Ah," Duke said, his face impassive. "You have that effect on people."

"Need to use your radio, too."

"Yeah?"

"I know. You're going to charge me to use airwaves now."

"Think of me as the local office of the FCC," Duke agreed. "But I'll be reasonable."

"Always a first time," Lucas allowed.

"Go ahead and let your horses drink. I'll have one of the boys get them some hay." Duke watched as Lucas dismounted. "Locos are all stirred up about you."

"Yeah?"

Duke eyed Eve. "Offering a big reward."

"No kidding. You tell them anything?"

He frowned. "What do you think?"

Lucas nodded. "Appreciate it."

"You're turning into one of my best customers. I feel like I've got a vested interest in keeping you alive."

"A regular Samaritan."

Duke grinned. "Runs in my veins. Can't help myself."

"Occupational hazard," Lucas agreed.

Duke turned serious. "Let's see the goods."

Lucas spread the gypsies' sad collection of AKs and pistols on the ground, and Duke eyed them with thinly disguised disgust. "Pile of junk."

"Seen better, won't argue that. But I don't want much for them, either. Some food. Few rounds of 5.56 ball. You'll come out ahead."

"Have to hang on to 'em till hell freezes over."

Lucas nodded. "Shouldn't be long now."

Duke issued a long-suffering sigh and motioned to them to accompany him into the building. "I'll send Aaron out for this mess. Don't want it stinking up my place."

"Diamonds in the rough. Little oil and elbow grease, they'll be good as new."

"I expect that sorry mule could drop better out of his backside."

"Mule? You mean the unicorn?" Lucas said, and both men cracked smiles.

They followed Duke inside, and Lucas nodded to a sleepy-looking Aaron. The Duke gave his man terse instructions, and Aaron went to gather the weapons. The trader padded to his customary seat and plopped down, rubbing a hand over his belly as he considered the newcomers. "Well, go ahead and take a load off. You're making me nervous standing around like that."

"Need as many dry goods as you can muster," Lucas said, lowering himself onto a threadbare sofa that smelled of mildew. Ruby sniffed at it and sat on the arm. Sierra and Eve pulled chairs from the dining set and sat to their left.

"Got a decent amount."

"Good. Could use another hundred rounds of 5.56."

"Cleaning me out of the stuff, huh?"

"Been busy."

"Target shooting, I expect."

Lucas shrugged. "Idle hands."

"That's it?"

"And the radio."

"Who you going to call?"

"Easter Bunny."

"I think he monitors channel seventeen."

Lucas and Duke prepared containers full of the dried jerky Duke prepared in a homemade smokehouse in the back, and when he was done counting out rounds for Lucas, they began the negotiations.

Lucas had to part with some of the AK magazines and ammo they'd scrounged as well, but all in all it was a fair trade.

The trader escorted Ruby to the radio and powered it on, and then moved aside, giving her some privacy. Lucas leaned into him as she adjusted the channel selector and broadcast a call.

"This reward you mentioned. The Locos stop by in person?" Lucas asked.

Duke nodded. "Like you thought they would. Bastards were downright impolite till I schooled 'em on their manners."

"How much they offer?"

"Enough so every lowlife in Texas will be after your scalps."

"If it's the same bunch that tried to bushwhack us in the desert, you'll be doing a fair business in coffins."

"Glass is always half full."

"They say anything useful?"

"Don't think they know about the girl, if that's any consolation."

Lucas nodded. "Was hoping they wouldn't. That's a break."

"Big guy who did most of the talking seemed awful anxious to find your girlfriend there. Looked like he'd fallen into a threshing machine face first. Name of Cano. Lots of prison ink. Tattoo matches hers," Duke said, tilting his head at Sierra. "Know him?"

"Can't say as I do. All the same in the end." Lucas waved a fly away. "Appreciate you sticking up for me."

Duke frowned an acknowledgement and looked away.

A tinny voice answered Ruby over the speaker, and she had a cryptic conversation that sounded like a foreign language to Lucas. When she was finished, she pushed back from the radio and stood. Lucas raised his brows inquisitively. "Well?"

"He's there. Said he'd be expecting me."

"That sounded like that kook up north, in Artesia," Duke said. "What's his name? Bill? Bruce? What you want with a nutter like that?"

"Got an electric razor needs fixing," Lucas said. "Appreciate it if you'd keep that under your hat."

"I see nothing."

Lucas shouldered the satchel containing the ammo and hoisted the containers with the food, and then Duke escorted them from the building. On their way out the front door, they were interrupted by Slim emerging from the back. The man nodded to Lucas and eyed Duke. "You need any help, boss?"

"No, I got it," Lucas said.

Slim's eyes roamed over Sierra and came to rest on Eve. He shrugged and cleared his throat. "Then I'm going back to bed."

"No problem. Got it handled," Duke said, and then they were outside in the swelter. Nugget and Jax were waiting expectantly; the gypsy horse looked stunned at having eaten as much hay as it could manage. Duke watched as they mounted up and shook Lucas's hand. "Be careful out there. I hear the natives are restless."

"That's the rumor," Lucas said. "Thanks again. Might not see you for a spell."

"Kind of figured. Probably best to lie low."

"Got that right," Lucas said, and then gently tugged Tango's reins. The big stallion spun and made for the gate, trailed by the women's mounts.

Duke watched them ride through the gate and shook his head as they disappeared from view. "*Vaya con Dios*," he muttered, and turned to the building, where Slim was standing in the doorway. "Thought you were hitting the sack again?" Duke asked.

"Have to use the can," Slim said, and walked to the outhouse, his face unreadable, his heavy steps those of a preoccupied man.

Chapter 26

A day after being found half dead in the dry wash, the Crew boss lay on the steel top of a conference table as a gray-haired man with a neatly trimmed Lincolnic beard and heavy black-rimmed spectacles dug pieces of shrapnel from his wounds.

The man had been working steadily for several hours and occasionally paused to wipe sweat from his brow with a grimy hand towel. The atmosphere in the room was oppressively hot even with the windows open and a fan consuming some of the precious electric power from the rooftop solar array. Other than the low hum of the fan, the only sound was the occasional clank of another piece of metal dropping into an aluminum trash can by the side of the table.

Luis entered and stood with arms folded across his chest, his face somber as he watched. When the man finished with the thigh he'd been working on, he wiped away the blood from Cano's leg with a rag, this one soaked with moonshine, and then stepped back from the table and took a deep swig from a bottle near the window.

"Steady the nerves," he said to Luis, whose face could have been carved from granite.

"What do you think?"

"That if he comes out of this coma, he'll wish he hadn't."

Luis's eyebrows rose. "You think he'll live?"

"He's tough as nails, so nothing would surprise me." The man took another swig. "That's both legs. I'll get to the arms next, and then his head. Don't think I can do anything about his left eye – you

133

can see it's filled with blood. That's above my pay grade."

"Not going to be winning any beauty contests, is he?"

"He can always join the circus."

The man dropped the pair of bloody forceps he'd been using into a tray filled halfway with alcohol, and made a face. A veterinarian who patched up cartel members when they were wounded, his knowledge of basic surgical procedures was better than anyone's in the area, but that wasn't saying much. He'd transitioned from cats and dogs before the collapse to being a human physician, catering to a crowd that wasn't particular about where it got its care.

"How much longer?" Luis asked.

"At least another couple, three hours. Don't want to rush it."

"Can you control the bleeding?"

"You're welcome to apply pressure wherever you want, but it's like playing whack-a-mole. He's clotting okay, though, so I don't see anything worse than the blood he's already lost."

Luis shook his head. "How the hell is he still alive?"

"The short answer is none of his vital organs were damaged, and other than the eye, the wounds on his face and head are flesh wounds. Doesn't look like anything penetrated all the way through his skull, and his body armor saved his lungs and heart. He probably won't be in a romantic mood for the next forever, but that's the least of his concerns."

"What about after you're done?"

"I'll pour another bottle of this fine elixir all over him, salve him with antibacterial ointment, and dose him with fish antibiotics for a week. If he doesn't die from that, none of his wounds will kill him. All of which is assuming his body can replace the blood loss – his pressure right now is almost nonexistent. I will say he must have the heart of a bull to have gone through this and still be breathing." The veterinarian grimaced. "Then again, looking at his older scars, this ain't his first rodeo. Man's been sliced and diced more than a few times."

"If you can save him, I'd owe you," Luis said quietly.

"I expect free drinks for the rest of my life."

"And you'll get them."

The man went back to work as Luis watched, methodically going over every inch of maimed skin, flushing the wounds periodically with either rotgut whiskey or boiled water, humming to himself as the fan blew tepid air through the stifling space. They'd brought Cano to the same hospital where the woman had been imprisoned only three rooms down, and the irony that their former captive had inflicted this damage on a prison-hardened Crew boss wasn't lost on Luis.

"If you need anything, call me. I'll be down the hall in the lobby. Too hot in here for both of us," Luis said.

"Not going to fight you on that one."

Luis made his way to the hospital foyer and stood at the open glass doors, where two cartel gunmen guarded the entryway. Bullet holes in the walls lining the corridor were a stark reminder of the recent battle fought there, which had cost the cartel more of its dwindling members. Already Luis had begun to hear grumbling from the remaining Locos that the locals seemed less docile – which, if allowed to escalate, would mean the end of the cartel's stranglehold over the survivors, whom they needed for growing food and doing the work that the cartel was too busy to do for itself.

He'd instructed his men that any act of rebellion or insubordination was to be greeted in the harshest possible manner, and that those suspected of agitating against the cartel were to be hauled into the public square in front of the courthouse headquarters and shot as a lesson to the rest. He had no compunction about carrying out executions, having done so for years as the number two Loco, but he feared the effectiveness might be temporary – when the two hundred or so surviving townspeople figured out that there were only a few dozen Locos and that the Crew gunmen weren't permanent, it could get ugly once they departed.

Luis's handheld radio crackled, and one of his men called his name from the tinny speaker. Luis pressed the transmit button and raised the radio to his lips. "What is it? Over."

"Bitch who sells us grain just back-talked me. Over."

Luis knew the woman. She was an older widow, hard as flint and short of temper. He also knew that she'd be hard to replace if they executed her. But if he allowed her to get away with dissing one of his men, the act could start a wildfire…

"Drag her to the square and we'll whip her until she's bloody," Luis ordered. The spectacle should serve the same purpose as a killing. The townspeople would see that the cartel was still in charge and would think twice about resisting. But that would only last so long. He needed to recruit more men, and soon.

"You going to come for the fun? Over."

"Wild horses," Luis said. "I'll be there in ten. Don't do anything until I get there. Over."

"Roger that."

Luis returned to the improvised operating room and took a final look at Cano. "I've got to get going. Have one of my men call me if he dies or if you need anything."

Another clank as a piece of shrapnel hit the bottom of the trashcan. The veterinarian didn't look up. "Will do."

Luis made for the door, where his horse was tied beside the front façade in the shade, anxious to get to the square before his men arrived with the woman for the flogging. He needed to keep up appearances, and he'd learned from Paco that nothing established pecking order like administering punishment in front of his men.

He reached up to where a bullwhip was coiled by his saddle horn, and his fingers grazed the woven leather.

Time to work up a sweat. If the woman survived, she'd carry the scars till her dying day and would never back-talk a Loco again. If she didn't, they'd leave her to rot in the square until the carrion birds had cleaned her bones, sending an unmistakable message to anyone who felt like crossing swords with the cartel: do so and perish.

Chapter 27

The trek to Artesia from Duke's trading post took two grueling days. The first night they camped northeast of Malaga, a ghost town south of Loving that had been abandoned after the collapse. They set up on the bank of the Pecos River, where Lucas and Ruby caught sufficient bass to feed everyone, if not in a particularly appetizing manner. The following morning they were underway just after dawn and gave Loving a wide berth, as though mere proximity to the site of the recent atrocities might contaminate them.

Nobody spoke as they rode past the town's walls in the distance. Lucas's mind filled with vivid recollections of the dead; his grandfather's face flooded his memory, and he blinked the image away, intent on spotting any present threats – there would be time enough down the road to grieve for Hal and the rest, and he couldn't allow his mind to wander.

The horses' hooves on the dusty trail drummed a relentless cadence as the sun ascended in the sky, and when they neared Carlsbad, they stuck to tracks that skirted the remnants of the town, preferring to pass unnoticed by the residents so as to leave no trail for the cartel to eventually follow.

The reward that Duke had warned him about would make life harder on them – if they'd broadcast it over the radio, then anyone could be a turncoat. Still, there were limits to the cartel's reach, and the further they traveled from Pecos, the less weight the group had.

His bet was that nobody would give them a second look once they were almost a hundred miles north of the Locos' stronghold, the offer of a reward an empty one to those who'd never seen one of the cartel members in their lives.

As they neared Artesia, Lucas and Ruby held a hushed discussion, riding side by side.

"He's expecting us tonight?" Lucas asked.

"No. He probably didn't expect us to push so hard. I'd guess tomorrow morning."

Lucas nodded. "Good. Then our arrival will be a surprise."

Ruby gave him a dark look. "I see this trip hasn't been good for your trust issues."

"I don't trust anyone."

"Exactly."

Ruby had assured him that her discussion with Bruce had been coded so any eavesdroppers wouldn't know what to make of it, but a coil of anxiety was wound tight in Lucas's stomach as they neared the man's spread on the outskirts of Artesia, a medium-sized berg that had been reduced to a fraction of its pre-collapse population. Bruce lived in a single-wide trailer surrounded by barbed wire, just inside of the perimeter fence the militia had erected to protect the town's border.

Two armed locals barred their way as they approached the entry to the inhabited area and advised the travelers to keep their hands where they could see them as they drew closer to the gates. It was nearly dark, and the men were clearly spooked by a party of three adults and a child materializing from the gloom.

"We're here for Bruce," Ruby announced.

"State your purpose," one of the men called out.

"Got problems with some electronics. We already cleared it with him."

The man checked a clipboard. "What's your name?"

"Ruby. He's expecting us."

"Says here you aren't comin' till tomorrow."

"Well, I'm here now. We made good time."

"Who're they?" the man's partner asked suspiciously.

"My daughter, and her husband and child."

"Don't say nothing about that on here," the first man said, eyeing the clipboard.

Ruby rolled her eyes. "That's Bruce for you." She hesitated. "Come on, guys. A four-year-old and her parents aren't going to take over the town. Give us a break…"

"I'm five," Eve protested, and one of the men smiled.

"Mine does that too," he said.

"Hard for grandma to keep everything straight these days," Ruby agreed. "Time sure does fly by, don't it?" she said, adding the folksy country homily as a sweetener. Who would turn away a grandmother and her charges?

"Well, we ain't supposed to let strangers in, but I suppose since you're together, and he's expecting you…" The man stopped when he saw Lucas's M4 strapped to his back. "Where'd you get that, cowboy?"

"What? The rifle? Traded a month's worth of moonshine to some crook who runs a trading post south of here," Lucas said, his tone friendly.

"Yeah? You make juice?"

"Best around. Grow my own corn. Nothin' like it," Lucas said, pouring on the *aw shucks* accent he knew well.

"Got any on you?"

Lucas eyed the guard. "I might."

"Reckon I could taste it? Always in the market for a new supplier."

Lucas nodded. "In my saddlebag."

The man smiled. "Go ahead. Won't shoot you or nothin'."

"Good to hear." Lucas dismounted from Tango, removed one of the jars of white lightning, and approached the men. He unscrewed the top and handed it to the first guard. "Just a taste. That's Bruce's payment there, so don't go heavy."

The first guard took a sip and let out a whoop. "Damn, that's got some fire to it!"

"Told you."

"Lemme taste it," the other guard demanded, and reached for the jar. The first one almost spilled it as he handed it over, and the second man took a small gulp and then exhaled loudly. "Sweet Lord, but that's clean."

"Secret's in the corn," Lucas said, motioning for them to pass the jar back to him. The second man took a long, rueful look at the moonshine and returned it to Lucas, who screwed the top on tightly and replaced it in his bag.

"Where you say you was from again?" the first guard asked. Lucas resisted his natural inclination to respond that he hadn't, and let Ruby field that one.

"Got a spread down south of Carlsbad. Out in the middle of nowhere. Just us and six more like him," she said, pointing at Lucas. "We do okay. Nobody messes with us."

"You had any trouble here?" Lucas asked.

"Nah, not for a spell. Maybe, I don't know, six months ago, bunch of highway thugs tried something, but we made short work of them. Been pretty calm, overall. You hear what happened down Loving way?"

"No. What?"

"Whole place burned to the ground," the second man said.

"Really? Who did that?" Ruby asked. "I traded some with them."

"Nobody knows. Guy riding north told us about it. Don't that beat all, huh? Spooked us good here."

"I'll bet," Ruby said. "When did it happen?"

"He told us almost a week ago. He didn't know for sure, but we saw smoke back around then, so that was probably it."

"Damn shame. Good people," Ruby said, and the men nodded.

"Well, you all can come in. You know where Bruce is at?"

"Not really," Ruby said.

"Over by the fence, about a quarter mile on the eastern side. Can't miss it. Only trailer there. Nobody but a damn fool would live on that stretch, I been sayin' for years, but you can't tell him nothin'," the first guard said.

Ruby nodded and rolled her eyes. "Tell me about it. Stubborn as my mule. But has a way with gadgets like nobody's business."

The men let them through, and they rode to Bruce's trailer, which appeared to be older than Ruby and in considerably rougher shape. Lucas and Sierra exchanged a look as they neared the rusting side of the dwelling, which for all its conspicuous faults, was well lit with outdoor LED lamps. On the roof, an array of solar panels provided free advertising for Bruce's talents. A motion detector tripped when they opened the gate and stepped onto the property, and the entire yard was illuminated by high-glare spotlights.

"Nice touch," Lucas conceded, squinting against the blinding light.

"He's playing for keeps," Ruby agreed.

The door of the trailer opened, and out stepped a man with a neatly trimmed goatee and dun-colored, dreadlocked hair in a ponytail, who appeared to be in his late thirties. The muzzle of a bullpup submachine gun was pointed directly at them.

"Ruby?" he asked when he saw the older woman. "You got here sooner than I figured."

"Never underestimate an old lady." She dismounted and moved toward him, indicating the others with her left hand. "This here's Lucas, Sierra, and Eve. Everyone, meet Bruce. Engineer and general troublemaker extraordinaire."

Lucas tipped the brim of his hat, and Sierra and Eve managed smiles. Bruce lowered his weapon and gave Ruby a small hug, obviously uncomfortable with the contact. "Wow. I'm totally unprepared. Sorry. You have anywhere to stay?" he asked.

"We were thinking we'd just camp out wherever you think is safe."

"I have a spare bedroom and a sofa. No need to camp, if you don't mind cramped spaces. It'll be tight, and I've got to move some stuff around, but it should work," Bruce offered.

"That's very generous of you," Sierra said, and Bruce returned her smile, his eyes lingering on her face.

"Nothing's too good for friends of Ruby's."

"Are you sure we aren't putting you out?" Ruby asked.

"Absolutely. *Mi casa* and all that. Go ahead and water your horses – and if they won't run off, they're free to graze the field. My nag can't keep it trimmed, so they'll be doing me a favor. Just shut the gate and we're golden."

Lucas returned to the barrier and swung it closed, and looked around slowly. "Nice spread. Big."

"Yeah, well, there's no such thing as property values anymore, so why not? Nobody else wanted it. Everyone's terrified of being on the perimeter, especially after what happened in Loving."

"Yeah, the guards told us about that," Ruby said neutrally.

"What's the world coming to, am I right?" Bruce shrugged. "Go ahead and unpack your gear. I'll make some room inside."

"Much obliged," Lucas said, and Bruce nodded.

"My pleasure."

Lucas removed his saddle and bags from Tango and then did the same with Nugget, Jax, and Sidney – Ruby's moniker for her new horse, based on an old boyfriend, she said. As they were finishing up, Bruce poked his head from the trailer. "Come on in. You can stow your stuff by the door. Need some help?"

Lucas nodded, and Bruce descended the two steps to the concrete slab that served as his porch and hoisted Sierra's tack. When Lucas followed him inside, the first thing that assaulted him was the sickly sweet aroma of stale marijuana smoke. Lucas glanced at the open windows and said nothing – it was none of his business how their host took the edge off.

Bruce dropped the saddle and bags by the door, and Lucas did the same, and then they went to retrieve Ruby's gear. Once they were all inside, the door bolted shut, Bruce gave them a ten-second tour of the trailer, which amounted to a central living room with adjacent kitchen, and a bedroom and bathroom at either end.

"Toilets work. I use a pressure tank on the roof. Gravity fed," Bruce said, pride in his voice. "And the battery bank will power everything for up to fourteen hours. But I obviously try not to run everything at once – just in case."

Sierra and Ruby admired his refrigerator and then moved to the living room, where he had a workstation set up with two large monitors and both a laptop and desktop computer. Bruce sat in a swivel Aeron chair and looked up at Ruby expectantly.

"Want to tell me what this is all about?"

Ruby gave him a brief summary of their situation, omitting that half of Texas was on the hunt for them, and handed him the note. He pored over it for several minutes and then shook his head. "Yeah, I don't see anything obvious. What did you have in mind, Ruby?"

"I can write a program that will try character substitutions. We can get into more involved cyphers later, if you can think of any, but that's the likeliest."

He stood and gestured to the chair. "It's all yours. I shall defer to the master."

She grinned. "Hardly. But I think I still remember how to write a code string."

Ruby went to work, her fingers flying over the keys, and Bruce plopped down on a sagging sofa and motioned to the rest of them to take a seat. They did, and Sierra sighed contentedly.

"So what is it you do here? Ruby mentioned solar panels?"

"Oh, yeah. It's been good to me. I can repair just about anything, and when someone wants to set up a rig, I get the call."

"Then business is thriving?"

"Used to be way better. Problem is that as stuff ages, it degrades. Like batteries. There's only so much I can do, and then they're just dead. But inverters, panels, radios, anything electric and most mechanical items, I can make work, assuming I can find, or create, the parts." He made a face. "Things have been pretty slow for the last six months or so, actually."

"Sorry to hear that," Sierra said.

Bruce shrugged. "It's not the end of the world. I mean, we already went through that, so this is gravy…"

Sierra laughed. "I guess we did."

"What's on the note?" Bruce asked.

"If we told you, we'd have to kill you," Ruby called from the keyboard.

"Seriously," Bruce tried again.

"Directions to a pot of gold," Sierra answered.

"Where did you get it?"

Lucas's smile was anything but friendly. "Leprechaun."

Bruce's eyes hardened as he met Lucas's eyes. "Ruby, I think I deserve an answer, considering I'm helping, don't you?"

"It might be dangerous for you, Bruce, or we'd tell you. This way you don't know anything."

Bruce snorted. "And how's that good?"

"You can't tell someone what you don't know."

"Who's going to ask?"

Lucas gave a noncommittal shrug. "Bad guys. Take your pick."

Bruce sat back with a frown. "That tells me nothing."

Lucas nodded. "Exactly." His tone softened. "Look, you really don't want to know. For your own good."

"All right, guys, this is freaking me out. What's going on?" Bruce demanded.

Ruby sighed and swiveled around to face him. "We think there's a message, obviously, we need to decode. It's supposed to have directions to a rendezvous point. But we want to keep it secret. There. Satisfied?"

"Rendezvous with who? For what?"

"That's part of the mystery," Ruby said. "We're hoping to learn more from the note."

Bruce's brow furrowed and he shook his head. "Wow. And I thought I was spun." He opened a small box on the coffee table and pulled out a pipe and some marijuana. "Want some?"

Lucas shook his head, and so did Sierra. Ruby returned her attention to the keyboard and called out over her shoulder, "Just take it outside, please. I can't concentrate if the room's full of smoke. And it's not good for Eve."

Bruce stood. "Now you're kicking me out of my own house? Fine. More for me."

The door slamming behind him sounded like a cannon, and Ruby hesitated before resuming her tapping. Sierra made to rise. "Is he okay?"

"He'll be fine once he chills out," Ruby said. "He's just high-strung. And he's got the kind of personality where a puzzle drives him crazy till he solves it. That's what makes him a good repairman and a great hacker."

"Hope so," Lucas said.

"I'll go talk to him," Sierra said. "Can't hurt to be nice."

Lucas didn't say anything, preferring to study his boots. Ruby muttered something unintelligible, and Sierra headed for the door. "Are we going to eat anything tonight?" she asked.

"Got jerky," Lucas said. "Unless Bruce there will let you raid the fridge."

"I'll try some friendly persuasion."

She left, and Lucas went to his saddlebags and withdrew a container of jerky. He passed two long strips to Eve, handed Ruby three, and took several for himself. They sat chomping the leathery meat in silence, watching as Ruby worked at the computer, Eve eyeing the lines of code with enraptured eyes.

Sierra and Bruce returned ten minutes later, laughing, the best of friends. He smiled at Lucas and Eve, his eyes now bloodshot slits, and gestured to the kitchen. "If you're hungry, you're welcome to what I have. Caught a bunch of fish yesterday, so that's fresh, and got some vegetables from my garden."

"Is that where you grow everything?" Sierra giggled.

Bruce laughed. "That's my little secret. You have yours; I have mine. Maybe we'll trade later?"

Sierra batted her eyes, and Lucas found himself struggling to choke down a rising anger.

"Maybe."

Bruce and Sierra prepared a meal while Lucas cleaned his guns, focusing on his task as he bit back any snipes that he felt like taking. He had no claim on Sierra, and they hadn't had time to discuss what had passed between them, especially with Ruby and Eve always around – not that Lucas had any idea what he wanted, if anything.

They ate while Ruby continued working, and several hours later, she sat back with a tired smile.

"There," she said. "Let's let it run tonight. I can't do anything more. The program will try pattern matching at increasingly complex levels, and go through every possible character substitution. We'll review the results tomorrow. I can't see straight right now."

Lucas yawned. "I'm with you." He looked to Bruce, who was talking quietly with Sierra. "Is it okay to sleep on this?" he asked, patting the couch.

"Oh, yeah, sure thing, dude." Bruce looked at the clock on the wall. "Didn't realize how late it is. I'm going to hit it, too." He offered Sierra a drugged half smile. "Unless you want a nightcap or something."

She returned his smile. "Rain check?"

"*No problema*," Bruce said, and stood. "Sleep tight. You know where everything is."

Lucas watched him walk to his bedroom and throw a final smarmy grin Sierra's way before disappearing inside. Sierra stopped smiling when his door closed and rolled her eyes.

"More flies with honey than vinegar," she whispered, and Ruby nodded.

"He seems to like you."

"He's kinda sweet, actually. Doesn't seem like he gets to talk to many people," she said.

"Go figure," Lucas said, and Sierra shot him a puzzled look. He didn't elaborate, and Sierra elected to lead Eve to the second bedroom rather than engage. Ruby lingered behind.

"I'll be there in a second," Ruby said. When Sierra was in the bedroom, Ruby leaned into Lucas. "She's a manipulator. Don't forget that. All useful information."

Lucas nodded. "So I see."

"In this case, it worked out well for us; but better to know what you're dealing with than make assumptions, Lucas."

"I'm not assuming anything."

"You looked about ready to skin Bruce alive at one point. Maybe 'assume' was the wrong word."

Lucas sighed and lay back into the sofa. "This thing stinks."

"Better than spending the night on hard rocks."

He sniffed and tipped his hat forward, covering his eyes, and swung his feet up onto the couch, his M4 by his side. "Don't know about that."

Ruby considered possible responses and then shook her head and made her way to the bedroom, leaving Lucas to his thoughts as the computer whirred and blinked, its fan sounding like a small turbine in the still, hot air.

Chapter 28

Slim sat in the sandbagged guard station at Duke's trading post, idly watching bats dart after mosquitoes in the gloaming, their movements jerky and fast yet with a strange grace to them. He shifted on the uncomfortable board seat and stared off into nothingness that stretched to a dim orange glow on the horizon from the setting sun.

He'd left the family ranch in search of adventure, bored to tears taking orders from his father and older siblings, and had jumped at the chance of being a guard at the trading post, visions of combat, showdowns, and making his fortune coloring his decision. Now, after little more than a week at Duke's, he'd settled into a routine of crushing boredom and taking orders from anyone senior to him, which meant all the others.

That wasn't what he'd signed up for, and he'd quickly realized that with Loving to the north now a deserted smudge and the highway a badland of wreckage and predators, traffic to the outpost was going to be a trickle. He'd merely exchanged one form of servitude for another. It was an improvement only in style, not substance, and he found himself filled with the same sense of dread and resentment that he'd had back home – only here he had to bottle it up inside and not show it, or he'd be fired and have to return to the ranch with his tail between his legs.

"Pride goeth," he muttered, remembering one of his father's often used expressions, and despised himself for his inability to have a more original thought than a repetition of the dogma that had been pounded into his head since childhood. The family had believed that the collapse had been the end of days prophesied in the Good Book and spent their time awaiting a rapture that was a long time coming. Slim didn't buy a word of it, but he'd been forced to play along or have his ears boxed by his larger, older siblings, all of whom had had survived the flu without contracting it, no doubt in part due to living like hermits who eschewed contact with the outside world.

That had been one thing the old man had gotten right – danger lurked around every turn, and their fellow man was a dangerous creature. But that didn't dissuade Slim, who was young and fearless; one thing he knew was that his chances of meeting a mate or of having an adventure more memorable than baling hay or shoveling slop were less than zero if he stayed with his family.

He'd always known he was meant for bigger things, but had nearly given up hope when Doug had ridden by the ranch to tell him of the opening on Duke's crew. Slim had been packed and on his horse less than an hour later, after a screaming match with his dad. Now, however, he wondered whether he'd chosen wisely after all. Latrine duty and grunt work weren't his idea of making his way in the world, and his visions of rousting hooligans and rescuing damsels in distress had evaporated when confronted with the mundane reality of the duty he'd signed up for.

Footsteps approached from the building, and Doug limped into view, his thigh wound nearly healed but the muscles still mending and sore. He handed Slim a tin plate with some sort of stew on it over white rice, the smell of which was less than appetizing.

"What is this slop?" Slim asked.

"Supposed to be rabbit. But I think it might have turned. Has something of a tang to it on the end, but it'll fill your belly."

"Why doesn't he let us go hunting for something fresh? Or at least fishing?"

"He's still paranoid about being attacked. Doesn't want to be caught shorthanded."

"So we've got to eat dog food?"

"It's not that bad." Doug's expression turned thoughtful. "At least, I don't think it's dog."

"Very funny."

Doug shrugged. "Enjoy your dinner."

Slim swallowed a chunk of mystery meat and choked down a spurt of acid that rose in his throat at the taste, the sour bile making him gag. He set the plate aside and swigged some water, disgusted at the gruel as well as his situation.

He needed to make a decision. He had information that the Locos had said they would pay handsomely for. All he had to do was seize the moment, take a single bold step, and his life would forever change.

His father's voice rang in his ear every time he contemplated selling out the woman, though. "Thirty pieces of silver," the old man snapped in his imagination. "Goin' price for Judas."

Slim tried another spoonful of the noxious concoction and then spit it onto the ground by the gate.

"Screw this," he muttered. He retrieved his gun and made his way to the stable for his horse, and was leading the animal out of the barn when Doug emerged from the main building.

"Where you goin'? You're on watch another three hours."

"I quit. That's where."

"You kiddin'? Duke's gonna flip out."

"Yeah, well, he'll get over it. I'm through."

"Best tell him yourself."

"Thanks for the advice, but I'm outta here."

Doug gazed off into the gloom beyond the gate. "Man could get killed riding at night."

"Better to die in the saddle than live like this."

Doug's voice softened. "What's wrong, Slim?"

"If I wanted to be everyone's bitch, I would have stayed home. I ain't cut out for this, Doug. So I'm gonna hit the trail, see what's over the hill."

"Just like that."

"Yep."

Slim unlocked the gate and slid it open. Doug watched him in silence as he swung up into the saddle and put the spurs to his horse, goading it to a gallop as he passed through the entryway. The sound of the horse's departure drew Duke from inside, and he peered at Doug from his vantage point on the porch.

"What the hell was that?" the trader demanded.

"Slim up and quit."

"He what?"

"You heard me. Said *hasta la vista* and rode off." Doug scratched his head. "Had a burr up his butt over something."

"Damn. That means we're shorthanded again. Looks like I'll have to take the bastard's watch." Duke paused. "Kinda strange that he rode away without even bothering to collect his salary, isn't it?"

"I didn't even think about that," Doug agreed.

"He say where he was going?"

"Nope."

Duke's expression soured as he turned and went inside to get his gun and flak vest. He'd never had a man quit like that before, especially not at night with no provisions and no warning. Although the youngster had been acting odd the last couple days. Should have seen it coming.

Duke stepped back onto the porch, an AR-15 in one hand and his body armor in the other. He trudged to the guard post, plopped down on the wood bench, and sniffed the discarded stew beside him. He eyed it and, seeing no flies, shrugged and picked up the plate.

"Waste not, want not," he whispered, and spooned a heaping portion into his mouth. He'd spent weeks living off rats after the collapse when the food chain had gone belly up and never missed a meal, knowing that in uncertain times any one of them could be his last. He chewed mechanically, wondering what had set the young man off, and then shrugged as he swallowed, the why less important than the inconvenience his departure would cause.

Chapter 29

The air in the hot room felt stifling, matching the searing pain being telegraphed from most of Cano's body as he drifted in and out of consciousness. He tried to move but lacked the energy, and barely managed to open his good eye. He looked down the length of his torso and saw that his arms and legs were wrapped in bandages, and he realized that one of the reasons he was so hot was that his face was also swathed in gauze and cotton, insulating him and retaining his body heat.

The last thing he remembered was a blinding flash as he rode into the canyon, senses tingling, and then the sensation of flying before everything went black. Cano tried to turn his head, and a lance of pain shot through his skull, the back of which felt like it had been run over by a bulldozer. He must have hit the rocks hard and concussed – even now, he could feel his temples pounding with pain from the impact.

How long had he been out? He didn't know. But he felt as weak as a newborn kitten, and his powerlessness and the vulnerability it implied were more disturbing to him than his injuries. He'd suffered near-death before; it went with the territory. But being prone, unable to move, at the mercy of anyone who would do him harm…that was frightening for a man who didn't scare easily.

He listened for any clue as to where he was, but heard nothing. Cano realized that he had no vision on his left side and raised his hand to his face. He felt the bandage over his eye and his arm fell back to his side.

The door opened, and an older man stepped into the room with a notebook in hand and a stethoscope draped around his neck. He regarded Cano in surprise when he saw that he was conscious.

"You're…you're up!" he said, moving to the bedside.

"Water," Cano croaked, his voice a harsh rasp.

"Yes. Yes, of course. Just a moment," the man said, and scurried from the room.

Two minutes later he was back with a plastic bottle, a straw, and a thermos. "Fruit juice. It'll help you build back your blood count," he announced.

"Just…water."

The man leaned toward him with the bottle and dropped the straw through the top. It stuck out a few inches, and the man bent it so he could sip. Cano took measured swallows, wary of drinking too fast, but even so drained the bottle in what seemed like a few moments. The man straightened and nodded.

"You're lucky to be alive. I really thought you'd be out a lot longer."

"Who are you?"

"The doctor who pulled a half pound of shrapnel out of you."

Cano digested that, and his heart rate increased. "How bad?"

"Arms and legs got the lion's share of it, but mostly surface wounds. No serious damage to the muscles. Your head, on the other hand…you've got a big gash on the back of it and probably a concussion. And of course, there's your eye – I couldn't save it, but it will heal over. Your biggest problem is blood loss, but that should rectify itself with time." He paused. "You need to drink the fruit juice. It will help."

Cano absorbed the news about his eye and grunted. "In a minute."

"Let me examine you and see how you're doing."

Cano allowed him to unwrap several of the bandages and check the lacerations. The doctor hummed as he worked and then listened to his heart with the stethoscope before clearing a section of his arm of gauze so he could take his blood pressure. Cano winced as the cuff tightened and the man eyed his watch, and then he was finished and removing it.

"Still low. Ninety over fifty-six. But that should come up as you rehydrate and get more calories into you." He set the cuff down and studied Cano. "You're healing relatively quickly. You have a strong constitution."

"How long have I been here?"

"They brought you in a little over a day ago. So the injuries are two days old."

"How long till I can move?"

"Probably not for another three or so, at least. Got to allow your wounds time to heal. Your head is another matter. No way of knowing how long that will take. Could be a matter of days or weeks."

"I don't have weeks."

The doctor frowned. "You don't have a choice. Your body will do whatever it's going to do. Best for you to stay out of its way and let it."

They were interrupted by Luis barging into the room, two-way in hand. "You said he's awake?" he asked the doctor, and then looked down at Cano. "Oh. Good."

"What happened?" Cano demanded.

"Grenade."

"I guessed that."

"We lost all the men except for myself and two others."

"Damn. And the woman?"

"Never saw anything but muzzle flashes and grenade blasts."

"Did you go back out?"

Luis scowled. "I'm about out of men, and yours won't listen to me. It's all I can do to maintain order over the town with the people I have."

"So she's gone," Cano said, disgusted.

"For now."

Cano closed his eye, exhausted, and took a deep, painful breath. The doctor and Luis exchanged a look, and Luis nodded.

"I'll leave you to rest. Glad to see you're going to make it," Luis said, and walked out of the room.

The doctor pulled up a chair with a sigh. "Let's try the juice."

"I don't suppose you have any morphine?"

"Sorry."

Cano opened his eye. "Whiskey?"

The doctor shook his head. "Can't. Thins your blood." He held out the thermos. "Can't give you aspirin for the same reason. But the pain should recede in another day or two."

"Great."

"At least you're alive."

Cano closed his eye again and exhaled forcefully. "For now."

Chapter 30

"Damn."

Ruby's voice woke Lucas. He rolled over on the couch and peered at her by Bruce's computer station.

"What is it?" he asked.

"The system crashed at some point last night."

"Great."

She tried to reboot the computer, but nothing lit up. Ruby fiddled with the plug and checked the surge protector. She glanced up at Lucas and shook her head. "Deader than Jim Morrison."

"Who?"

"I forgot. Before your time."

He stretched. "So, nothing?"

She held up a USB drive. "I had it auto-save the results every hour to this dongle, just in case. So the record should be on here." Ruby plugged the small device into the laptop's port and opened a folder on the screen. Lucas moved to her side and checked his watch.

"You're up early."

"You know the saying about worms."

He smiled. "Doesn't work so well if you're the worm."

"Nobody tells them anything." She tapped a command and then scanned a readout of possible decryptions of the character string. It didn't take long. "Well, that amounted to a big bag of fresh squat."

"So what now?"

Her shoulders slumped. "I'm sorry, Lucas. I put everything I could think of into the program. If it isn't a substitution cypher, I'm out of ammo."

"You don't have a plan B?" he asked incredulously.

"I'm not a code cracker, Lucas. I'm a programmer who's good at writing software, but that only translates so far. I'm not Mata Hari. A code that's something other than replacing one letter with another, or every third or fourth letter with another, can take months or even years to crack. Without knowing the basis of the string, all we can do is look for patterns. The program didn't find anything intelligible."

"You sounded pretty confident last night," he observed.

"Looks like I was wrong."

The door opened and Sierra stepped out, eyes puffy from sleep. "Did you decrypt it?" she asked.

Lucas shook his head. "Blew up the computer."

Ruby swatted his arm. "No, it didn't. I mean, technically, it might have overheated or something, but that's not the code's fault. This system's old."

"Well, can't you use the other one?" Sierra asked.

"No point. The results are in, and they're gibberish."

Sierra gaped at Ruby, her mouth hanging open, while Lucas walked into the kitchen and opened the refrigerator. "Think this water's safe to drink?"

Bruce's voice rang out from his bedroom doorway. "Of course it is. What's all this about blowing up my CPU?"

Ruby glanced at Bruce. "System failed. I can't get it to restart."

"Crap," he said, moving across the room and kneeling down to study the box. He fiddled with it for a few moments and then retrieved a screwdriver from a coffee mug filled with tools and opened the back. Ruby watched as Lucas poured himself a glass of water and drained it.

Sierra walked to the door. "I need some fresh air," she said, and slid the bolt wide. She stepped outside, and Lucas followed her out, leaving the tech gurus to figure out what had gone wrong. Sierra sat on a collapsible lawn chair and Lucas took the seat beside her. She looked over at him and he found himself unexpectedly lost in her eyes, a thrill running through him like a live wire. "We're screwed," she said, obviously unaware of the effect she was having on him, and the moment passed.

Lucas nodded, his face giving nothing away. "Seems that way. Maybe she can pull a rabbit out of her hat, though. Never know."

"She didn't sound positive."

"Nope."

"Damn."

"Sometimes that's how it goes."

"We have to do something."

He eyed her. "Like what?"

"I was thinking. One man knows how to get in touch with Shangri-La. He may still be alive. If he is, he's our only hope of reaching them. He could set up another rendezvous."

Lucas shook his head. "The scientist in Lubbock? I thought you said he was probably dead."

"I said he might be. But I don't know that. I was just guessing that they might have figured out he helped us."

"Was there any evidence linking him to you?"

"Not really."

His tone hardened. "That's not the same as 'no.' It's a pretty straightforward issue. Either there was, or there wasn't."

"I…I don't know whether anyone knew we had a thing. If not, then there'd be no reason to think he was involved." She hesitated. "We kept it secret, so unless he told someone, he might be fine."

"Might. Kinda like might not."

"If he was planning to help us, it doesn't make any sense he'd advertise the connection, does it?"

"You're the one who thought he'd be dead."

"I was just being pessimistic. I honestly have no idea."

Lucas sighed. "What are you saying, Sierra?"

"We need to return to Lubbock. Find him, if he's still alive. Get him to help us again."

"Take Eve back into the heart of enemy territory and risk handing the devil the fate of the world, you mean?"

"There has to be a way, Lucas."

He thought for several moments. "There is, and we both know it. If I go, nobody knows me. I could find him, assuming he's alive, and deliver the message. Set up a meet somewhere." He remembered Ruby's admonishment about Sierra's manipulative talents, and part of him understood what she was doing – but there really was no other way he could see if they were to find the sanctuary, given that Ruby was out of gas and Bruce's talents seemed better suited to rolling joints than decoding cyphers. "Tell me everything you know about him."

"We…we had a fling. He was lonely, and so was I. We were both stuck in a horrible situation, against our will, and…he's a good man."

Lucas studied her face as though looking for a lost puzzle piece. "Would he be easy for them to replace?"

"I honestly don't know. I mean, he was a specialist, so probably not."

"He's the one who got in touch with Shangri-La? Directly?"

She shook her head. "Through someone else. He just told me it was a rebel group."

"He was the conduit." It wasn't a question.

"I suppose." She studied her feet. "The research facility is heavily guarded, but the staff quarters across the street aren't. If you could get into those, it's doable. You could find him and talk to him."

"What's his name? How would I recognize him?"

"His name's Jacob. Thirties, black short hair, glasses, a little shorter than you. He looks like a teacher or something. But there aren't a lot like him at the facility. Most of the staff are…like me."

"Tell me about the security. Everything you can."

"It's a big place. The University Medical Center. They have a wing set up where all they do is work on this project. There are guards at all the entrances and roving security that do spot checks during the day. I imagine they've tightened things up since we escaped, too."

"Why?"

She furrowed her brow. "What do you mean? Because we escaped!"

"Are they holding anyone else?"

"Well. Oh. I see what you mean."

Lucas thought for a moment. "So that's where he is during the day. Tell me about the staff housing."

"It's adjacent to the Medical Center, across the main boulevard to the north. They used to be apartments, but are now set up as living accommodations for the high-level workers."

"Guards?"

"A couple. Not nearly as many as at the main campus."

"Can you draw me a diagram of the layout?"

"Sure." She paused. "You're really thinking of doing this?"

"Barring a miracle, I don't see any other option, do you?"

"I could go. You could stay here with Eve."

He made a face. "Not very practical, considering they know what you look like and have the whole state on the lookout for you."

"I just hate that you have to put yourself at risk again. For us."

"Beats sitting around here watching Ruby spin her wheels."

Sierra reached out and placed her hand over his. "You're a remarkable man, Lucas. I...I wish we had more time to get to know each other. We need to make some when you get back."

Neither of them said anything, and then the door opened and Eve burst through. "Auntie Sierra! I had a bad dream. You were gone," she said. Sierra stood and hugged the little girl, and Lucas also rose.

"Sooner you draw that for me, sooner I can be on the trail," he said.

He went back inside to find Bruce shaking his head, hands on his hips, a look of frustration on his face. "I don't know. I think it's the power supply," he said. "I can scrounge around and see if I can find another one — a lot of the homes here are abandoned, and nobody's got any use for computers with no Internet or electricity. But this is the second one that's blown, so it's a long shot."

Lucas interrupted him. "How far is Lubbock from here?"

Bruce frowned. "Oh, I know that. It's...about a hundred and sixty miles."

Lucas's expression matched his. "Three hard days, if no problems."

Sierra came in with Eve and sat down at the small dining room table, a cheap glass and wood affair, the top chipped from hard use.

"Morning, Bruce. You have any paper? And a pencil or pen?"

He looked confused by the question. "Um, sure. Why?"

"I could use a couple of sheets."

He brought her a notebook. "Go ahead and take whatever you need," he said, handing her a pencil. She thought for a long moment and then began drawing a series of lines, connecting them into a rough blueprint.

"Damn," she said after five minutes, and tore the page out and started over. Lucas watched her wordlessly. The next time she got it to her satisfaction and nodded. She carefully removed it from the notebook and handed it to Lucas. "That's the overview. I put an X where Jacob's room is, or at least used to be, and a G where the guards were stationed."

"That's good," Lucas said, considering the drawing before folding it and slipping it into his back pocket. He glanced at Bruce. "Your shower work?"

"I told you. Pressure tank. And a solar heater," Bruce said with pride.

"Think I'll go freshen up before I hit the trail."

"The trail?" Ruby asked.

Lucas didn't comment, just made his way to the bathroom and closed the door behind him. Ruby fixed Sierra with an expression that could have frozen fire. "What did you talk him into?"

"Me? Nothing," she protested. "You should know by now you can't talk him into anything he doesn't want to do."

"Where's he going?"

Sierra shook her head and looked at Bruce before returning the older woman's stare with equivalent intensity. "That's not for me to say. If Lucas wants to tell you, he will."

Ruby got the message – no discussion in front of Bruce. She grudgingly backed down and busied herself with preparing breakfast.

Bruce came into the kitchen and watched her beat some eggs.

"I forgot how nice it is to have someone around who knows how to cook," he said.

"If you don't watch out, you may have us for a while."

"There are worse things."

"Careful what you wish for." Ruby inspected her concoction and smiled. "Where do you get them from? The eggs?"

"Got a few dozen chickens. I'm not a complete wire head, Ruby. I've learned along with the rest of them."

"No question." She sighed. "Been a long time since I've made an omelet."

"Like riding a bike, isn't it?"

"Let's hope I don't fall off."

Lucas emerged from the bathroom to the aroma of eggs. Ruby offered him a plate, and he polished it off in a few gulps, obviously anxious to get going.

"Those were delicious, Ruby."

"You going to tell me where you're going?"

"Should be back in a week."

"A week!"

"About that."

"What are we supposed to do in the meantime?"

"Stay put." Lucas looked at Bruce. "That okay with you?"

Bruce looked uncomfortable, but Sierra stepped into the gap with a sunny smile. "We'll stay out of your way."

He nodded. "I...I guess." His eyes never left Sierra.

She offered him another beaming flash of teeth and then approached Lucas, fiddling with a leather cord around her neck. She slipped it over her head and handed it to Lucas. "He'll recognize this and know you're my friend and that it's not some kind of setup."

Lucas inspected the medallion hanging from the cord: a cheap green and white yin yang symbol embossed on an enamel disk. He removed his hat and slipped the necklace over his head, where it hung tight against his throat.

Ruby eyed him, not understanding. "Who will recognize it, Lucas?

What are you thinking about doing?"

Lucas glanced over his shoulder at Eve, who was watching him with childlike curiosity – and something more, that maturity he couldn't put a proper name to. He sighed, resigned to yet another ordeal in a never-ending series, and turned back to Ruby.

"Going for a ride."

Chapter 31

Slim's horse stumbled for the third time in the final stretch leading to Pecos, and he eased up on the animal, having pushed it to the breaking point all night. It would serve no useful purpose to drive the creature to the brink and have him collapse before they reached the town. The beast slowed to a walk, breathing hard, its mouth foaming, and Slim felt a twinge of remorse, which he brushed aside, as he had all his earlier misgivings. Victory went to the bold, the meek inherited nothing but misery, and winners took big steps and did what was necessary to cross the finish line first. If his horse had to pay, he'd get another one – no, he'd get fifty of them with the wealth he would demand from the cartel for his information.

His head had swum all night with visions of forbidden pleasures – beautiful young women, scarce food, the finest alcohol, a protected compound where he was waited on like a medieval prince. As day broke over the arid landscape, he could almost taste the fruits of his triumph, and he had to remind himself not to goad the horse faster to get to his destination, whose promise shimmered like an oasis just over the horizon.

He tried not to think about what would happen to the woman and Lucas when the cartel caught up with them – that was none of his concern. It was their beef, and they could figure it out. Cano had promised the bearer of meaningful news anything he wanted, and Slim believed the Crew boss would follow through. He'd seen in the man's face the desperation, the need to locate her, and Slim had heard stories of the Crew's riches, such as their possession of a slew of southern states, vast resources that would have made their territory one of the wealthier countries if it had a national boundary around it. Anything Slim could ask for would be a pittance, and he had increased his price a dozen times on the ride, originally starting out with a modest demand, but by now, having increased it to a real eye-opener.

He guided the horse along a trail that paralleled the highway for the final leg into Pecos, and pulled up short when a voice called from a guard post as he neared a bridge on the outskirts of town.

"Stop, or I'll shoot."

"Easy. I'm here to trade," Slim said.

"Let's see your hands."

As Slim raised them, the guard, his face tattooed, stepped from behind a pile of sandbags. Slim waited as the cartel gunman looked him over, and was relieved when the man appeared to relax.

"What you got to trade?"

"Information."

The man regarded Slim with a puzzled expression. "Come again?"

"You heard me. I'm here to see…Cano."

The man's eyebrows rose. "Cano," he repeated.

"That's right. He's with the Crew."

"Oh. Sure. That guy." The guard waved him past. "Headquarters is over at the courthouse. Know where that is?"

Slim's eyes flitted to the man's gun and then back to his face. "I've been there before."

"All right, then. On your way. Just keep your hands off your weapons till you're out of sight," the guard warned, obviously jumpy.

"You got it."

Slim's first obstacle successfully negotiated, his confidence increased with each tired step his horse took. The stallion ambled toward the brick edifice, and Slim stopped at another guard post in front of it. The Locos there were a sight more alert than the drowsy border guard.

"I'm here to see Cano," Slim announced.

"Yeah? Who're you, homeboy?"

"Name's Slim."

"Slim, huh? There's a classic for ya," one of the guards said to his companion, slapping his chest with the back of his hand and laughing. "Slim here wants to see Cano. Isn't that right?"

Slim's certainty wavered, but he didn't let it show. "That's right. Where is he? He'll want to talk to me."

"He will, huh? And why's that, Slim?"

"I've got information he's after."

The guards exchanged a glance. "Is that so?"

"Yep."

One of the men shifted his gun so it was pointing at Slim. "Why don't you tell us, and if it sounds legit, we'll take you to him?"

Slim shook his head. "I only tell him."

"You're pissing me off, boy. Bad idea. Spill the beans."

Slim swallowed the knot that was threatening to strangle him. "He's looking for someone. I know where she is."

"She?"

"The woman."

Another surreptitious glance and the men stood, brandishing their weapons. "Is that so?"

Slim nodded. "It is."

"Where is she?"

"I told you. I only talk to Cano. That was the deal."

"Deal? You're going to make a deal with him?"

Slim didn't like the way the exchange was going, and dug in. "That's between me and Cano." He paused. "He's not going to be happy to hear you didn't take me to him immediately."

"Is that a threat?" the guard asked the other, and then studied Slim. "Sounds like one to me."

"Look, I have no beef with you. I came to talk to Cano."

"Oh. Sure. Sort of like, 'Take me to your leader.' Except by some hayseed shit-kicker." The Loco flipped off his weapon's safety. "Now tell us where she is, punkass. I'm running low on patience."

Slim shook his head. "I want to see Cano."

The Loco looked to his companion. "Take his guns. We'll do this the hard way."

Realization of the situation he'd gotten himself into struck Slim with the force of a blow, and he tried to turn his horse, but the cartel thug was already reaching for the bridle. The exhausted stallion panicked as the gunman tried to grab it and reared on its back legs, lashing out with its front hooves and striking the Loco, knocking him to the ground, one of the hooves caving in his skull like a porcelain doll.

Slim fought to bring the horse under control as the remaining Loco raised his gun. Slim reached for his to protect himself, and the Loco's AKM barked on full auto, stitching Slim's torso with rounds and blowing the horse's brains all over him in a shower of blood and bone shards.

Rider and horse collapsed, the stallion dead before he hit the ground, and Slim's life ebbing as his dreams of riches seeped from ragged holes in his chest, the flashes of searing pain replaced by a cold so profound it took his final breath away.

Chapter 32

Two days into the ride to Lubbock, Lucas was questioning the wisdom of his decision. It had seemed like the only alternative when he'd awakened to the idea, vivid as a kiss on the lips, but now, with the reality of over fifty miles a day of sunbaked slog across barren plains where decrepit oil pumps loomed like petrified giants on a lunar landscape, he wasn't so sure. Maybe he should have waited another day or two to see whether Ruby or Bruce could pull a rabbit out of their hat?

He'd camped west of the city of Lovington on the first night, staying clear of the town's bonfire glow, not wanting to invite questions or attack. He wasn't sure where the Crew's territory began, but he was taking no chances and was operating under the assumption that anyone he encountered would be a threat. He'd slept uneasily under the stars, unwilling to risk even a small fire for fear of drawing hostiles, the song of distant coyotes his lullaby as the night's chill descended like arctic breath.

The next morning he'd pressed Tango until Lovington's skyline was a speck on the horizon behind him, and then settled into a steady walk across the flat expanse, the big horse soldiering on without complaint. As he approached a rusting yellow sign announcing the New Mexico-Texas border, he calculated that he would have one more long day's ride before he arrived in Lubbock. With a hundred miles under his belt, he was dog tired, and his heart went out to Tango, who was grazing without complaint near a rural well as Lucas sized up the location's viability for a campsite. Situated at the end of a dirt road near the bones of a farm, the area was deserted, and as the wind blew from the east, carrying with it an all-pervasive red dust that invaded every crevice and cranny, he decided to make camp there. He again avoided a fire, dining on smoked jerky and water.

Lucas inspected the bullet wound on his arm and was relieved to see that it had healed. The new skin was pink and tender as a baby's, but there was no sign of infection. He flexed his bicep and didn't feel any pain, so that was one concern he could check off his list. Going into enemy territory on a suicide mission, he had plenty on his plate to mull over without his body betraying him. He waited until it was completely dark and then used the well water and a soiled shirt to clean the worst of the sweat and road dust from his body, his naked form pale as a ghost in the light of the rising moon.

The wind strengthened to a howl as the night wore on. Lucas snatched sleep when he could, but was awakened multiple times by tumbleweeds blowing by and the moan of sustained gusts through the bones of the farmhouse. When he packed his bedroll away just before sunrise, fatigue still wore heavily on him, and he again was overcome by a wave of misgiving. He'd chosen to put his life on the line based on a slim chance of success, violating every precept that had kept him alive through the post-collapse anarchy. In the crisp predawn luminescence, he shook his head in a kind of wonder at how crazy his actions were. Maybe it was a delayed response to Hal's passing, or the loss of the ranch, or the death of an entire town's good people, but if he kept making poor decisions, he'd join them in eternity sooner than later – and he wasn't ready to shed his mortal coil quite yet.

The truth was that the idea of Shangri-La, of a sanctuary where the madness of the outside world was held at bay, had infected him, corroding his pragmatism and leaving something far more dangerous in its stead: hope. For years he'd avoided thinking of anything but the present, living day to day, never expecting to wake up the next. But now there was a chance of a better future than one of mere existence, and he'd drunk the Kool-Aid like it contained the antidote.

And since he was being completely honest with himself, there was also Sierra and Eve. The little girl had touched something he'd thought dead in his core, and for better or worse, he felt an unusual bond with her. As to Sierra, he understood that she was cunning in the way a survivor had to be, but she was also the first woman he'd seen in forever that had stirred his interest – and reached a part of him he'd believed had vanished forever with his wife's death.

"I'm a weak man," he whispered to Tango, who passed judgment with inscrutable eyes. "Ready for another day in hell?"

The horse stood motionless as Lucas climbed into the saddle, and by the time the sun rose, they were miles along the trail that stretched east to Lubbock, where he would hopefully find the answer to questions that he'd never known existed until a few days earlier.

Toward midday, as he was crossing a vast oil field dotted with rusting pumps, he spied a dust cloud straight ahead. He raised his binoculars and scanned the horizon until he could make out the source: a group of six horsemen, all heavily armed. Their plate carriers, assault rifles, and facial tattoos alerted Lucas that he was now in Crew country.

"Come on, Tango, let's make tracks," he said, dropping the glasses back against his chest and wheeling the horse around to the north. Lucas wasn't interested in discovering how the Crew treated new arrivals into its territory – Sierra's account had convinced him that was a pleasure best skipped. He urged the horse to a trot, just fast enough to put some distance between himself and the patrol but at a moderate enough pace that no dust was stirred up. After half an hour, the dust cloud passed behind him, the group riding hard for some unknown destination.

Lucas stopped and allowed Tango to take a breather. He watched the unending fields with his spyglasses until the dust was out of sight, and when he remounted the horse, any fatigue was gone, replaced by an adrenaline buzz from the near miss. If there were regular patrols from here on out, it would be slower going, and he'd need to be extra vigilant the remainder of the way to avoid discovery.

The dry scrub turned greener as he neared Lubbock, and he

PURGATORY ROAD

paused regularly so Tango could munch grass for ten minutes at a
time while he relieved himself and stretched his legs. He began seeing
signs of life as he drew closer to the city: smoke rising from chimneys
and the occasional boom of a small-gauge shotgun as hunters bagged
dinner. In one section, the sky was thick with partridges, and his
mouth watered as he debated risking shooting one himself so he
could dine on fare other than jerky. Ultimately, the risk wasn't worth
it, and he discarded the idea and continued on, stomach rumbling in
protest.

Twilight arrived with swarms of flies and mosquitoes, and he
spent the final half hour of daylight swatting at them like a man
possessed. When darkness fell, the high plain glowed in the distance
from the lights of Lubbock, and he recalled Sierra's description of the
wind farms the Crew had harnessed for power.

Because of the town's size, it was unlikely the entire perimeter was
guarded, so to enter the city, he'd just need to avoid the obvious
outposts and find a way in someplace secluded. Once there he would
find the hospital; and then the difficult part of the operation would
begin. He'd reconnoiter the grounds and get a sense of what he was
up against – how alert the guards were, where they were stationed –
and then search for Jacob after midnight, when most would be
asleep.

What he would do if the man's quarters were empty was another
matter; one that had haunted him on the journey east. If the scientist
had been killed, they had no options – they'd be destined to run from
constant pursuit until the inevitable day their luck ran out. The
thought made his stomach muscles tighten to the point where they
were sore, and he willed himself calm. He patted Tango, preferring to
focus on the immediate future rather than speculate on what would
soon be obvious.

"We can do this, boy," he said, unsure whether he was talking to
Tango or himself. He gazed through his binoculars at the amber
radiance, faint silhouettes of buildings framed against the glow, and
then coaxed the horse on, the final five or so miles likely to be the
most treacherous.

Chapter 33

Cano studied the stucco walls of the hotel room where he was convalescing. The stained surface had bubbled in places where water had leaked through the roof in one of the area's infrequent storms, forming patterns strangely similar to a collage of stylized human faces. He blinked away the vision, his good eye roaming the baseboards that rodents had chewed much of away. He could hear them at night, their tiny feet scrambling across the linoleum floor, and for the first few days he'd been unable to sleep for more than a few minutes at a time, the conviction that they were going to dine on him while he was defenseless consuming his thoughts.

He was better now; his wounds had scabbed over, and his strength was returning by the day. He'd avoided reporting his state to Magnus for fear of his injuries being interpreted as an early failure on his part. Cano knew the price for disappointing the great one, and he'd seen no reason to give Houston an update, preferring to allow them to think he was still in the field, on the quarry's tail.

The doctor had warned him not to push it, and Cano had reluctantly obeyed the instruction, there being no obvious trail to follow. He'd sent out a party to circle the crest from which he'd been ambushed and look for tracks, but had little hope that they would find anything significant. With him out of commission for almost a week, the trail would have gone cold, and the woman could easily be in Canada by now.

The thought wasn't a pleasant one. Magnus wouldn't be pleased, and he wouldn't care about the details. He'd made that clear.

Cano's plan was to recuperate another few days and then get back into the saddle and resume the hunt. His head was now clear, and he'd grown accustomed to the blindness on his left side. Physically he was healing remarkably fast, but mentally he was still shaken, and he gave the wall another sidelong glance, from where the faces seemed to be mocking him.

"Another couple of days," he muttered.

The worst part of his self-imposed bed rest was that he was going stir-crazy. Cano was a man of action, and he didn't do well on his back, waiting. He had a strong urge to suit up in his plate carrier and ride out despite the doctor's warning, but he resisted it, there being no place to go. He closed his eye and willed himself to rest, knowing that every hour of recuperation would pay dividends later.

Outside, his men were playing cards, laughing and swearing as the level of their bottles sank and their luck changed. Inertia was also bad for them, Cano knew – left to their own devices, they would quickly lose their edge, and soon the fights would start.

He needed to get back into the field.

"Soon," he whispered. "Soon."

~ ~ ~

Duke spied motion in the darkness and hit the switch for the floodlights, his AR-15 in hand as the compound's periphery lit up for two hundred yards in all directions. Doug was approaching on the main trail and waved to signal his presence. Duke looked through the telescope and then leaned back to take a swig of water and extinguish the lights, the rider identified.

Doug waited outside as Duke opened the gate. He dismounted and walked his horse through, and after tying him to a hitching post by the water trough, gave Duke an abridged report on his recruiting effort.

"Not many able-bodied men around in a mind to leave what they got to come to work, Duke. Word's spread about Loving and Pecos, and it's got people on edge."

"There's got to be somebody. Don't want to keep having to do four-hour stretches. Like death by a thousand cuts, once you get to be my age."

"I hear you. Maybe we'll have more luck tomorrow." Doug hesitated. "I did stop by Slim's place. They ain't seen him."

Duke set his rifle down. "Kind of weird, dontcha think?"

"He was glad to be rid of the ranch. Can't see him excited to return."

"Wonder where he went off to?"

"No tellin'. Boy always had a restless streak, long as I known him. A real mustang when he got it in his head."

"Not many places to get to, though, are there?"

"Sometimes even nowhere's better than where you are."

"And he didn't mention anything to you about wanting to leave before he skedaddled?"

"Not a word."

"Go on in and grab some chow. Aaron caught some fish. Still on the stove."

"Don't mind if I do."

Duke watched him make his way to the main building, and his brow creased with mounting worry. Was it possible Slim had gone to the Locos and sold them out? He hadn't seemed like the type, but what did Duke really know about him? And where else could he have gone? It wasn't like West Texas was a hotbed of opportunity waiting for a young man with big expectations to come along.

He followed the thought through to its conclusion: if Slim had done as he feared, the trading post was toast. It would just be a matter of time before the cartel rode in and flattened it for lying to them about the woman – and worse yet, not alerting them when there was still time to catch her.

It wouldn't be about picking up her trail, although he was sure they'd delight in torturing him to learn whatever he knew. It would be revenge, pure and simple, brought to him by the same forgiving folks that had slaughtered an entire town without hesitation.

Duke didn't back down from a fight, but he wasn't delusional and understood that if the cartel came loaded for bear, his defenses would fall and they'd prevail. His usefulness as a trading conduit wouldn't save him from their wrath – especially not that of the tattooed demon who'd searched his place. No, if Slim had sold them down the river, Duke was already on borrowed time.

So the question was, did he feel lucky?

He looked around the compound. Duke had a hideaway up in the mountains where he could lie low for a while. Near a stream flush with fat bass, far from prying eyes. He could get most of his high-value items into the wagon and leave at first light; tell the boys he was headed for greener pastures. Aaron would probably accompany him. Doug, likely not. Which was fine. He didn't know the man all that well, anyway, and wouldn't miss him.

"Nothin' lasts forever," he murmured, eyeing the building and already running an inventory of what would stay and what would go. That the outpost would be looted was a given, but there was only so much damage that could be done to cinder block and dirt. He'd miss the solar and considered how many of the panels he could fit in the wagon.

He glanced at the time. Another hour, and then it would be Aaron's watch.

Duke would break the news to him then.

Doug, he'd tell in the morning. He didn't want to take the chance of a mutiny.

That this stage of his life was over didn't bother him as much as he would have imagined, but then again, he'd always been resilient.

He'd radio the kook up north and see if he could get hold of him before he left. No way was he going to take the chance of being overheard before that. Of course, the chances that the man was monitoring the airwaves twenty-four seven were slim and none, but he had to at least try. And he'd have to phrase things carefully so an eavesdropper from the cartel wouldn't understand the warning he was giving, or it could do more harm than good.

Composing it would require some thought.

Duke sighed as he looked out into the darkness. At least he had plenty of time to do so.

Chapter 34

Lubbock at night was a study in contradictions. As Lucas rode into town unchallenged, he passed groups of indigents gathered around fires, their skeletal forms bent by premature aging from the ravages of hunger and disease and dressed in little more than rags. Their gaunt faces watched him in silent misery as he guided Tango along the streets. At one of the fires he spotted the unmistakable carcass of a skinned dog roasting on a spit, and hot bile rose in his throat. The stench of sewage and rot greeted every step further into the city, which appeared to be a nightmare vision of privation – until he neared the town center.

There, where the Crew occupied most of the better buildings, electric lights burned brightly. Groups of gang members cruised the streets, well fed and radiating danger, and many of those he saw were apparently drunk, high, or both. He skirted everyone, sticking to deserted streets as he wended his way toward the medical center campus, which he could see on the far edge of the city, its multistory towers dark against the star-filled sky, its outline familiar to him from a prior visit with his wife.

If stopped by anyone, Lucas would pretend to be a trader looking for a watering hole – a likely enough cover, Lubbock being a reasonable hub for those wishing to travel west. Magnus, like any of the other regional warlords, needed commerce to keep his population of de facto slaves prosperous enough to afford whatever the Crew was selling – chiefly protection, drugs, clean water, and electricity.

Trading accomplished that. Unlike small strongholds like Pecos or Artesia, larger towns had porous borders too large to guard, so rather than attempt to impede entry and exit, the gang profited from it indirectly, taking a bite of every transaction via a tax on the outposts, and then downriver from sales of its wares to the residents. The end result left the population with just enough trading wealth to be willing to continue working while the Crew took most of the juice.

Not so much unlike the pre-collapse governments, Lucas reasoned. Most had been originally set up to provide services to the populace – in the case of the United States, to build roads, deliver mail, defend against attack, and the like – but had morphed into tyrannical rulers that sucked the marrow from the citizenry, ruled it with a set of laws the elite members of society didn't follow, quelled rebellion with a police state that would have been the envy of industrialists at the turn of the century executing union organizers on behalf of the corporations, and generally drained the prosperity of the nation via hundreds of hidden taxes…in addition to one on income.

Magnus had simply removed the pretense of free will from the equation. He supplied the same services of protection and punishment, taxed the survivors for his efforts, and fleeced them of most of their earnings over time with the threat of force while delivering as little as possible. He'd stepped into the gap left by state and federal entities and imposed his own kind of order that recognized no rights he couldn't dispense with at will, and the inhabitants of his territory had tolerated it – anything to survive.

Lucas was drawn out of his musings by the sound of hooves pounding down one of the adjacent streets. A cry was answered by two shots and then laughter, followed by the clip-clop of horses moving away. He didn't need to investigate what had happened to understand: one of the unfortunates had crossed the Crew and had paid the ultimate price. Nobody else would have dared discharge a weapon in Lubbock with so many of the gang there; ergo it had to be them, enforcing their rule with a bullet.

It wasn't his problem. He had to stay focused on his objective, which was to make it to the staff housing, find a way past any guards, and identify whether Jacob was still alive. Lubbock would take care of itself, for better or for worse. Still, the part of him that had carried a badge rankled at the injustice of the situation.

He cut east of the medical center campus and made his way to the boulevard, which was dark as pitch, only a few lights on at the hospital guard stations. After confirming that there was nobody nearby, he lowered himself from the saddle and freed his M4 to look through the night vision scope. A quick scan of the street revealed two gunmen at the front of the apartments near the hospital, exactly where Sierra had said they'd be, blocking the entryway into the horseshoe-shaped complex.

Lucas had thought for three days how to best get into the apartments undetected, and had come up with creating a diversion as the safest way. To do that, he'd need a bottle of his grandfather's white lightning and a shirt that had seen better days. He bundled the jar of moonshine inside the shirt and stuck it under his arm and, after tying Tango beneath a tree at the back of a vacant lot two blocks away, set off for the apartments on foot, M4 at the ready.

He eased himself past an overflowing dumpster that hadn't been emptied for years and crept up an alley that ran between Jacob's complex and the next in the line, which Sierra had said was abandoned. When he arrived at the midpoint of the span, he stopped at a window and peered into the darkness. The room appeared empty, and he tried the window, which was locked. He studied the aluminum frame and spotted screws connecting the vertical piece to the top and bottom.

Three minutes later he'd removed them with his bowie knife and pried the vertical bar loose until it slid with a soft scrape to the side. Inching the glass free was easy from there, and he placed it carefully on the ground, listening for any indication that the guards were taking a lap around the building. Confident they were still at their post, he pulled himself into the apartment and stood motionless for a few moments in case the sound of his entry had given him away.

Nothing but the smell of mildew and rat droppings.

A sweep of the room with his NV scope revealed a vacant dining room and kitchen, the cabinets and baseboards chewed away, explaining the vermin infestation. According to Sierra's map, he was six apartments from Jacob's, which was on the second floor. He'd decided he couldn't go to Jacob, so he needed a way to force the scientist to him.

The moonshine was the key.

He dowsed the kitchen with alcohol and then stuffed his rolled-up shirt sleeve into the half-full jar until it had absorbed much of the fluid. He removed a disposable lighter from his flak jacket, lit the garment, and threw it against the cabinets, breaking the glass and spraying the area with flaming liquid.

Lucas was back through the window in a flash. He watched as the flames licked at the wood and the sheetrock and then crawled up the partially exposed struts. Within moments the apartment was blazing, smoke and tongues of fire flitting from the window, and he ran to the dumpster and waited behind it, ignoring the nauseating odors wafting from it.

A voice called from the front of the apartment complex. "Fire! Shit. It's going up. Hey, wake up! Fire! Get out of your rooms!"

The guards reacted predictably and were rousing the residents as the flames spread along the wood-framed structure. Lucas heard doors being thrown open and confused cries of alarm as the guards raced the fire. There was a fifty-fifty chance that they'd come down the alley to investigate, but once the residents of the apartments emptied onto the street, it wouldn't matter.

Smoke billowed from the ground floor as another unit caught, and then the first footfalls sounded on the pavement – probably one of the guards by the sound of it, given that the residents had been sleeping and wouldn't have had time to don heavy boots. A burly gunman jogged past him toward the area he'd lit, and Lucas sprang from his hiding place and drove his Bowie knife into the back of his neck before the man had a chance to register his presence.

The razor-sharp blade severed the gunman's spinal cord at the C3 vertebra, and the man dropped like a sack of wet manure, limbs limp and torso twitching. His AK-47 struck the ground, but the sound was lost in the growing cries from the complex. Lucas wiped the knife on the man's leather vest and sheathed it, and then dragged his body to the inferno and hoisted it through the window, wincing from the effort and the withering heat.

When the guard's body was found, the fire would have obliterated the evidence of the cause of death. But he was running out of time. It was just a matter of minutes before reinforcements arrived from the nearby medical center, and they'd easily spot a stranger, even in the dark.

Lucas ran to the mouth of the service alley and looked around the corner. There were maybe a dozen people, men and women alike, standing in the street and watching their home burn. Lucas removed his hat and propped it on the barrel of his M4, and then shrugged out of his plate carrier and stashed it along with his weapon behind the dumpster. His hope was that in the confusion he wouldn't look alarming enough to be registered – and in a pinch, he still had his Kimber.

He took a deep breath and rounded the corner. The other guard was in the courtyard, screaming a warning at the remaining staff, leaving Lucas the opening he'd been hoping for. He looked over the spectators and spoke in an urgent voice. "Oh, my God. It's going to burn to the ground. Jacob! Has anyone seen Jacob?"

One of the women, who looked half asleep, motioned to a man a few yards away on her left. "Don't worry, he made it out."

"Thank goodness," Lucas said, and moved away as she turned back toward the blaze. He sidled toward the man, who matched Sierra's description, albeit in sweat shorts and a collegiate T-shirt that looked decades old. When Lucas was beside him, he leaned in. "Jacob?"

The man tore his eyes from the burning spectacle before him and gave Lucas a blank look. "Yes?"

Lucas tapped a finger against the medallion hanging from his neck. "A friend sent me to make sure you're okay."

His eyes widened and his mouth formed an O, and Lucas shook his head. Jacob quickly regained his composure and nodded understanding. He looked around, his attention fixed on several Crew members jogging from the medical center campus. He nudged Lucas and whispered to him, "How is she?"

Lucas followed his stare and frowned. "Not here. We need to talk."

Jacob matched his expression and nodded. "There's a brick house a block north. Empty. White chimney. Wait for me there."

"When?"

"Later. Get out of here."

Lucas didn't need to be told twice. He moved back toward the alley and ducked out of sight as the guards arrived. He leaned down to retrieve his weapon and hat and then took off at a dead run for the opposite end of the walkway, the roar of the fire now covering any sound from the clomping of his boots on the pavement, his shadow long and wavering along the far building's wall, backlit by the flames.

Chapter 35

Lucas waited across the street from the brick house, Tango tied a safe distance away. He had his M4 trained on the structure, watching it through the NV scope. A part of him was troubled by how easily he'd knifed the Crew guard; it worried him that he could kill so easily now. Then he remembered the stories he'd heard about the Crew – the pedophilia, the rapes, the atrocities – and his doubts melted away.

His rumination was cut short by Jacob cutting from shadow to shadow as he made his way toward the house. When he was at the entry, Lucas shifted his focus from the building to the street to see if he was being followed. After verifying they were alone, Lucas rose from his position and darted to the house, little more than a wraith in the dim moonlight.

Jacob was obviously startled when Lucas materialized in the doorway. Lucas stepped inside and immediately sized up the fields of fire he would have if they were attacked and positioned himself accordingly. Jacob watched him in silence, and when Lucas was crouched in the shadows with the M4 clutched in both hands, he finally spoke.

"You have Sierra's medallion."

"That's right. She sent me. There's been a problem."

"I heard. Nobody showed up at the rendezvous. You have no idea how worried I was. And Eve?"

"She's fine. They both are."

Jacob gave a slow sigh. "That's a relief. But why did you come?"

"They told me about Shangri-La. They don't know how to get there."

"Of course they don't. Almost nobody does."

Lucas nodded. "You mentioned a rendezvous?"

"That's right."

"We need to set up another one."

Jacob studied Lucas in the gloom. "Who are you? What's your connection to them?"

"Their entourage was cut down. I saved their lives."

"How do I know this isn't a trick?"

"I have the medallion. She wouldn't have given it to me if she didn't trust me."

"You could have taken it against her will."

Lucas shrugged. "Sure. Anything's possible. But take a hard look at me. I've been riding for a week. Why would I do that? Just to trick you? To what end?"

"You could be working for...for them."

"The Crew? Don't you think if I was, you'd be in a hole somewhere, begging for your life?" Lucas sighed. "Look. They're safe, but the Crew has people hunting them. You know why as well as I do. They're not going to give up. So everything you've done, all the risks you've taken, will have been in vain if they catch them – which they will, eventually, because they'll throw as many men at it as they need to." Lucas let that sink in. "Unless I can get them to safety. To Shangri-La."

Jacob mulled over Lucas's words, and Lucas gave him time to process. He could understand the hesitation. The scientist had thought he was out of the woods, and now he was being asked to put it all on the line again.

"Where are they?" Jacob asked.

"New Mexico."

"Ah. So they made it that far, at least."

"Yes. Where was the rendezvous supposed to happen?"

"Roswell."

Lucas nodded again. "We could make it, no problem."

"You say her escorts were cut down. Can you be more specific?"

"Sure. A bunch of scum that call themselves the Raiders attacked them. Ambushed them in a gulch. They were after their guns and animals. They do it all the time."

"Damn."

"Yup. They manage to escape only to be taken out by scavengers. Bad luck, no doubt." Lucas glanced at his watch. "No offense, but won't the guards notice you're gone?"

"Probably. I mean, eventually." Jacob regarded him skeptically. "The fire. Was that you?"

"I had to find a way to get you where I could talk to you."

"You burned down the entire building just for that?"

Lucas shrugged. "Didn't see a lot of alternatives."

"Good Lord…"

"Look, Jacob, I've ridden a long way, and I'm playing for keeps. I'll do whatever's necessary to get the job done. That was necessary. End of story."

Jacob eyed him. "You have blood on your sleeve."

"You're short one guard." Lucas exhaled impatiently. "I need you to radio your people and set up another meet. Either that, or tell me how to decode the note."

"You have that too?"

"And the USB drive."

"Thank God. That's almost as big a piece of the puzzle as Eve is."

"So same game plan, just a different inning. Where's your radio?"

"I'm afraid you've misunderstood. I don't know where Shangri-La is or who they were supposed to meet. I just know it was in Roswell. I don't have any contact with the sanctuary. I go through a cutout who speaks with them."

"So you can't call them?"

"No. I also don't know how to decode your note or what it contains. Probably just directions to the rendezvous, which will do you no good – the contact is long gone by now."

Lucas's shoulders sagged. "Then this was all for nothing. They're never going to make it, you know. I'll do my best to keep them safe, but the odds are lousy."

Jacob was silent for several moments.

"I can get in touch with my cutout," he said softly. "It's worth the risk of another broadcast." Jacob trembled slightly at the prospect. "The Crew monitors the airwaves. They're not stupid, and they're sophisticated enough to be able to locate a transmitter. Every time he broadcasts, he's jeopardizing all of us."

"Stakes are pretty high, I'd say."

Jacob began pacing. "We were fairly close to developing a vaccine, but we can't without Eve." His eyes met Lucas's, and Lucas saw a haunted soul in them. "Magnus can't be allowed to get the vaccine. It would be...it would be worse than the collapse."

"I know. Sierra told me."

Jacob stopped and squared his shoulders. "Okay. I'll do it. Where are you staying?"

"I'm not."

"What does that mean?"

"It means I rode here to find you. I did. Once you set up the rendezvous, I ride back."

Jacob adjusted his glasses and considered Lucas for a long minute. "What's your background?"

"Used to be a Texas Ranger."

Jacob nodded. "It makes sense. You guys had quite a reputation."

"Ancient history. We going to do this or not?"

"What – now?"

"Got any reason to wait?"

"I...I suppose we could try."

"That would be good." Lucas straightened. "Let's go talk to your contact."

"Oh. Well. I mean, he...I'll go, and meet you somewhere later."

"No. Too risky. Let's do this right now, the two of us. No stalling or thinking things over. They're following Sierra's tracks as we speak. There's no time to lose."

"I...I don't know. It could compromise him."

"I risked my neck riding all the way here, Jacob. You want Eve to get to this sanctuary of yours, you need to get off the pot. Your apartment's burned to sticks, there's confusion – this is your chance."

Lucas could see the hesitation in the scientist's eyes, and then he nodded again, the thick lenses of his glasses glinting from reflected moonlight as he moved to the door.

"Okay. We'll give it a try." Jacob stopped. "What's your name, anyway?"

Lucas transferred his M4 from his right hand to his left and tipped his hat brim in the dark. "Lucas. Where are we headed?"

"Back to the hospital."

"Are you kidding?"

Jacob shook his head. "No. He lives there."

"How do we get in?"

"Let me worry about that."

Jacob brushed by Lucas and stepped out of the doorway onto the deserted street. The sky glowed orange from the apartment's flames. Lucas followed him out, wondering how the situation could get any worse than going into the most heavily guarded building in Lubbock, and then stopped himself.

The creeping dread in the pit of his stomach warned him that he might soon find out.

Chapter 36

Bruce sat at his computer station, LED work lamp illuminating the living room. Eve and Ruby were asleep in the bedroom. Sierra was relaxing on the couch across from him, unable to sleep even long after dark. Bruce had been unable to find a power supply for his CPU and had griped on and off for the last three days about the far slower processing power of his laptop.

They'd continued trying to decrypt the note, but with no success, making Lucas's decision to ride to Lubbock appear more prescient with each passing hour. Bruce had been pestering Sierra and Ruby for more information on the cryptic note ever since Lucas had departed, and was becoming increasingly truculent at their stonewalling.

Sierra was reading one of Bruce's prodigious collection of paperback sci-fi novels, the pages yellowing at the edges from age – this one about a planet far away where spice was the currency of the empire. She shifted and sighed as she flipped a brittle page, and Bruce swiveled around and faced her.

"Sierra, I've been thinking about this a lot, and I have a right to know what's going on. You're taking advantage of my hospitality, my resources, and you're treating me like an adversary. It's not fair, and I don't like it, and frankly...it's pretty shabby," he said, the speech obviously one he'd been polishing in his mind for some time.

Sierra set the book down beside her and looked him in the eye. "Bruce, I totally get what you're saying, and I want you to know that I appreciate everything you've done for us. We'll find a way to pay you back. I swear."

"You could start by being honest."

"That's not my call to make."

He frowned. "Whose is it, then? Aren't you an adult?"

She shook her head. "Lucas made me promise."

"Lucas? Does he own you? What does he have to do with anything?"

"We're in this together."

Bruce looked around. "Funny. I don't see him here, do you?" Bruce softened his tone and sat forward, an earnest expression on his face. "Look, Sierra, I can't put myself at risk if I don't know what's at stake. I know that I'm doing so by the way you and Ruby are acting, and it's a crummy way to repay me for letting you stay here."

"What do you mean, how we're acting?"

"Come on, Sierra. You hardly go outside at all, and when you do, you spend ten minutes checking through the windows to make sure nobody's around to see you. Do you really think I'm that much of an idiot?"

"I…I can't."

His expression hardened and his mouth narrowed to a thin line. "Then I'm afraid you're going to have to go tomorrow. I'm sorry. I truly am."

"Go! Go where?"

Bruce shrugged. "Not my problem. All I know is that I'm either your friend or your enemy, and I've been treating you like my friends, and you're rewarding me by acting like I'm your enemy. This is my place, so I get to make the rules. I'm sorry."

"Come on, Bruce, that's blackmail."

"No, it isn't. It's telling you that the condition of staying here, under my protection, is being honest with me. Christ sakes, Sierra, hasn't it occurred to you or Ruby that I can't do a decent job of it if I have no idea what to expect?"

Sierra chewed her bottom lip. "You can't tell Ruby I told you anything, Bruce. You have to swear."

He smiled for the first time. "I promise."

"We're trying to get somewhere, but we don't know where it is."

"Why?"

"Because it's safe there."

"Safe from what?"

She looked away. "Everything."

"Could you be any less specific? Come on. This is bullshit. You're not telling me anything I couldn't have already figured out from your little talks with Ruby." He sat back. "Oh, you think I don't overhear you two? You really do think I'm oblivious, don't you?"

"We're trying to find out the location of a place called Shangri-La. A refuge. It's supposed to have electricity, water, food, and is well defended – and not like here. I mean really well defended."

He stared at her incredulously. "Shangri-La? As in the mythical Himalayan valley where people live forever? You realize that's a myth, right?"

"I didn't name it."

He studied her face. "You believe this crap?"

"It's a real place, Bruce. If we can get there, we'll be…everything will be good."

Bruce's tone quieted. When he spoke, it was as though to a child. "Sierra, I hear versions of this all the time on the radio and from travelers who pass through and need something repaired: that there's a place with chocolate rivers and unicorns and rainbows, where everything's different and special. It's a common fable throughout history because it's so attractive to believe. Who doesn't want to believe that if they just put out a little effort, they can live in paradise? Believe me, I get it. You think I like living in this shithole? This town's slowly dying for me – there's less I can do to fix people's stuff as time goes by, and I can't source parts. I can tell you how that's going to end up – with me trying to eke out a living however I can in a place that isn't exactly the land of plenty. If I thought for a minute there was someplace where I could go and have it all different, I'd be on it like white on rice." He stopped. "But there isn't. I get that. Because I'm an adult, and that's just the way things are."

"I don't care whether you believe me or not, Bruce. You asked what we're doing. I told you. You think it's BS, that's your prerogative. I'm not looking for validation, I'm just laying it out, as you asked."

He shook his head. "I can't believe Ruby bought into this. She's smarter than that."

"That she did should tell you something," Sierra snapped back.

"It tells me that people get strange ideas into their heads, especially as they get older."

Sierra shrugged. "Whatever. Think what you like. I'm not asking for your pity. We're waiting for Lucas to get back from finding out where it is."

"Will he be riding in Santa's sleigh?"

She picked up the book. "Sounds like this discussion is done. I told you what you wanted to know. Is there anything else?"

He nodded. "You left out the part about who you're afraid of."

"There's a gang that thinks I'm their property. They don't take no for an answer, okay? So they're after me."

"A gang? Which one?"

"Why? What does it matter? There's a bunch of filth that wants to use me until I'm broken, and they don't like that I got away. They have the same in store for Eve. You want to throw us out and give them a shot at us? Is that how this is going to play?"

"I didn't say that…"

"The hell you didn't. You threatened it. Don't pretend you didn't, Bruce. Own it."

"I said I didn't want you staying here if you weren't going to be honest with me. That's not unreasonable. Because it's what you don't know that can get you killed. Now you've told me, so consider that settled. Although it would help to know who to be on the lookout for."

"Take your pick. The Locos. The Crew out of Houston. The Raiders. Anyone who would treat us as slaves because they can."

"They're *all* after you?" Bruce said, his face draining of color.

"I used them as examples," Sierra backtracked, aware that she might have said too much.

"So they aren't after you?"

Sierra sighed and stood. "Just assume everyone in the world is, Bruce. You've never been a woman, so you have no idea what it's like to be treated as property, but that's what it's like most places these days. The reason we're interested in finding Shangri-La is because that's not how things are there. If you think looking for someplace better is crazy, that's fine, you're entitled to your opinion, but until you've been passed around like a joint at a concert by a bunch of scum you'd rather die than..." She ran out of breath and shook her head in disgust. "You think you've got it tough here, Bruce? I'm not dissing you at all, but you have no frigging idea what tough is. And I want better than that for Eve and myself. End of story."

Sierra turned and stormed to the bedroom, leaving Bruce watching her departure with an open mouth.

"Damn, girl, you're something else," he muttered after the door closed behind her, and reached for his pipe and a pinch of marijuana to steady his nerves.

Chapter 37

Jacob led Lucas down an empty street, a tributary to the main artery that fed onto the hospital campus. They'd agreed it best to leave Tango well away from the medical center in order to reduce the chances of their being discovered; a big bay stallion was likelier to be spotted than a couple of men moving stealthily in the gloom.

The scientist had been tight-lipped about his contact, other than to say that he was a character and that the Crew depended on him to keep the lab operating. Lucas hadn't pressed for more information, figuring that if it made Jacob feel more secure to keep the man's identity a mystery, that was fine – as long as Lucas could conclude his business that night and be rid of Lubbock by morning, they could talk in code and wear masks for all he cared.

The only good news in the scenario so far was that Jacob appeared to be taking the adventure seriously, and he didn't strike Lucas as the flighty type. That lent credibility to the possibility that they could actually make it to Shangri-La and that it would be as worthwhile an endeavor as Sierra hoped. The skeptical part of Lucas was still doubtful that an enclave could evade detection by powerful foes for years, but judging by Jacob's reactions, it seemed more likely. Now that he'd met the man, he could tell that he was dead serious about the risks involved in contacting his cutout, which meant that he believed attempting to organize another rendezvous to be worth it.

For Lucas's sake, he hoped that Jacob was right.

That Sierra had been intimate with Jacob didn't faze Lucas as much as he'd thought it might. Her explanation had made sense once he'd met the scientist – he had a kind of quiet magnetism, and he could see how she might have been drawn to him, especially given the circumstances. Neither of them seemed shattered to have moved on, so it couldn't have been all that deep a connection – not that he had any proprietary claim on her.

They reached the north parking lot, which was larger than several football fields, and Lucas paused next to a tree to scan the area with his scope while Jacob waited beside him. He spotted three guards by the main building, a six-level monolith with several multistory connected structures of mammoth proportions.

"There are gunmen at the entrance on this side," he whispered.

"Not unexpected. We're going to cut over to the east side, through the health sciences building. It's not being used, and there are a number of subterranean passageways, even though they've blocked off the ones at ground level."

"Why don't they lock the passages?"

"Maintenance. Some of the equipment's shared."

"They don't guard it?"

Jacob shook his head. "From what? Main reason they guard the hospital is because of the lab. The health sciences building's been looted – there's nothing left worth stealing you wouldn't need a forklift to move."

"You're sure?"

"I'd have been told if anything changed," Jacob said.

Lucas followed him across the expanse to the health sciences entry, which was boarded up. Jacob glanced around and then slid one of the plywood slabs aside just far enough so they could squeeze through. Lucas pushed the board closed behind him, and they stood beside each other in utter darkness.

"Got a flashlight?" Jacob asked.

"What would you do if I didn't?"

"I have a lighter, but I'd rather not waste the fuel."

Lucas removed his penlight from his plate carrier and switched it on. He handed it to Jacob, who led the way through the wreckage of what had been the lobby and then down a flight of service stairs that smelled of long-dry urine and general rot.

"There were some squatters in here a few years ago," Jacob explained. "Before Magnus set up the lab. His men took care of them."

Lucas didn't have to ask how.

"Why didn't you try to get to Shangri-La too?" Lucas probed. "Sierra told me you were...close."

Jacob shook his head. "That's not my role. I have to stay here and do what I can to sabotage Magnus's vaccine effort. That's the most important thing I can do – they already have adequate know-how in Shangri-La."

"You weren't tempted?"

"I wasn't invited. Besides, I know what I have to do. If I'm successful, Shangri-La will still be there, and the world will be a better place for everyone."

Their soles crunched on broken glass and bits of ceiling tile that had been ripped out for access to the copper wire above. Next they entered a long basement hall with dank air, the walls sweating through battleship gray paint. Jacob stopped at one of the metal doors, listened, and then swung it open and motioned for Lucas to enter.

They entered a room lined with huge steel pipes, each with wheeled handles at junctions where they continued on in narrower runs. Jacob walked to a small opening on the far side of the room and gestured for Lucas to follow him through. They both had to crouch to get through the vandalized duct gap, and then they were in a tunnel with bundles of heavy wiring running its length, a two-foot wide walkway stretching down the middle.

They made their way to the end, and Jacob twisted the handle on a corroding steel door at the top of four cement stairs. He walked through and Lucas ascended, the hair on his arms standing up at a thrumming sound coming from ahead of them.

"AC compression lines and the pump rooms are up ahead," Jacob explained. "Not much farther to go."

They were in another corridor, this one with a polished concrete floor and ivory walls painted in high gloss. Above them, emergency lighting flickered, though only a few of the bulbs were still working. Jacob handed Lucas back his flashlight and whispered, "No need for it from here on. This section has power."

The scientist picked up his pace and turned into a dark hall before stopping at a green steel door with *maintenance* stenciled on it. He glanced at Lucas and rapped softly. A muffled voice called out from inside.

"What the hell do you want at this hour?"

"Eddie. It's me – Jacob."

The sound of a bolt opening filled the hall. The door opened ten seconds later and they found themselves facing a gnome of a man in orange coveralls, no more than five foot two, his white hair askew, his blue eyes puffy but the whites almost luminescent.

"What's wrong?" he asked, unable to keep the fear from his voice, and then registered Lucas standing behind Jacob. "Who's this?"

"Sierra sent him."

The man's expression changed and he sized Lucas up. "Yeah?"

"She's safe," Lucas said, his voice low.

"Who're you?"

"A friend."

The little man looked down the hallway and stepped aside. "Get in here before you draw the guards," he snapped. "I could hear you a mile away."

Jacob and Lucas stepped into a chamber as long as a boxcar and stacked to the ceiling with boxes of parts, pieces of machinery, tools, bails of wire, and various gizmos Lucas couldn't identify.

"Lock it," the gnome said.

Lucas obliged, driving the bolt home with a solid thunk.

"This way," the man said, and led them through the clutter to another room, this one wider but equally stuffed with junk. He moved to a seat and sat beside a desk with a computer monitor in the center of it and stacks of papers on either side of the screen. He swiveled around and faced them, his bulldog face raised pugnaciously to Lucas. "You have two minutes to explain," he barked.

Lucas recounted his story in half the allotted time and, when he was finished, stood silently waiting for a response. Eddie looked him up and down, taking in his dusty boots and pants, the dried blood on his sleeve, the fatigue lines and discoloration beneath his eyes, and slowly nodded.

"I can make a call. How long will it take you to get to the Roswell area?"

"Figure four days, if I turn around now and start riding."

"And your interest in the woman and child?"

"I promised I'd help them reach Shangri-La. After that, I'm out."

Eddie's eyes softened. "You said you rescued them both?"

"I was the only one around to do it."

"The Native Americans believed that you became tied to those you saved. That there was a bond you couldn't shake."

"I'm not Native American."

Eddie eyed him skeptically. "Might be something to it, is all."

Lucas nodded. "Could be," he allowed.

Eddie stood and motioned to two sorry-looking metal chairs with red vinyl seats. "Take a load off. I'll go see if I can raise someone."

The little man trundled to another door at the back of the room, unlocked it, and then disappeared inside. Lucas checked the time, fidgety, and Jacob steepled his fingers and leaned forward.

"He's a little rough around the edges, but Eddie's good people."

"What's his story?"

"He keeps the place running. He was the head of maintenance before the collapse. He holed up in here while the world fell apart around him, and was on his last legs when the Crew took over the town. They pressed him into duty, and he's been here ever since. Hates them, but what can you do?"

"He could disappear."

"Man's sixty-seven this year. Wouldn't last long out in the world."

"You'd be surprised. One of my friends is about that age, and she's doing fine."

"Eddie isn't like everybody. He's got diabetes. Magnus keeps him supplied with insulin, and he stays put. Bargain with the devil, he calls it."

"Where does the Crew get insulin?"

"We make it in the lab. For trade. Same with a few antibiotics and painkillers. You'd be surprised how much the desperate will pay for those." Jacob glanced at him. "Or maybe you wouldn't."

"Never seen a U-Haul behind a hearse. What's the point of having something if you can't use it to save your life?"

"True words."

"So he's working behind the Crew's back to sabotage them?"

"Nothing overt. That would be too dangerous. But he can be eyes and ears, and when they brought Eve and Sierra here and set up a vaccine lab, that launched a whole series of events in motion, which culminated in their escape."

"And nobody suspected you two?" Lucas asked.

"They suspected everyone. But what are they going to do, absent any evidence? Kill the two people that run their operation? And then what? Who's going to keep the lights on or the meds made?"

"From what Sierra told me about Magnus, they easily could have. She didn't describe him as a deep thinker."

"There's risk to everything," Jacob agreed.

"Dangerous game."

Jacob gave him a grim smile. "So's the one you're playing."

"Got that right," Lucas conceded.

"Then we're in the same boat."

"Not really. I can leave."

Eddie reappeared and approached Lucas. "All right. There's another meet set: four days from now at dusk. Place called Bitter Lake, northeast of Roswell."

"Bitter Lake," Lucas repeated. "Never heard of it."

"There's a makeshift bar the locals built out of pallets and whatnot at the water's edge. Bartender's name is Colt. He's your man."

"Colt. Bitter Lake. Got it," Lucas said.

A pounding sounded from the hallway door, and a loud voice called out, "Open the door. Now – or we'll kick it down."

Chapter 38

Jacob looked around, eyes wild. Eddie's expression hardened with determination. "Damn. They must have been able to triangulate the broadcast. Come on. This way," he said.

The little man led them to the room from which he'd emerged. Inside was a storage room with a small bathroom in the near corner. Eddie raced to the bathroom door and yanked it open, and then moved to the shower stall. He fiddled with one of the faucets, cursing. A soft click echoed from behind it, and he heaved on the stall and slid it toward him.

"Inside. This leads to a storage room on the upper level. From there you can make it back down the stairs to the basement on the far side of the hospital, and Jacob can show you the way out." Eddie pointed to iron rungs leading up to a hatch in the ceiling. "Good luck."

"What about you?" Jacob asked.

"Someone's got to open the door."

Jacob's face hardened. "They'll kill you."

"For what? There's nothing to find. Radio's up in the other room. I'm the only one with the keys. And I'm in here." Eddie frowned. "Now go. I'll take my chances."

Lucas didn't hesitate, and Jacob tailed him into the small space. The shower snicked back into place behind them, and Lucas switched on his penlight. Clenching it between his teeth, he climbed the rungs and then pushed the hatch up.

The storage room was piled with discarded machinery, and Lucas pointed at a corner as Jacob scrambled through the gap in the floor. "He's pretty tricky. That must be the radio. If I didn't know what to look for, I'd assume it was being used for parts."

The radio sat on a crate, sans cover, just a metal frame and a bunch of wire and electrical components. The giveaway was the microphone and a pair of small computer speakers, as well as a power cord stretching into the darkness.

"I hope he'll be okay," Jacob said.

"Let's worry about us for now." Lucas flashed the light on the far door. "I assume you know where we are."

"I think so."

Lucas removed his hat and pressed his ear against the steel slab. After several moments he replaced it, shut off the flashlight, and switched his scope back on.

"I can't see," Jacob said.

"I can. Once we're out, which way?"

"Left. It would have to be left."

"Hang on to the back of my flak jacket. Ready?"

"Yes."

Lucas twisted the handle and eased the door open. There was a wide hall he could make out in the scope. He whispered what he was seeing to Jacob, who whispered back.

"There should be a stairway at the end of the hall."

Lucas nodded and then inched from the doorway with cautious steps, doing his best to avoid any noise. Jacob was right behind him, shuffling along with smaller strides to keep from tripping while hanging onto Lucas's vest. They heard muffled voices behind them, but they were further away in the building, the sound echoing off the walls, and the absence of light confirmed that they hadn't been spotted.

At the stairwell, Lucas led Jacob down to the lower level. When they exited into another hall, Lucas murmured to the scientist, "We're on the basement level. There's a hall going straight and one to our right. Which way?"

"It would have to be right." Jacob sounded tentative.

"You sure?"

"It's been a while since I was down here…" He swallowed. "Yes, I'm sure."

"Then come on."

Lucas picked up the pace, and within a couple of minutes they were at another stairway, this one leading up. When they were at ground level, Lucas stopped.

"Can we use the flashlight now?" Jacob asked.

"Risky. Why?"

"I need to see where we are."

Lucas checked the M4 safety and then offered the weapon to him, the night vision scope eyepiece glowing green. "Look through there. Takes some getting used to, but not that much."

The scientist took the rifle from him, clearly unfamiliar with the feel of a weapon, and peered through the scope. He grunted and motioned left. "This way."

Lucas shadowed him to the foyer of the health sciences building. They approached the plywood covering the entry, and Jacob handed the rifle back to him. They listened at the barrier for a solid minute, and when there was no movement outside, Jacob slid the loose panel open and stepped into the night.

They sprinted across the parking lot, afraid gunfire would erupt from behind them at any moment, and breathed a sigh of relief when they neared the trees at the edge of the lot. They stopped and got their bearings, and then Jacob grimaced in the dim starlight and offered his hand to shake.

"This is where we part ways. Good luck," he said.

Lucas took the scientist's hand and shook. "You too." He paused. "You think Eddie will give you up?"

"Not willingly, but if they apply enough pressure…"

"You should bail."

"I can't." Jacob looked away. "It'll be fine. They don't have anything on him."

Lucas didn't press the point – Jacob was an adult and knew the risks.

Jacob hesitated, and when he spoke, his voice was soft. "Tell Sierra I…tell her she's missed, would you?"

Lucas swallowed hard, but his face remained unreadable. "Sure thing."

"I appreciate it. We didn't really have any time to talk the night she left…"

"Right."

They split up, and Lucas trotted north toward the brick house as Jacob went east. There was nothing Lucas could do for either of the men who'd helped him, although deep down he had the urge to return to the hospital, guns a-blazing, and take out the guards. He knew even as he thought it that it was foolhardy, but if the old man or Jacob told the Crew the details of the rendezvous…

At that point it would be a footrace – it would take them as long to reach Roswell as it would Lucas, and he would have a considerable head start.

He'd have to chance it and hope that the interrogation went long, assuming there was one.

Then again, the radio was well hidden and Eddie didn't strike him as stupid. He had to be clever to have worked against his masters for years without being caught. Perhaps he would get away with it this time.

Lucas shook away the second-guessing.

Either he would be questioned and tell them what he knew, or he wouldn't. Regardless, nothing changed for Lucas. He still had to get to Bitter Lake by dusk in four days with the women, whether with the Crew on their tail or not. Everything else was theoretical. What Lucas did know was that horses could only cover so much ground per day, and Tango, with the ability to make a solid fifty, was better than most, especially if the Crew didn't use theirs for long distances with any regularity. In that case they might get forty if they were lucky, slowing as the days went by and the animals wore out.

No matter what the case, Shangri-La had transformed from an

ambiguous possibility to a certainty in Lucas's mind – one he wasn't going to allow to pass them by.

He spied Tango's dark form at the tree where he'd tied him and increased his speed. They would be well clear of the city by dawn, and they could rest more in the heat of the day, once Lubbock's skyline had faded into the horizon behind them.

Tango sensed Lucas's arrival and gave a welcoming snort. Lucas smiled in spite of the dire situation and allowed the horse to nuzzle him before climbing into the saddle, his weariness heavy as a lead blanket, and directing the stallion west.

~ ~ ~

Jacob rounded a corner on the way back to the gutted apartment complex and almost ran headlong into three crew gunmen. He recognized one of them – a guard at the lab – and nodded a greeting.

The man scowled at him. "You been at the hospital tonight?"

"What are you talking about?"

"Why are you out in the middle of the night?"

"Where have you been? My apartment burned to the ground. Where am I supposed to go?"

The guard eyed the scientist the way a crocodile eyes a lamb and then glanced at the man on his right.

"Take him to the hospital. I'll be there shortly. Don't let him talk to the other one."

Jacob bit back his protest when he heard the final words. *The other one.* So they'd somehow placed him with Eddie. He had no idea how, but they obviously had, which meant his time on the planet was limited to hours, barring a miracle. His knees threatened to buckle, but he held firm, resolved to continue his pretension that he had no idea what they were talking about as long as possible in order to buy Lucas time.

Because regardless of what happened to him, Magnus couldn't be allowed to get his hands on the girl.

Jacob would go to his grave to prevent that.

Chapter 39

Ruby and Sierra were in the kitchen, preparing breakfast from eggs Bruce had collected, when someone pounded on the trailer door. Ruby froze, skillet in hand, above the flickering flame from the modified wood-burning stove Bruce had shoehorned into the dwelling.

Bruce came out of his bedroom and peeked out of the side window, and then turned to Sierra. "Don't worry. Just a couple of customers. Stay out of sight."

Ruby moved the skillet well away from the fire and set it down as Sierra made for their bedroom, where Eve was dozing. Ruby followed her in, and Bruce opened the front door as they disappeared into the room.

Three men stood at the steps, the middle one with his hands on his hips, the others with their arms folded across their chests. All had rifles hanging from shoulder slings, and none looked particularly happy.

Bruce offered a smile. "Tom. Wesley. Hank. How're you guys doing today?"

"Been two weeks, Bruce. Tired of waiting. Either give us what you promised or return the goods."

"I told you it could take a while. Hard to find parts for the panels anymore. But I've been looking."

"You took half the payment in advance, Bruce. You done half the work?" Hank, the largest of the three, growled.

"Doesn't work like that. More than half the work is finding the right stuff. I explained that up front."

"Getting mighty tired of doin' without power, Bruce," the man in the middle said. "Maybe you should give us your panels and see how you like it for a while."

"Yeah," Wesley agreed. "Why don't we do that and see how it sits? Even trade. Our busted ones for your workin' ones."

"Guys, come on. I can't repair your stuff without power," Bruce countered.

"Don't much matter if we got yours," Hank observed. "I'm likin' that idea a whole bunch."

Bruce's voice hardened. "It'll be another week. Sorry, guys, but that's the best I can do. I can't materialize parts out of thin air. Be reasonable."

"Then how about you give us back all the ammo we traded you, and we take our panels and find someone else?"

"There is nobody else. You know that."

Tom elbowed Wesley, an ugly expression twisting his meaty features. "Betcha he don't have the ammo, either."

Wesley took a step closer. "Think we want our ammo back, Bruce. Now."

"I had to trade most of it to get wire for your inverter. The other stuff was fried, shorting out all over the place. Sun had baked the insulation – that was a part of your problem."

"Told you," Tom said. "I knew it. Bastard robbed us, and now he's tryin' to stall."

The men freed their weapons and held them loosely in their hands, the message more than clear. Bruce's face blanched and he shook his head.

"No need for that, gentlemen. I'm good for it. But don't you really just want your stuff fixed rather than your ammo?"

"Nah. We want your array. Fair's fair, you friggin' pothead," Hank growled. "Don't think we haven't seen you lyin' around here stoned instead of workin'. Makes me sick thinkin' 'bout it. You think you can screw us and get away with it? That what you think?"

"Nobody's screwing anyone, Hank. There was a slight delay. That's all."

"You told us less than a week originally."

"You mean when you came here begging me to help? Told me to bump my other jobs and you'd make it worth my while? Is that when I told you?" Bruce countered.

"Damned fools to think you would," Tom snapped.

"Look. You can't have my array. That was never part of the deal. I told you I'd repair yours and gave you an estimate of how long I thought it would take. It's running longer than I'd hoped. For which I apologize, but I can't change that or find parts before I find them. You can threaten all you want, but it's not going to get the job done any faster."

Wesley's face flushed with color and he raised the barrel of his gun. "Playin' with fire, boy."

The side window slid open and the snout of an AK-47 appeared. Ruby's voice rang out from behind the thin gauze curtains.

"There a problem, Bruce?"

Bruce eyed the men and tried not to smile. "No, I don't think so. Is there, boys?"

Wesley looked like he'd been kicked in the balls. "Why, I oughta—"

"You oughta get out of here and let me work before you discover you aren't bulletproof, boys," Bruce warned. "I've been pretty civil, but I don't appreciate the bully tactics, and if you think you're going to draw down on me while on my property, ask yourself how you'd react if someone did the same to you." Bruce let that sink in. "Now I'm going to repair your gear and get it back to you as fast as possible. The alternative is I can give you back the panels and inverter, and I'll scrounge up some ammo in a day or so. But you're not going to threaten me, and you're not taking my array – or you're going to have some serious problems, and the town will back me for defending myself. We both know that."

"You're makin' the mistake of your life, punk," Hank spat.

"Gentlemen, I'd suggest you get on home before my friend here gets nervous. An AK on full auto can be touchy. You don't want nervous fingers on the trigger. Hate for an accident to happen, so lower your guns, move off my property, and come back in a week."

Wesley did as instructed, clearly not prepared to be staring down the barrel at death that morning. The other two men followed his lead and shouldered their guns as they backed away.

"You best sleep with one eye open. You ain't the only one can have accidents around here," Hank warned. As they turned and trudged off, Bruce's eyes seared holes in the backs of their jackets.

When the men had disappeared, Bruce resumed breathing and closed and locked the trailer door. He glanced at Ruby and nodded his head to her. "I didn't realize what customer service talent you had. You've been wasting yourself on computers."

"Seemed like you could use a hand there."

"Yeah, welcome to my world. It's been getting worse. Everyone wants it now, or sooner, and they don't care about the details." He exhaled slowly. "Anyway, thanks."

"Think they were serious about coming back at night?"

"Nah. That was bluster. There's still nobody else who can repair their crap."

"Sounded awful convincing. Hate for one of them to get drunk and put a few rounds through the side of this tin can. Not with Eve around."

"They won't."

Ruby looked at him skeptically. "You one hundred percent sure?"

"Do I smell eggs?"

She shook her head and closed the window. "Don't get us into any more trouble than we're already in, Bruce. Just promise me that."

"Might have to carry your luggage for you if things keep going this way," Bruce conceded. "Neighborhood's turning chillier by the minute."

"Lucas will be back in a few days. That's all we need."

"Then that's what you shall receive. Now let's get some of those eggs cooked so I can keep my strength up. I'm hungry as a horse."

"You should cut back on the loco weed. I hear that's hell on the appetite."

Bruce ignored her barb and strode to his room. "Call me when it's ready. I need to go empty my pants now."

Ruby couldn't help but grin. "I'll bet."

Chapter 40

Jacob stood shivering in a lower-floor room of the hospital in spite of the warm temperature, stripped naked and hanging from an eyelet in the ceiling by his bound wrists, his feet barely touching the floor. His left calf had cramped several times, adding to his discomfort, and the complete darkness in the dank chamber further isolated him and increased the sense of surrealism of the experience.

He'd always known this day might come, but all the intellectualizing hadn't prepared him for the grim reality. The guards had marched him to the hospital and led him downstairs, and then gone to work on him with their fists until he'd lost consciousness. When he'd come to, he'd been in his present state, his jaw and cheekbones throbbing from the beating, one eye swollen partially shut, and a trickle of blood drying beneath his broken nose.

He inhaled through his mouth, every breath a gasp that sent lances of pain shooting through his chest from several broken ribs. He tried to imagine the bones splintered, the ragged edge of one puncturing an organ, the hemorrhaging causing him to black out a final time and sparing him the ordeal he knew was to come, but he knew he wasn't fatally injured – the Crew thugs had seen to that.

For Magnus's men to have beaten him, Eddie had to have given him up – there was no other way they would jeopardize the vaccine effort to the extent that Jacob's demise would cause. True, he had subordinates who knew how to make the antibiotics and other products they manufactured, but the vaccine held its own complexities. The virus's composition and penchant for mutation was unlike any he'd seen before, its genesis unknown other than its startling resemblance to Spanish flu.

That he would be replaced was obvious, but it would mean significant delays as the new director came up to speed, checked all prior work, and familiarized himself with the failed attempts they'd made and the leaps in understanding that had resulted. Jacob had deliberately stalled the project at every turn, knowing there was nobody watching over his shoulder capable of catching the subtle sabotage. That would change when his replacement came in, and would bring Magnus closer to being able to generate an effective vaccine – an eventuality that Jacob and Eddie had risked their lives to prevent.

The Crew guards had demanded to know what the broadcast meant as they'd beaten Jacob bloody. They went about their work with detached determination, taking care to deliver blows that would cause maximum pain without endangering his life. They'd promised to break his fingers and toes on the next round, and to cut his ears, nose, and more sensitive appendage off should he fail to tell them what he knew, but Jacob had resolved to continue pleading ignorance right up until the time he expired.

That he would die was a foregone conclusion. After spending five years under Crew rule, he had no doubt about that. He was far too familiar with their tactics to believe any promises of mercy – if he did tell them anything, they would simply increase the damage to him in order to see if he changed his story.

A door opened and the room flooded with fluorescent light. He blinked at the unexpected glare, and then his eyes focused on a small form lying in the corner in a fetal position, orange jumpsuit and white hair as distinctive as a fingerprint. Eddie's eyes were frozen wide in death, his face gray and his mouth open in an expression of pained surprise. Jacob could make out his tongue, cyanotic and swollen, and looked away, the image an indecent violation of his friend's eternal rest.

A man entered and Jacob's heart sank. He recognized Kyle, one of

Magnus's especially mean-spirited lieutenants, and braced himself for what was to come. To Jacob's surprise, the door remained open, and Kyle approached until he was only a few feet from Jacob – close enough for the scientist to make out a thin sheen of sweat on the network of tattoos that covered his face and head, the iconic Eye of Providence in the center of his forehead exactly like that of his master's.

"Well, well. Seems you and your little friend have been very naughty boys, Doctor," Kyle hissed, his voice raspy from an injury to his voice box in some prison fight. "Funny that we should find ourselves like this, isn't it?"

Jacob had made no secret of how much he despised the man, and he now regretted his hubris. Kyle would take special delight in making Jacob's final hours the most agonizing of his life, he knew.

"Why are you doing this?" Jacob managed between broken teeth and mangled lips.

"Oh, let's not pretend. Your buddy there told us enough before he died. Little turd had a heart attack early on, but before he did, he confessed that you were his partner in crime. He told us it was he who made the broadcast we intercepted, and he told us what it meant. We need you to confirm he told us the truth."

"You believed him? He hated me. Hated all the staff."

Kyle smiled. "I don't think so. He was very convincing, and my experience with those about to go to their graves is that they tend to find honesty in their last words."

"He tricked you, and now he's gotten what he wanted, obviously – to get rid of your lead scientist. Not very smart, are you? He played you, and you fell for it."

Kyle sighed, as though fatigued. "You're very good. Really, you are. If I didn't know better, I'd believe you."

"Because it's the truth."

"I'll save us all a little time, Doctor. I intend to hurt you in ways you never thought possible. I'm talking Biblical, Inquisition-level shit. You'll be drowning in your own blood, begging for death by the time I'm done with you. But I'm in a hurry, so I'm going to give you a choice: a quick death or the drawn-out version."

"Have you spoken with Whitely? There's no way he'd allow me to be taken out of the game. We're too close to a vaccine."

"Whitely doesn't matter. Magnus ordered it. You know what that means."

Jacob's heart skipped. He did indeed know what it meant: there was no possibility of relief.

"I can't tell you what I don't know," he tried.

"I guess we're going to do this the hard way. That's fine." Kyle turned to the open door. "Bring in the stuff."

Two guards wheeled in a rolling mechanic's table with an array of nightmare tools on it – wire cutters, saws, vices, surgical instruments. Kyle smiled at the sight of Jacob's face and reached to select a thin, twelve-inch-long glass rod.

"You have no idea what this is going to feel like," he said, eyeing Jacob's genitals. "The hammer blow that shatters it inside you will feel like an angel's kiss compared to what follows. You really don't want to experience it, or so I've gathered from watching tougher men than you cry like baby kittens by the time I'm done."

"I swear I have no idea what you want to know. You're making the mistake of your life. You'll never get the vaccine if you kill me, and Magnus will ultimately blame you for carrying out his orders. You know how that will work. You'll be on the receiving end before you know it."

Kyle studied the glass rod like it held the answer to a mystery, and then sighed again. "I was afraid of that."

"What?"

"You're ready to endure anything, aren't you?"

"You're mistaking not knowing anything with something else."

Kyle nodded once. "I was right. I told them it wouldn't work."

Jacob felt a tremble of relief. Maybe he'd managed to save himself…?

"Don't do this," he whispered.

Kyle snapped his fingers and called to the doorway. "Bring her in."

Two guards half-dragged a woman into the room, her eyes terrified. She screamed when she saw Jacob and dropped to her knees sobbing when the guards released her.

"Sarah!" Jacob screamed in a tortured voice.

"That's right, smart guy," Kyle snarled. "Your sister. You're obviously willing to undergo just about anything, but let's see how you feel about subjecting your sister to the punishment intended for you."

"She's innocent," Jacob protested. Sarah was a technician at the Dallas facility. They must have run her over in a vehicle, using some of their precious fuel, to get her to Lubbock that quickly.

"Of course she is. That's the whole point. We'll see how your convictions hold up when she's raped repeatedly in front of you – while you know you're responsible for her misery and could save her at any time. Sodomy, rape, a good enthusiastic beating, and then we'll start carving her face." Kyle gave him a cold smirk. "You really want that?"

Jacob closed his eyes, willing himself dead. It was an impossible choice. Sell out and condemn his species to an existence of living hell under the rule of a demon; or betray his sister and watch her violated and tortured.

"You can't do this," he screamed, choking on the last word.

"Oh, Jacob, of course I can. And you will eventually tell me what I want to know. The only question is how much you're willing to allow to happen to your flesh and blood before you do."

Kyle raised an eyebrow and offered the grin of an unrepentant sadist. Jacob believed him. He would follow through, probably was aroused at the thought of the horror he was going to perpetrate, and was hoping Jacob would refuse to tell him what he asked.

"If I tell you, you'll let her go?"

Kyle nodded. "You have my word."

"How do I know I can believe you?"

"You don't. Makes it more fun, don't you think?"

Jacob took a deep breath. "The broadcast was arranging a rendezvous," he began.

An hour later he was gagging on his own vomit after watching his sister systematically ruined, the lump of bleeding, burned flesh quivering on the floor in front of him unrecognizable as human.

Kyle closed the door behind him as Jacob's strangled shriek reverberated off the walls, the rod broken. The real amusement was only about to begin.

Chapter 41

Lucas watered Tango from one of the plastic bottles, his eyes on the distant intersection of the sky with the plain, watching for any evidence of pursuit. He'd ridden from Lubbock and hadn't stopped until noon other than to allow Tango to rest and to take an occasional bearing. Now, as the heat rose, he debated snatching a few hours of sleep – he'd established sufficient lead and had left no trail to follow, so he was confident that nobody was tailing him.

He could go only so long without slumber, though, and then his senses would begin playing tricks on him. He'd miss some critical tell or, worse, misinterpret or invent one, which could be disastrous. And Tango, for all his fortitude, wasn't a machine; pushed too hard, he would eventually misstep and hurt himself, which would leave them dead in the water.

Lucas spotted the remains of a maintenance building at the edge of one of the oil fields and led Tango to it on foot. The interior was in ruins, but there was shade to rest in and sufficient grass for the horse to feed. Lucas could see endless green stretching in all directions, so he'd be able to spot any riders from far away – although he hadn't spied a single one all day and, given the heat and absence of any nearby destinations, didn't expect to.

He decided to risk it and unfurled his bedroll and lay down inside the building after setting Tango loose to graze. He closed his eyes and was asleep within moments, his body in desperate need of recharging.

Lucas awoke to Tango nudging him with his nose. He rolled over and peered at the time, and then sat up. He'd been asleep for four hours – two longer than he'd planned. He swore at his carelessness as he rolled up his bedroll and, after setting his hat on his head, exited the building. A study of the horizon to the east with his binoculars revealed nothing new, and he relaxed a bit as he swept the remainder of the area, pivoting in a slow circle until he'd scanned everything.

He mounted up and Tango strode forward; the much-needed respite had done them both good. Lucas resolved to keep moving after dark to make up the time, the first twenty-four hours the most critical.

An hour after nightfall, he heard four riders galloping from the south. He estimated that they were no more than a half mile away, likely from Plains. He had to assume that the Crew also had night vision gear, so he couldn't rely on the cover of darkness to avoid them, which left only two options: finding a hiding place or taking them on.

The old saying from his law enforcement days came back to him as he mulled over the choices: you can't outrun a radio. Perhaps he was reading too much into the hoofbeats, but he couldn't imagine a lot of reasons for hard riding at night.

Of course, they had no idea how much progress he might have made since departing Lubbock, so they were oblivious to his actual location. At least, that was his hope.

He raised the M4 and activated the scope, and then looked through it in the direction of the commotion. Lucas could barely make the riders out and adjusted his guess of a half mile away upward to more like a mile – good for him, as it bought more maneuvering time.

Lucas twisted in the saddle and eyed the towering shapes of the oil pumps that stretched westward, each roughly a quarter mile apart. He had earlier crossed the highway that ran northwest from Plains that the riders were following, which gave him another advantage: they were sticking to the road, so the further he could get from it, the likelier he was to evade them. He selected a pumping rig a half mile

217

off the thoroughfare at random and urged Tango toward it. The big horse broke into a trot, and by the time the riders passed, he and Tango were concealed by the pump's wide steel base.

He watched through the scope as the patrol moved beyond his position and absently smoothed the horse's mane with his free hand.

"Easy, boy. We'll get out of here in a few," he whispered, and wished he had an apple or some other treat for Tango, who had performed thanklessly for weeks.

He would remedy that when he made it back to Artesia.

That he would, he didn't question. Searching for a single rider on the plains, absent a spotter plane or helicopter, was looking for a needle in a haystack.

When the riders were out of sight, he mounted Tango and spurred him west, reconciled to riding most of the night. The more miles he could put between himself and the Crew, the greater his chances of survival, and he'd push until they were both ready to drop and then sleep when he could. Lucas knew the approximate location of the Crew's checkpoints on the main highway from his inbound journey and would, as he had then, stick to open fields far from them. That Magnus's goons believed anyone in their right mind would use roads was a relief to Lucas – it showed that they were approaching things from an urban perspective rather than with rural expertise that would be useful on the plains, another edge he would use to his advantage.

Lucas thought about Jacob and Eddie as he rode, trying to imagine what they had been put through, but flushed away the images that sprang to mind. Whatever they had endured, it was over by now. Lucas was no stranger to atrocity – the Mexican cartels, even back in the pre-collapse days, had been expert in torture and disfigurement, leaving mutilated corpses for discovery with messages of warning for their adversaries. It was no shock that the prison gangs who were now in control had adopted their brutal tactics – in times of flux, brutal tactics inevitably carried the day.

That his fellow man could be so loathsome was disheartening but unsurprising, and he again wondered that his species had managed to rule the planet without wiping each other out for as long as they had.

The collapse was just a trip back in time to a period when roving hordes of conquering barbarians would descend on a target and slaughter all but the women. For all mankind's pretense of having evolved past that point, the truth was far more disappointing: a despot like Magnus had far more historical precedent than not.

And history taught that the bad guys usually won.

"Maybe not this time," he murmured, swaying in the saddle, his eyelids heavy. The trail spanning into the distance glowed white in the moonlight, the tall grass on either side of it wrinkled by the dry wind.

Chapter 42

Luis looked up as his radio operator entered his office and neared with a slip of paper. The bottle of tequila on his desk was halfway gone, as was Luis, his sorrows only somewhat drowned by the acrid liquor, though his rage was blunted.

"What is it?" he slurred.

The man set the paper in front of him. Luis groped at it with fingers that felt dead and then sat back, disgusted. "Read it," he ordered.

"It's for Cano. I thought you'd want to see it first."

Luis nodded. "Okay. So read it."

"Rendezvous planned for three days from now, sunset, Kola bar, Bitter Lake. Woman and child will be there."

Luis digested the message and sat up straighter, the sudden rush of adrenaline coursing through his system sobering him somewhat. "Bitter Lake? That's…where is that?"

"They said it's by Roswell. In New Mexico."

"The UFO place?"

The operator nodded. "That's the one."

"Shit. You have a map of the area?"

"I found an atlas. It's three days' hard ride. Maybe four."

"Damn." Luis did the math, his brain foggy from the alcohol. "We could make it, but just barely. Horses would be near dead by the time we got there." Luis thought for a minute. "Why don't they send a patrol from Lubbock?"

"Same distance. Guess they think Cano's a better bet than whoever they have there."

Luis pushed back from his desk and stood unsteadily. He glanced at the bottle and pushed it away. "Well, it was nice while it lasted," he muttered, and held out his hand. "Give me the message."

The operator did as instructed and left. Luis scowled at the note like it was a venomous snake. He considered delaying presenting it to Cano or just never telling him, but shook off the idea as soon as he had it. The truth would eventually come out, and then he'd be feeding the buzzards out by the latrine trenches. No, he had to alert the man and then be ready for three grueling days to follow.

Luis grunted to himself and walked to the door. The hotel where Cano had set up camp was only two blocks from the courthouse headquarters, and the walk might help him work off some of the booze. He already knew that they'd be riding all night and much of the following one – the math required that they get in at least fifty-something miles per day, which would likely kill a few of the horses if they weren't careful. They'd have to travel light and see if they could commandeer more animals on the way north.

But it was possible to do it.

They'd just all be about as beat as their steeds by the time they arrived.

Luis's boots thumped against the dusty pavement as he walked, the stars slim illumination in the midnight sky. His head was clearing as he neared the hotel, but still, he nearly fell face forward when a voice called out from the darkness by the entry.

"Stop, or I blow your head off."

"I'm here to see Cano. It's Luis."

"He's asleep."

"It's important."

A Crew thug stepped from the gloom, his eyes slits in a face that had taken a lifetime of punches, with a Kalashnikov in hand, its snout pointed at Luis. "He's third room from the end on the lower floor. Better be an emergency, for your sake."

"Thanks for the warning."

"It's a promise."

Luis followed the path along the peeling wall until he found the door. He rapped authoritatively and waited. Cano's distinctive voice rang out. "Good way to get killed."

"Cano, it's Luis. We got a radio message from Houston. It's important."

The door opened. Cano stood shirtless in the darkness, his wounds now completely healed. Green ink snakes writhed along his abs, satanic symbols adorned his chest, and a stylized grim reaper grinned from one shoulder, scythe in one bony hand and a skeletal finger pointing with the other.

"Better be. What is it?"

"Something about a rendezvous at a lake north of here. The woman and girl."

"What?" Cano exclaimed. "Give me the message."

Luis fished in his vest and handed him the slip of paper. Cano read it twice by the moonlight and glowered at him.

"When did this come in?"

"Just a few minutes ago."

"You know where this lake is?"

Luis nodded. "A long way."

"Be specific," Cano barked.

"About a hundred sixty miles. In New Mexico." Luis told him what he knew and answered several terse questions about the logistics involved in getting to the rendezvous point in time.

Cano nodded. "Get a dozen of your best men ready to ride. I'll round up the same of mine. I want to be on the trail within the hour."

Luis grunted assent, unsurprised by the order. "It might take longer to secure provisions and ready the horses."

"See that it doesn't."

The door slammed in Luis's face. He turned, livid at the summary dismissal, and all of his earlier resentment came flooding back. If this was how the next three days were going to go, where he was expected to act as Cano's lapdog, it would take more than tequila to quell his fury. He considered confronting the Crew boss on it now, before Luis was surrounded by his men to watch his embarrassment, but thought better of it. If they found the woman and child, Cano would be out of his hair, and things would return to normal. If they failed, Cano would depart in disgrace. Either way, this was a temporary situation he'd just have to grin and bear.

Luis slid his two-way from his tactical vest and radioed his orders to his lieutenant, who greeted the news without comment. He retraced his steps to the courthouse and compiled a mental list of everything they would need, and wondered how in the hell he would get it all collected in an hour. He decided to take the approach smart leaders had been using since time immemorial: Luis called his lieutenant into his office, ignoring the man's sleepy expression, and delegated most of it.

When the man trudged off, Luis took a final swig of the tequila and set it aside, resigned to an almost impossible ordeal where everything would have to go perfectly for them to reach the lake by the appointed time.

Chapter 43

Lucas arrived at the Artesia fortifications well after dark and obtained permission to enter the town after the wary guards checked with Bruce to verify his bona fides. He was beyond tired from the six days of riding to and from Lubbock, and he was looking forward to a hot meal and a decent night's sleep. He'd calculated that if they left at dawn, they could easily make it to Bitter Lake by dusk, the distance do-able even with plentiful rest stops.

Lucas entered Bruce's property and the floodlights blinked on. Ruby and Sierra burst from the trailer's front door as he neared, and he offered a weary smile as he dismounted. Sierra drew near, her intent to hug him obvious, and he shook his head.

"Let me take a shower first. Been a long ride."

She hugged him anyway. "I don't care."

Ruby watched without comment from the entrance. Lucas glanced at her and she nodded to him. "Nice to have you back. Trip uneventful?"

He pulled away from Sierra reluctantly. "About what I expected."

Sierra's face fell. "Then he...he wasn't alive?"

"Didn't say that," Lucas said, unstrapping his saddle and lifting it off Tango, along with his saddlebags.

"Then he was?"

Lucas led the horse to the water trough and removed the bridle. The stallion drank greedily while Jax and Nugget ambled over to greet him. Lucas turned to Sierra and nodded.

"Yes. We've got a meet set up for tomorrow at sunset. Going to have to ride all day, but it's done."

"What! Why…that's awesome!" Sierra exclaimed. "Where?"

"Up by Roswell."

Bruce appeared at the door. "Did I hear Roswell?"

Ruby nodded. "Yes. Why?"

"Oh. Well, it's kind of dicey up there if you don't know your way around and have an in with the locals…"

"What do you mean, dicey?" Sierra asked.

"They have the reputation of being a shoot-first bunch. Why? You planning a trip?"

"Could be," Lucas said, his tone guarded.

"Then I best go with you, or you might not make it."

"Done okay so far," Lucas said, his face a blank.

"But if all of you are headed there, you really want to take a chance with them?" Bruce shot back, glancing at the women.

Sierra studied her boots and then met Lucas's eyes. "I told Bruce about Shangri-La, Lucas. He had a right to know."

"You what?" Ruby blurted.

"He cornered me – he said we'd have to leave immediately if I didn't. What was I supposed to do?" she protested.

"Point is, I know all about it, Lucas," Bruce said. "So there's no reason to keep me in the dark."

Lucas fixed him with an icy stare. "Takes a special sort to threaten to throw women and a kid into the wild."

"I wasn't going to do it. But I have every right to know what I'm involved in. Even if *you* believe everyone's just here to be used by you to advance your interests," Bruce said. "If I'm at risk because of something you're involved in, and you're staying at my place, that's reasonable."

"Didn't realize you were so philosophical," Ruby said.

"Come on, Ruby. I wouldn't show up at your place asking you to hide me and then stonewall. I get why you did it, but that doesn't make it right." Bruce paused. "Besides, it's done, and you can't put the toothpaste back in the tube, so maybe we should be discussing the future, not the past?"

"How was…you know who?" Sierra asked quietly.

"Good," Lucas replied, still staring holes through Bruce.

"That's it?"

"That's all for now," Lucas said, his tone indicating that there would be no more discussion about it with Bruce around.

"Lucas, I can help you get through Roswell safely," Bruce said. "Don't snub me. There's no reason to."

"Why are you feeling so helpful?" Lucas asked, his skepticism obvious.

Bruce sighed. "Business is terrible. This place is dying for me. I had no real reason to stay except that there was no better option." He shrugged. "Now that I know about your destination, there is. I thought that would be obvious."

Sierra's eyes narrowed. "I thought you said it was all BS?"

"Sure. Most stories like it are. But if you're meeting someone who will take you there, that moves it from the pile of idiocies that circulate constantly and into the real world." Bruce favored Lucas with a complacent expression. "I'm a pragmatic guy. If you're off someplace better, I'll pull my weight to be part of the group. I know this area, I have a lot of gear that could be helpful, and I can repair anything."

"What kind of gear?" Ruby asked.

"Portable solar chargers. Medical supplies. Spare parts for that AR-15 of Sierra's, that will also work with Lucas's rifle. Batteries. Lighters. You want me to go on?"

Lucas and Ruby exchanged a glance. "That's an impressive list," Ruby admitted.

"Plus, I know where you're headed. So you'd be stupid to leave me behind. I might tell someone."

Nobody spoke. When Lucas finally nodded, it was with clear reluctance. "I could always shoot you on the way out."

Bruce shook his head. "You don't strike me as the type."

"Always a first time."

"People don't change who they are. Come on, Lucas. I know you don't like me much, but you don't know me. I can help. Anytime you meet someone who can, why would you turn them down? That makes no sense."

Lucas carried his saddle into the trailer, and Ruby toted the saddlebags behind him. Bruce brought up the rear and closed the door and bolted it once they were all inside. Lucas set his gear down by the door and knelt to say hello to Eve.

"How you holding up, Eve?"

"Good," she said.

"You been behaving?"

"Always," Sierra said.

"She's a little angel," Ruby chimed in.

"We're going for a ride tomorrow. You want to come?" Lucas asked.

Her blue eyes swiveled to his and he felt the odd electric current sensation throb through his skull. "Yes, please."

Lucas looked up at Sierra. "At least that's decided."

"What about me?" Bruce asked.

Lucas blinked twice, obviously irritated. "Let me get something to eat and rinse off while I think about it."

Bruce looked ready to argue further, but wisely held his tongue when Sierra gave him a small shake of her head.

"I'll make you the biggest omelet you've ever seen, with rabbit stew inside. Sound good?" Ruby offered.

"You have no idea," Lucas said, and made for the bedroom, freeing the Velcro fasteners of his flak jacket as he walked.

Sierra and Ruby prepared the meal while Bruce sat on the couch, staring glumly at his computer station, lost in thought. Ten minutes later Lucas emerged wearing new pants and a fresh shirt, his face shaved clean, burnished the shade of an old penny from the sun. Sierra gave him a beaming smile as he sat at the cheap dining table and placed a plate in front of him.

"You clean up pretty good," she said.

Lucas dug into the meal without comment, eating like a starved man, washing down the heaping portion with a liter of water. When he was finished, he sat back and eyed Bruce.

"Let's be clear. I don't like the tactics you used on Sierra."

"I got that."

"But you're right that we could use any help we can get. How are you with a gun?"

"Good as any, I guess."

"You ever been in a firefight?"

"I've had to shoot my way out of a few situations," Bruce said.

"Like what?"

"Guys tried to rob me couple years back."

"You ever kill a man?"

"One of them died."

"Could you do it again?"

Bruce nodded. "In a heartbeat. It was either them or me. In that kind of situation, you do what you have to."

Lucas returned his nod. "Fine. We're going to ride at daybreak. Pack everything you'll need as though you were never coming back. Because you'll probably never see this place again. You got any problem with that?"

Bruce shook his head. "Music to my ears. I'll be ready."

"What kind of weapons you have?"

"AR-15, modified to full auto. H&K 9mm. Six spare magazines for the rifle, three for the pistol. Flak vest. Whole nine yards. You don't have to worry about me."

"You do the modification yourself?"

Bruce nodded again. "Of course."

Lucas yawned, the long hours on the trail suddenly hitting him hard on a full stomach. He looked to Sierra and Ruby as he stood. "I'm sorry. I'm beat. Let's get some sleep while we can. Tomorrow's going to be a hard one."

They followed him into the bedroom, Eve holding Sierra's hand as Ruby fetched his bedroll from his kit and joined them. She spread it on the floor beside Sierra's, and Lucas kicked off his boots and lowered himself with a grateful sigh.

"You going to tell us what happened in Lubbock?" Sierra asked.

Lucas gave them the short version, and by the time he was finished, both women looked shocked. Ruby shook her head and eyed him. "I swear you have nine lives, Lucas. But you've used up about ten."

"Sometimes it feels that way," he agreed.

"Do you think Jacob will be okay?" Sierra asked softly.

"He seemed to think so. I have no way of knowing," Lucas dissembled, reluctant to share his conclusions with her if he didn't have to. She seemed to accept the response, and he let the discussion die there.

On that note, he closed his eyes, and within thirty seconds he was snoring softly, the women beside him as they settled in for their last night of sleep under a roof for the foreseeable future.

Chapter 44

Readying the animals for travel and packing everything took longer than Lucas would have liked, and the sun was already painting the sky tangerine by the time they got under way. Lucas eyed the western horizon warily. A band of dark clouds loomed over the Guadalupe range, flashes of occasional lightning illuminating their mass. A gentle wind carried the scent of rain and ozone as they finished their final checks and mounted up, Lucas in the lead.

Bruce moved to the gate and opened it, only to freeze when Wesley's voice called out from the road beyond.

"And where the hell do you think you're goin'?" he demanded, shotgun in hand.

"Wouldn't be plannin' on sneakin' out on us, would ya?" Hank asked.

"Boys, I've been thinking," Bruce said. "I can't find the parts, so you're free to take my array. In fact, take anything you find inside – there's a lot of stuff. Radio, inverter, batteries, the whole shooting match."

"He *is* sneakin' away," Wesley said. "I knew it. His crap probably doesn't even work."

"It's all fine. And now it's yours. I've had it with this one-horse dump. You're entitled to it," Bruce said. "Including the chickens and the garden."

"What if we don't want 'em?" Hank asked belligerently.

"What are you talking about?" Bruce countered, shaking his head in wonder. "That's what you came for. It's yours. You win, and I quit. How dumb are you that you don't get it?"

"I think he just called you an idiot," Wesley snarled.

"There a problem here, fellas?" Lucas asked, guiding Tango into view.

"What's it to you?" Wesley barked.

"You're holding me up, and I need Bruce here to fix my rig. I've got a lot of road to cover, so I'd appreciate it if you boys settled your differences and moved aside."

"You don't tell us what to do," Hank growled. "This is our town."

"Which you're entitled to. But Bruce here is going with me, and he won't be coming back. You have a beef with him, he's leaving you plenty to make up for it. So I'd say you're more than even." Lucas adjusted the shoulder strap of his M4 and let his hand trail to his hip holster.

"Don't like your tone, stranger," Wesley snarled.

"My grandpa used to say something pretty smart. Stayed with me," Lucas said. "Always ask yourself if this is the hill you want to die on before you pick a fight. If it is, and you're ready to meet your maker, then continue. If not, let it go. Wise man, he was."

"You threatening me?" Wesley asked, raising the barrel of his shotgun toward Lucas.

"Another thing he said was if you point a gun at a man, better be because you plan to use it."

The sound of Ruby chambering a round in her rifle before riding into view, her gun leveled at Wesley, surprised Wesley and Hank.

"Your grandpa was indeed a smart one," Ruby said. "You fellas want your lives to be over this morning, or you figure this isn't worth dying for?"

Lucas drew his Kimber while the two men were absorbing the sight of Ruby with an assault rifle pointed at them. He drew a bead on Wesley's head. "This here's a .45-caliber Kimber with hollow-point rounds. When one hits a man's skull, it puts you in mind of a melon smacking the sidewalk. Ain't pretty. Ask me how I know that."

"Our fight ain't with you. He screwed us," Hank called from

behind Wesley, his gun now raised as well.

"That may be," Lucas conceded. "And now he's giving you everything he owns. So you need to decide whether you want what brains you have in the dirt, or are smart enough to walk away." Lucas shrugged, his gun hand steady as a rock. "Ruby, you take the loudmouth behind this one – full auto. I got our friend here."

"Okay."

"So fellas, like I said: I'm in a mite of a hurry, and you're holding me up. What's it going to be?" Lucas asked, cocking the Kimber hammer, his eyes barely visible beneath the brim of his beaver felt hat.

"Ain't right, is all," Wesley said, lowering his shotgun.

"You gonna let 'em just walk?" Hank demanded.

"Shut up, Hank," Wesley said. "Put the gun down. We won this round."

"Appreciate it if you boys would toss your pieces inside the gate," Lucas instructed. "You can get them back once we're out of sight."

"Now you're disarming us?" Hank called, his rifle still raised.

"Don't want to get back shot. Only two ways to do that. One's blow your heads off. The other's to lock your guns in here so it takes you some time to get 'em. You're trying my patience something fierce."

The conflict ended when both men tossed their rifles to where Bruce stood. He toed them onto the grounds. Lucas eyed the pair. "Pistols, too."

Wesley reluctantly removed a Glock from a belt holster, and Hank drew a long-barrel Colt revolver. They lobbed them past Bruce with angry expressions.

"There," Bruce said. "Everybody gets to live to see another sunrise. That wasn't so hard, was it?"

"Wouldn't push it," Lucas warned. "Close up after us, and let's git."

Bruce scrambled to comply as Sierra and Ruby trailed Lucas off the grounds. Bruce led his horse past the waiting men and then returned to close and lock the gate with the padlock hanging from the bolt. If looks could kill, Bruce would have been dead and buried, but he ignored the duo and mounted his horse.

"See you around here again, ain't gonna go like that," Hank growled to him. Bruce flipped him off as he gave his horse the spurs. The man reddened as he and Wesley made for the gate and the guns beyond it.

Lucas breathed a sigh of relief when they were on the road, and led them off the highway once the town had faded in the distance. There were well-defined game trails that paralleled the highway, and the horses settled into a comfortable pace Lucas estimated at between three and four miles per hour.

"Think we're going to outrun the storm?" Sierra asked from beside Lucas.

"Hope so. Might blow itself out over the mountains. They sometimes do."

"That would suck. I mean, riding in the rain. As if covering this much distance in a day isn't bad enough. Can you imagine?"

Ruby spoke from behind them. "Don't tempt fate. The universe hears you, it might get ideas."

"Little rain never hurt anybody," Lucas said. "But it would slow us down some." He peered at the clouds. "Doesn't seem to be moving. Cross your fingers."

"So who are we meeting?" Bruce asked.

"A guy," Lucas responded.

"Are we back to that again?"

"Look, Bruce, you're riding with us, okay?" Lucas snapped. "Let's get to Roswell and see how things shake out."

"Where exactly in Roswell is it we're meeting this…guy?"

"At a lake north of town."

"I know the place you're talking about. Not much out there."

"Like it better that way."

Lucas spit to the side of the trail, signaling the discussion was over, and kept his eyes on the trail ahead, M4 in one hand and reins in the other, his back straight as he scanned the surroundings. An occasional low rumbling of distant thunder from the mountains reminded them all that they were far from in the clear, and it was with distinct apprehension that they rode toward uncertainty, thoughts filled with imaginings of what was to come.

Chapter 45

Their luck ran out as they skirted Roswell. The heavens opened, dropping raindrops the size of quarters, instantly soaking everyone. If Lucas was deterred, he gave no indication, checking the time occasionally as he navigated the trail and confirming with Bruce that they were headed in the right direction. Sierra wrapped a horse blanket around Eve to help shield her from the rain as they soldiered on through the storm, the rain hammering them relentlessly.

Bitter Lake was a dark strip a little over half a mile long and provided water for Roswell, as well as ample fishing and hunting of the animals that made their way to it in order to quench their thirst. Bruce told them that the bar they were going to had been built as a stopping point for townspeople out for the day, providing a cool destination when the heat became unbearable.

They traversed a dirt road and Sierra pointed to a sign barely visible in the downpour. "Look. Bitter Lake, one mile."

"Good. Horses need a break. Harder slog in this muck," Lucas said. The horses' hooves pulled free of the mud with an audible sucking sound, every step a chore with the additional resistance, especially at the end of a demanding day.

They followed the road and slowed when they came around a curve and found themselves at a barrier, facing two men with assault rifles sitting beneath a lean-to with a tarp over it that sheltered them from the deluge. One of the men stood and approached them, his rifle on Lucas.

"Place is closed 'cause of the storm," he announced. "Sorry."

"We're supposed to meet someone," Sierra said.

"Yeah? Who are you?"

"My name's Sierra."

The man's expression changed and he nodded. "He's expecting you."

"So it is open?" Bruce asked.

The gunman eyed him and then Ruby and Lucas. "For some."

The guard turned to his companion and motioned to him. The second man climbed from the shelter and opened the gate. He pointed into the rain at a single-story shack at the top of the rise. "Up there. He's inside."

Lucas nodded, his eyes unblinking as water ran from the brim of his hat. "Much obliged."

"Hell of a thing, the rain, ain't it? Came outta nowhere."

Lucas grunted. "It'll do that."

He guided Tango toward the shack and saw as he neared that it was larger than he'd first thought. The walls had been fashioned from pallets nailed together, and several long slabs of corrugated metal mounted above the wood served as a makeshift roof. When he reached the entrance, he dismounted and waited for the others to do the same, and then tied Tango to a hitching post. The women followed suit. Bruce took his time lowering himself from the saddle with a grimace.

"Damn, that hurts. It's been a while since I've spent that much time in the saddle," he said.

"Best get used to it," Lucas said. "No planes headed to wherever we're going."

The hinged board that served as the front door was open, and Lucas entered the building. The rain beat a steady tattoo on the metal roof. Sierra and Eve mounted the single step after him, and Ruby accompanied Bruce inside, glad to be out of the rain.

A man stood looking out at the lake through a window opening at the far side of the room. He turned at the sound of their arrival and looked them over with eyes like a bird of prey's, his face angular, all planes and sharp edges.

"You made it just in time," he said.

"Had to ride a ways," Lucas said.

The man's gaze lingered on Eve, and it was with obvious reluctance that he pulled his eyes away and focused on Lucas.

"It'll be dark soon. Storm's almost over, you can tell. Couple more hours, tops, which is good. We'll be riding some tonight, until we're well clear of Roswell and it's safe to make camp." The man hesitated. "Name's Colt."

Lucas made introductions. "You're our guide, then?"

"Not for this leg. I'll be riding with you, though. We have to meet a Native who will take us through his tribe's territory."

"Apache?"

Colt nodded. "They control a swatch about sixty miles deep that we have to cross. Take a dim view of trying without one of their own."

"Where are we meeting him?" Sierra asked.

"There's a truck stop just before the freeway junction northwest of here."

"How far?" Bruce asked.

"About six miles."

"And from there?" Ruby asked.

Colt smiled. "From there, we'll make camp on the other side of the intersection. That delineates the end of Roswell's territory and the beginning of Apache land."

"You sure we'll be safe?" Bruce asked. "I heard about that last time I was here. Nobody goes north of the freeway, or they're never seen again. I thought it was all BS…"

"Nope. They mean business. But it's okay. The tribe knows we're coming."

"They do?" Sierra said.

"Not who or why. Just that there's a party headed north. They were paid a pretty penny to allow us through, so there shouldn't be any problems."

"And where to from there?" Ruby asked.

"We'll be riding for a long time, let me put it that way."

"You can't tell us where Shangri-La is?" Sierra asked.

"I've sworn to keep its location secret. I'd go to my grave without revealing it. It's better that you don't know until we've reached it."

"How do we even know it exists?" Bruce asked.

Colt stared at him impassively. "Who is this?"

"He helped us get here," Ruby said.

An uncomfortable silence settled over them as they sized one another up. Lucas checked his watch and looked to Colt. "What's your role in this?"

"Pretty simple. I don't want to see the world ruined any worse than it is. We weren't meant to be at each other's throats like we are, living from day to day, killing to survive. Way I see it is this is a fight between light and darkness. I'm on the side of light."

Bruce tried to stifle his smirk, but Colt caught it. "Something strike you as funny?"

"Um, no—"

Gunshots from down the hill interrupted them, and Colt bolted for the entrance. Lucas joined him there, binoculars raised to his eyes. He lowered them a moment later and looked to the bartender.

"Get them out of here. The Crew is on its way."

"What?" Sierra cried.

"Come on," Lucas ordered. He pushed into the rain, making for Tango with hurried steps. He removed the Milkor and the bag with its grenades, slid four additional magazines for the M4 into his flak jacket, and then untied Tango and handed Ruby the reins. "Take him with you. I don't want him hurt."

"You're not coming?" Ruby asked.

"You'll never make it unless I can hold them off."

She frowned. "I'll stay too."

"Don't argue. Get out of here now."

Sierra grabbed his wet sleeve, her eyes frantic. "Lucas…"

"Sierra, keep Eve safe. That's what's important. Now go."

Ruby touched Sierra's shoulder and led her to Nugget. Lucas couldn't tell whether the liquid streaming down Sierra's face was just the rain or not, but decided that it didn't matter – he had bigger issues to deal with than a budding attraction.

They untied the animals and leapt into the saddle, and then vanished into the downpour with Colt in the lead as Lucas loaded the Milkor, eyes glued to the gate, where at least twenty riders were jumping over it on horseback, guns in hand.

Chapter 46

Lucas slammed the Milkor magazine home, loaded with six grenades, and squinted through the sight at the gunmen. When he estimated them at five hundred yards, he pulled the trigger, launching the first with a whump. It exploded harmlessly about forty yards short of the men, and he adjusted his aim and fired as fast as he could, emptying the weapon by the time the first grenades exploded near the gunmen.

It was hard to make out in the rain, but a quick glance through his binoculars showed at least ten men and animals down, with the remainder milling on the other side of the gate. Gunfire rattled from their weapons at the bar, but only a few rounds whistled past, most punching harmlessly into the pallets or throwing up splashes of mud, the three-hundred-yard accuracy of the AKs proving to be a critical limitation for the horsemen and a saving grace for Lucas.

He ducked through the doorway and reloaded the grenade launcher with the last six projectiles and then loosed them from one of the windows. Blossoms of orange flame and black smoke erupted from around the gate, but Lucas didn't wait to see the result of his final onslaught, instead dropping the Milkor and bringing his M4 into play. He squinted as he tried to fix the iron sights on a target, but the rain made it almost impossible, and he didn't want to waste rounds. After two bursts that did nothing he could make out, he looked through his binoculars to see how many of the Crew gunmen had survived.

He swore as seven of the riders leapt the barrier. Five peeled off into the woods, leaving two to ride into his fire. Lucas dropped the binoculars to his chest and took aim, gritting his teeth as the riders neared, a vision of naked aggression and bloodlust that would have been perfectly at home in a film about Mongols charging enemy lines.

When the riders were no more than a hundred yards from the bar, he began shooting, the M4 stuttering the distinctive bark of its three-round burst, and the lead gunman pitched backwards with a scream Lucas could hear through the rain. Lucas shifted his aim to the second man before the first had hit the ground, and fired again and again. Four of the bursts missed as the rider dodged and weaved, but the fifth found him, and a fountain of crimson blew from the man's back as his body armor gave way.

The man fell from his horse, still squeezing the trigger of his AK, and landed facedown in the mud, the pool of water beneath him marbled with ruby tendrils as he struggled for breath. Lucas drew a bead on him and ended his life with a final burst, and then ejected the spent magazine and slammed another into place.

He swept the trees with the scope but saw nobody. The five riders had vanished, and now things would get messy – it was rifle against rifle, with his adversaries having the benefit of the cover of the trees, whereas Lucas's position was known to them.

The first thing he had to do if he was going to survive was to get away from the bar and find a location he could defend until he could slip away once night fell.

He sprinted through the bar and made for the window that faced the lake. A sound behind him was all the motivation he needed, and he threw himself through the opening as fire erupted from the area in front of the bar, peppering the flimsy pallet walls and sending rounds tearing through the half-rotten wood.

Lucas landed hard on the wet ground and drove himself to his feet as the shooting continued. Let them waste their ammo on an empty building. He ducked low and ran toward the bluff that overlooked the water. The lake's surface was dimpled by a million raindrops, and his boots slid on the muddy terrain.

He spotted a promising tree – a pine with a trunk thick enough for him to hide behind, which would provide cover from enemy fire. A glance at his watch told him he only had a few minutes before the dim glow of remaining daylight faded behind the storm clouds, and he'd be in the clear.

The area lit with a brilliant flash of lightning, followed by a deafening boom of thunder nearly directly overhead. His ears popped from the pressure change and the wind switched direction, driving sheets of dense rain into his eyes and slowing his progress.

He was almost at the tree when an assault rifle chattered behind him and the ground around his feet churned. Lucas veered left as the stream of bullets neared him, and then launched through the air in a bid to get to the tree before the rounds stitched across his legs.

The wet ground rose up to meet him and knocked the breath out of him as he slammed into it and slid toward the trunk. He ignored the pain in his chest from the impact and pulled himself along, and then he was behind the tree only moments before rounds whistled past him, shredding the nearby leaves.

Lucas removed his hat and collapsed the top and, once flattened, slid it into his vest. Free of it telegraphing his movements with the brim, he peered around the trunk and spotted a dark form running toward him. He fired two bursts from the M4 and cut the assailant down, the man's only exclamation a surprised grunt as he collapsed.

The forest around him erupted with orange muzzle flashes, and another peal of thunder shook the ground. The storm's fury seemed to intensify with the shooting, and the next cloudburst sent a blinding sheet of rain at the earth – buying Lucas the opening he needed, as the air was suddenly so thick with water he could barely see a few feet in front of him.

He pushed himself up and tore off as fast as he could, running away from the gunmen; his death was assured if he stayed and tried to battle it out, one against four. He was nearly at the outcropping of rocks at the edge of the bluff he'd spied when the shooting from behind him zeroed in on him, and bullets punched into the earth to his right. He dodged left along the edge of the bluff and was almost to the rocks when his foot slid out from under him on a patch of slick mud, sending him sailing through the air, falling toward the surface of the lake below.

Cano raced for the spot where the shooter had disappeared. Luis was only footsteps behind him, and both fired as they ran. They reached the edge of the bluff and saw nothing but the lake below. Cano screamed in rage and emptied his gun into the water, and Luis did the same as the two surviving Crew gunmen joined them.

"Did he dive in?" the nearest one asked, and Cano turned to him, his face distorted with fury.

"No. It looked like he slipped and fell."

Luis took several steps and knelt down by the edge, where there was a clear impression left by the man's body sliding over the precipice. He held up his hand and two of the fingers were red with blood.

"Maybe he didn't slip. Looks like at least one round hit him."

Cano watched as the rain rinsed Luis's hand and nodded. "Did you see anyone else?"

"No. I think it was just him."

"Damn. Where are the others? I saw them up by the bar."

"They must have escaped."

Cano glared at his men and then at Luis. "Get the horses. We can follow them," he fumed. "Hurry. We're losing the light."

The pair of gunmen ran to obey, and Cano led Luis back to the front of the bar.

Luis cursed as they studied the tracks that led away from the decrepit structure. Cano leaned to look at the prints, the impressions already almost obliterated by the storm, and then stood. "They can't have gotten far."

A sound like a jet on takeoff filled the clearing and the area around the shack brightened as white as a phosphor flare. Lightning struck the big pine the man had used for cover and it split in two. A massive fireball exploded into the sky, sending the men reeling, arms covering their faces, the air suddenly searing, steam rising from the ground near the tree as thunder deafened them directly overhead.

Cano recovered first, his ears ringing, and staggered toward the tree to look at the damage as Luis picked himself up and wiped mud from his face. When Cano turned to face him, for the first time since he'd laid eyes on the man, Luis saw what might have been defeat – it was hard to tell in the dimming twilight. Luis looked back at the tracks and saw that they were now indistinguishable from the surrounding earth, large pools of water forming as the ground saturated. Cano walked heavily toward him and, following Luis's stare with hooded eyes, roared at the sky with a clenched fist, the sound that of a mortally wounded animal in its death throes, otherworldly issuing from a human throat.

Chapter 47

Colt rode at a moderate pace on a trail that ringed the lake, and the others followed close behind. Only a few moments after they had gotten under way, there had been a series of loud explosions, and Ruby had leaned toward Sierra.

"That's the grenade launcher. Lucas is laying waste."

"Do you think he'll be okay?"

"He's got heavy artillery. If anyone can pull it off, it's him."

Bruce listened in silence as the rain pelted them with the ferocity of a jilted lover. He was about to speak when rifle fire exploded from behind them. Colt picked up his speed. Sierra looked over at Ruby.

"If they're shooting, that means he didn't get them all, Ruby. We need to go back and help him."

"If Lucas had wanted us to put ourselves into harm's way, he would have told us to stay. He didn't. We need to honor his wishes."

"But he's hopelessly outgunned."

Bruce finally spoke. "It was his choice. He bought us time. You should be grateful."

"I am. But I don't want him to get himself killed."

Ruby's voice had steel in it. "Sierra, your job is to get Eve to Shangri-La, not to take risks every time you get a new idea. Bruce is right. Lucas knew what he was doing, and he made a good call. If you want to be useful, try offering a prayer that he makes it."

"Makes it how? We have Tango!"

"He can walk to the truck stop," Colt said over his shoulder. "It's not that far. Maybe three, four hours, tops, on foot. We can wait for him. If he shows, fine. If not, at least you're safe." He didn't have to say that was what mattered the most.

"I just wish there was something we could do."

The sound of the gun battle continued, and then, as the sky darkened, fell silent. Colt led them off the lake trail and onto a dirt road that led west, toward town. He slowed and twisted to see them. "Keep quiet from here on out. Roswell has guard outposts. I know where they are, and we're going to pass within a few yards of two of them. Not a word, or there'll be trouble."

"Why would they hassle us?" Sierra asked.

Colt exhaled loudly. "Last thing I'm going to say. We don't want to leave a trail of our passage. So nobody can see us. Now, all due respect, zip it, and no more questions. Not a peep. Understand?"

Sierra nodded, and so did Eve.

The rain grew lighter after the first hour and settled into a drizzle, now an annoyance rather than an impediment to their passage. Colt pointed to their left as they neared a grove of trees and held an index finger to his lips, reiterating that they had to be silent. They passed the outpost without incident and, forty minutes later, skirted the second without being spotted.

The truck stop was a dark warehouse-size structure with a rusting roof, its windows broken out, the interior stripped by looters. Abandoned freight containers loomed in the darkness along the perimeter where they'd been dropped so the trucks that had pulled them could travel longer on the same fuel. The building was cavernous, they could see as they rode up to it, and after glancing around, Colt signaled for them to dismount and tie their horses where they could.

Colt walked into the interior. The only sound was water dripping from holes in the roof. He looked around as the others followed him in and, once his eyes adjusted, smiled at the shadows.

"You're here," he said.

A man with long, gray hair and a lined face stepped from the gloom and returned the smile with a grimace. "Of course I am." He looked at the women, Eve, and Bruce. "This is everyone?"

"No. We're waiting for one more."

"How long?"

"We'll give him…how long before we absolutely have to move?"

"Four hours, on the outside. We want to be well into the territory before we make camp."

Colt turned to the women. "This is Frank. He's our guide."

Ruby introduced them and offered a smile of her own. "So we'll be with you for two days or so?"

Frank nodded. "About that. Depends on how much ground we cover each day." He yawned. "I'd advise you to get some rest while we wait. We won't get much when we camp – we'll be moving again at first light, so this is your chance."

"Good idea," Colt said. "There's cover from the rain, and the locals avoid this place like the plague."

"Why?" Sierra asked.

"This is kind of a no-man's land between the outer boundary of Roswell and the beginning of Frank's people's territory," Colt explained. "There's nothing here but bad memories, so no reason to come. And the truck stop and other buildings have been used by bandits in the past. It's got a dangerous reputation."

Frank pointed at a dry area relatively free of debris near the entrance. "You can set your bedrolls there. I'll keep watch." He patted a lever-action Winchester rifle hanging from a shoulder sling.

Five minutes later they had their rolls placed and had settled in to the lullaby of occasional thunder and the patter of rain as they waited for Lucas, an Apache stranger looking out for them at the edge of civilization.

Chapter 48

Lucas hit the water with a loud splash, M4 gripped reflexively in his hand. The impact knocked the wind out of him, but even as he sank, he had the presence of mind to shrug the rifle's sling over his shoulder, freeing his arms to swim. The water's cold chilled him to the bone. He saw light from off to his right and assumed he had gotten disoriented when he'd entered the lake. He pulled hard with his arms and broke the surface to gasp near the overhang of a willow tree's branches, protected somewhat from the rain.

Shooting erupted from his right, and he slipped beneath the water after a large gulp of air, thankful that he'd broken the surface near the shore and not further out in the lake where the men above were directing their fire. He figured they would exhaust their ammo shortly, and it would be completely dark due to the storm, so all he had to do was stay alive a couple more moments and he would be safe.

He remained underwater until his lungs were burning, and when he poked his head from the lake again, the darkness was total and the shooting had stopped. Still, he didn't want to allow overconfidence to ruin his tenuous advantage, so he treaded water as best he could beneath the tree's cover in case anyone was still watching from above.

A massive explosion of thunder shook the surroundings as a brilliant flare lit the lake, and Lucas took that as his cue to make for the shore. He swam underwater parallel to the steep bank for fifty yards, the effort nearly killing him; the weight of his body armor and magazines felt like he had a rucksack filled with bowling balls strapped to him. At last he dragged himself from the lake onto a rocky shore, the wind howling as waves of rain washed over the lake.

Lucas didn't allow himself the luxury of resting. The women were on horseback and, even at a slow pace, would make better time than he could on foot. He needed to find the truck stop and get there before they left, which meant he was already at a disadvantage, given that he had no idea where it was, other than the brief description offered by the bartender.

What was it that he'd said? Northwest? Question was how far north and how far west?

He shook his head to clear the fogginess in his mind, no doubt an artifact from the shock of the cold water and the fall. Think. What had Colt said?

That it was just before the major highway intersection, which he guessed meant south of it. The best course of action would be to find the highway as it stretched north of town and follow it until he reached the truck stop.

He removed his compass from his vest and took a bearing, and then quickly fieldstripped his M4 and dumped the water from it. He did the same with two magazines, figuring he'd deal with the others later, and finished with the Kimber.

All things considered, it could have been worse. He was still armed, had all his fingers and toes, and had stopped any pursuit.

Lucas removed his hat from inside the vest, restored it to a semblance of its prior glory, and fit it onto his head. He grimaced as he forced himself to his feet. His entire body was sore from weeks of hard riding and now the fall into the lake. After a glance around the area, he began trotting along the shore, wishing his NV scope wasn't in his saddlebags, but reminding himself that if it hadn't been, it might well have been rendered useless by the protracted submersion.

No, he'd have to do this the old-fashioned way, using his compass and watch. He remembered what Bruce had said about the good citizens of Roswell and the hospitality with which they greeted strangers, and made a mental note to dodge any patrols – there would be no asking directions from friendly natives.

He came to a dirt access road, now a muddy wash down which brown runoff coursed, and lumbered up the slope. Lucas pushed himself to a faster clip, painfully aware that at least a few of the Crew had survived and that the further he could get from the lake, the better his odds. His leg muscles protested the exertion, but he continued without pause, driving himself hard for half an hour until light-headedness forced him to slow.

The rain had lessened and was now a third of what it had been an hour before. He stopped near a tree and stood with his face upturned, mouth open, consumed by thirst. He adjusted his Kimber, and his hand brushed the bottom of his vest and came away covered with warm fluid.

Lucas looked down at his fingers and saw blood, black in the nearly nonexistent light. He probed the area above his hip and winced when a searing jolt of pain shot from his waist.

He'd been hit but, like many combat vets had described, hadn't even realized it until adrenaline and shock had worn off.

Lucas stripped off his plate carrier and noted with dismay that his entire right leg was slick with blood. That explained his weakness and dizziness – it was a wonder that he'd made it that far without passing out. He felt the wound and exhaled in relief; the bullet hadn't hit any organs or bone, but rather had passed clean through the flesh just above his belt.

He tore one of his long shirtsleeves off at the shoulder, and then repeated the maneuver with the other, and created a crude pressure bandage around his waist to clot the blood. When he was done, he re-donned his flak jacket and drank some more rain, but as he was doing so was struck by a fatigue so total he couldn't force himself to go another yard.

Lucas barely made it to the base of the nearest tree and sat beneath its branches. He'd have to rest a few minutes, allow his body time to recover. Only a few, he reasoned as he closed his eyes, shivering in spite of the moderate temperature, his mind filled with images of charging tattooed furies – and of Sierra, whose kiss still tingled on his lips as he passed from this world into the void.

Chapter 49

The rain had increased again as the tail end of the storm passed over Roswell, and waves of water lashed the outside of the truck stop as the group huddled inside. More thunder had awakened them a few minutes earlier, and they were now sitting around a small fire Frank had built deep in the interior, where its flames wouldn't be seen from the outside, given the downpour.

Ruby and Sierra, Eve's head in her lap, stared at the fire as though in a trance, the smoke drifting to the rafters before finding a hole to escape through. Frank stood by the entrance, gun in hand, protecting his night vision from the firelight. Colt and Bruce were further away, Colt busying himself cleaning his weapons, and Bruce contenting himself with watching everyone else.

"Poor horses. They're getting soaked. Maybe we should bring them in?" Sierra asked.

Frank shrugged. "They don't mind. Not like they have umbrellas in the wild. It rains, they get wet. Then they dry off. They're hardier than we are."

"You mentioned that we'll be traveling through your tribe's territory. What makes it theirs?" Ruby asked.

"We took it back after the collapse. Mescalero Apache. Everything north of Roswell to just south of Albuquerque." Frank paused. "People forget that originally this was all ours. Everything. The settlers and the white man's army came and slaughtered the Native Americans so they could confiscate our land. All we've done is taken back what we can defend. We charge a toll to travel north, and east to west, or vice versa."

"It's reasonable," Colt agreed.

"What's funny is that since the collapse, our lives haven't changed that much – if anything, they've improved," Frank said. "We weren't tied to the cities, to the grid, so we were better prepared to return to the old ways. That collective knowledge has served us well."

Ruby nodded. "I would imagine so. We've seen that with other places. The rural towns have fared better than the cities."

Frank smiled, the expression creasing his face with sadness. "Cities are unnatural. It always struck me as funny that people wanted to crowd together on top of each other when there's so much space. Don't get me wrong, I spent some time in them when I went to college, but I never felt comfortable. Claustrophobic."

"What did you major in?" Ruby asked.

"Geology. Kind of a childhood obsession."

"Ah."

"My people are very protective of their newfound land, and nobody crosses it without paying the toll. You've paid, so you'll pass through without problems."

Bruce rose. "I gotta use the can."

"World's your toilet," Frank said, indicating the drizzle outside.

Bruce pushed past him and Colt's eyes followed him into the darkness. "Where did you pick him up?"

"He's a tech guy – can repair anything. I've known him for a while. We stayed at his place in Artesia while we were lying low," Ruby explained. "Why?"

Colt shrugged. "More bodies means more resources required. That, and they're very picky about who they let in." Colt didn't mention Shangri-La in front of Frank. "Not sure he's got the kind of attitude they like."

"He grows on you," Sierra said. "Like fungus."

They all laughed, and then a shot rang out. Frank dropped his rifle and opened his mouth to speak, and blood gushed from it down his chin. He pitched forward, eyes wide, gasping on the filthy ground like a beached fish, and Bruce stepped into the building with his H&K pistol in hand.

"What the hell—" Colt said, reaching for his gun.

Bruce was on him in a split second and slammed the butt of his pistol into the bartender's temple. Colt went down, eyes rolled up into his head, and Bruce leaned over and scooped up his weapon, his gaze on Ruby and Sierra, the younger woman clutching Eve to her chest protectively.

"Bruce—" Ruby started.

"Shut up." Bruce shook his head. "You're really not all that smart, are you? Doesn't surprise me. Did you know the average IQ in America is ninety-eight? I Googled it once. I don't know why I keep expecting people to be smarter."

"Why?" she whispered. "Why shoot Frank?"

"Why shoot Frank?" Bruce mimicked. "He was the most dangerous of the bunch, and he's got no value. Colt there, maybe. Sierra and Eve? A ton."

"Value?"

Bruce smirked. "Do you really believe that I didn't hear the broadcasts offering a reward for you?"

"You'd turn us in to those...those animals?"

Bruce shrugged. "It's nothing personal. Strictly business. You're worth a lot alive, and I have you. That makes me rich."

"But Shangri-La," Sierra began.

"You mean the magical kingdom where chocolate rivers flow and the sky's filled with marshmallow clouds?" He shook his head in disgust. "You people are truly delusional."

"It's real, Bruce."

"You're really out of your minds is more like it. Let me tell you what's real: the big fish eats the smaller one, and then another even bigger one comes along and eats him. That's real. Some Disneyland ideal in a hidden valley? Let me guess – the earth's flat and aliens rule the world. Am I close?"

"You're making a big mistake. They'll kill you," Ruby said.

"The only mistake I made was letting my handheld radio get wet in the saddlebags. Now I've got to wait for it to dry out to alert your boys to come collect you." He held up a small radio. "But that's okay. Not like we're in any hurry. You're not going anywhere, and Frank sure as hell isn't." He laughed harshly.

"You don't know the Crew, Bruce. They'll put a bullet in you the second they have us," Sierra said.

"They have no reason to. I give them what they're looking for, plus the bonus of another nutcase who believes in fairy tales, and they pay me. Simple transaction. Who knows? Maybe they could use someone who can repair anything. By the sound of it, they're increasing their reach, so it could be a growth opportunity."

"You make me sick. There's more to life than money," Ruby spat.

"Spoken by an old crone who's at the end of her runway. Do you have any idea what it's like to live in a trailer in Hicksville, surrounded by morons? Are those the people who I'm supposed to believe my life would be better spent respecting than looking out for myself? Like I said, you're delusional." He shifted his aim to Ruby. "And frankly, you're also valueless in this equation."

"That's all we are to you? Pawns in a transaction?"

"That's all you've ever been to anyone. You talk about sickening – you're the ones who've been living in a dream world. You really believe that the machine you obeyed before the collapse saw you as anything but sheep to be fleeced? Come on. You couldn't cross the street without permission. You lived in a police state with twenty-four-hour surveillance. You had to pay most of what you earned to a government that couldn't have cared less whether you lived or died, except for what it meant to its bottom line. Where did you get all these high-minded ideas about your value? You were just worker ants then, and you're worker ants now. Only I'm the one who will benefit from your cluelessness instead of them. You? You're in the same position."

Sierra looked past Bruce. He followed her eyes and spun just in time to avoid Colt charging him. Bruce slammed him in the head with his gun again, and Colt crumpled, his hand to his skull.

"Another one that doesn't learn," Bruce said, and then turned back to Ruby, gun raised. "Been nice knowing you, but I'm afraid it's time to go to Valhalla, or whatever bullshit you think happens when you die."

This time Ruby looked over Bruce's shoulder, but instead of turning, he smirked and held his weapon steady. "Won't work this time. Oldest trick in the book. Make your peace."

"Drop the gun," Lucas's voice called from the entryway.

Bruce's pupils contracted to dots as he pirouetted, gun in hand, crouching low as he turned. Lucas's Kimber barked three times. The hollow-point rounds slammed Bruce backwards, exiting in bloody divots the size of tennis balls. Sierra screamed and held her hands over Eve's ears as she clutched the little girl to her, shielding her eyes from the gruesome spectacle. Bruce staggered sideways and then toppled like a felled tree, his gun clattering by his side.

Lucas stepped through the doorway and holstered the Kimber. Sierra leapt to her feet and ran to him while Ruby comforted Eve.

"You're alive!" Sierra cried, and then they were kissing, water running down Lucas's face onto hers. Lucas was surprised by the measure of passion he felt, but told himself it was relief, even if he suspected it was something more.

"Took you long enough," Ruby said from beside the fire.

Sierra pulled away, and Lucas gave a lopsided smile. "Got a flesh wound that kinda held me up."

"You're wounded? Where?" Sierra demanded.

"My side. But it's not going to kill me." He exhaled a measured breath. "Would you get the first aid kit out of my saddlebag and patch me up? And then we need to get out of here – the gunfire's going to draw the bad guys, as well as the town patrols, even in this soup." Lucas looked down at Colt. "You okay?"

"Going to have a headache for a few days, but nothing fatal," Colt said, sitting with his hand to his head.

"Got a pretty good gash there. Make that two patch-ups, and then we're gone." Lucas turned to where Frank lay dead. "Who's that?"

"Our guide."

"That going to be a problem?" Lucas asked.

"Maybe," Colt responded.

Lucas considered the dead man. "We'll deal with it when it is. Those shots will draw everyone we don't want. Let's get some bandages on us and ride. You know the way, right?"

Colt nodded. "Up the road."

"The way Frank made it sound, without a guide to take us through, it's going to be hell trying to make it," Ruby observed.

Colt grunted. "Maybe not hell, but if the Apaches don't buy our story, maybe purgatory."

"And from there? Then what?" Lucas asked.

"We'll cross that bridge when we come to it," Colt said, ending the discussion.

Sierra returned with the kit, and Lucas removed his sopping flak vest and shirt. Sierra made short work of the bullet wound, which, using Ruby's penlight, she verified had done no significant damage other than drain Lucas of blood. After wiping it clean, she closed it with butterfly stitches. A final application of antibacterial ointment and a bandage finished the job, and then she turned to Colt, whose injury only required a couple of sutures and some salve.

"You're going to have an ugly bump for a couple of days, but other than that, looks like you got away light," she informed him.

Colt glanced over at Frank's corpse. "I'll say."

They gathered their things and Lucas said a prayer over Frank and even Bruce as they stood with heads bowed. Their amen, at least for Frank, was heartfelt, and then they collected Frank's rifle and were out in the drizzle, riding through the darkness toward the intersection, and from there, the unknown.

Chapter 50

Cano drew his horse up short when they reached the truck stop, drawn by the sound of the shots, and dismounted outside of the main building, AK-47 in hand. Luis followed him through the entrance, and they stopped at the sight of Bruce's and Frank's corpses lying in the rubble.

"There's your answer as to who was shooting," Luis said.

Cano nodded. "But what does it mean? Two dead men – and no way of knowing whether they're even related to our woman."

"Awfully coincidental."

The Crew boss frowned. "I don't know that it's that coincidental. We're a long way from the lake. A pair of drifters get knocked off five hours later? Could be unrelated. We should go back to the lake and continue searching for a trail to follow."

"Wonder where their guns are."

"Whoever shot them probably took them."

Luis strode to the remains of the fire, his boots crunching on debris underfoot, and felt it. "Still warm."

"Not surprising. We know the shots were only a half hour ago." Cano moved to something on the ground, pulled a flashlight from his plate carrier, and flicked it on.

"What is it?" Luis asked.

Cano picked up the long strip of bloody fabric and examined it before dropping it on the floor and straightening. "Looks like a man's shirt soaked with blood. Or at least the sleeves." He walked over to the dead men and played the beam over their bodies. "Not one of theirs."

Luis joined him. "Shine your light over there," he said, pointing to an area near the remains of the fire. Cano did as asked, and Luis nodded. "See that? Looks like someone cleared that spot so they could lie down there. More than one person, by the size of it. And recently – there's no dust on the cement floor."

"The two dead men could have done that."

"True. But then where did the bandage come from?"

Cano's face darkened with realization. "From whoever we wounded at the lake. Damn." He made for the doorway, and Luis rushed to follow him.

Outside they looked at the wet pavement of the truck stop parking lot like detectives searching for clues. One of the Crew gunmen had a flashlight, and they split up, walking the perimeter of the lot. After ten minutes it was obvious that there were no tracks; the rain had wiped any traces clean, and the road north to the intersection was wet asphalt, so of no help.

When Luis joined Cano at the horses, the Crew boss's expression was unreadable.

"What now?" Luis asked.

"Let's assume this was them. The bandage seals it – the blood's relatively fresh, and I agree that a wounded man wandering around the same night we hit someone at the lake isn't coincidental. So what's now is that we need to figure out where they went."

Luis looked around at the drizzle. "How?"

"I didn't say I know. I just told you what we need to do," Cano snapped. He began pacing in the rain, his face a mask of rage. Luis said nothing, reasoning that Cano's botched mission was his to work through. He'd already seen ample indications of the Crew leader's violent temper on the ride from Pecos, and he didn't want to have the man's anger taken out on him.

Eventually Cano stopped pacing and retraced his steps to the truck stop interior. Luis called after him. "What are we doing?"

"Get in here and try to rest. We'll wait until morning and then quiz the locals about this pair. Maybe someone knows them – there could be a clue in their identities. Right now, there's nothing we can do. We're screwed until daybreak and this storm blows by."

The pair of surviving Crew gunmen tied their horses to a pole and Luis followed suit. He followed them in with his bedroll and spread it on the flat area near where the fire had recently blazed. Cano sat with his back to the wall at the edge of the cavernous space, gun in his lap, his eyes boring holes in the night. Luis called out to him as he adjusted himself on his pad.

"How are we going to get the locals to cooperate with us?"

Cano laughed, the sound harsh and humorless. "We'll find a way to convince them."

Luis leaned back and closed his eyes, his head swimming at the implication of Cano's words, and wondered for the umpteenth time what he'd gotten involved in with his alliance with the Crew, and whether a life as a de facto servant to them was worth it.

As though reading his thoughts, Cano called out from the darkness. "We'll call for reinforcements tomorrow at dawn. They won't escape. We'll follow them to the ends of the earth, and when we find them, they'll wish they'd never been born. There's no way in hell they get away. None."

Luis closed his eyes and sighed.

He believed him.

About the Author

Featured in *The Wall Street Journal*, *The Times*, and *The Chicago Tribune*, Russell Blake is *The NY Times* and *USA Today* bestselling author of over forty novels, including *Fatal Exchange*, *Fatal Deception*, *The Geronimo Breach*, *Zero Sum*, *King of Swords*, *Night of the Assassin*, *Revenge of the Assassin*, *Return of the Assassin*, *Blood of the Assassin*, *Requiem for the Assassin*, *Rage of the Assassin* *The Delphi Chronicle* trilogy, *The Voynich Cypher*, *Silver Justice*, *JET*, *JET – Ops Files*, *JET – Ops Files: Terror Alert*, *JET II – Betrayal*, *JET III – Vengeance*, *JET IV – Reckoning*, *JET V – Legacy*, *JET VI – Justice*, *JET VII – Sanctuary*, *JET VIII – Survival*, *JET IX – Escape*, *JET X – Incarceration*, *Upon a Pale Horse*, *BLACK*, *BLACK is Back*, *BLACK is The New Black*, *BLACK to Reality*, *BLACK in the Box*, *Deadly Calm*, *Ramsey's Gold*, *Emerald Buddha*, *The Day After Never – Blood Honor*, and *The Day After Never – Purgatory Road*.

Non-fiction includes the international bestseller *An Angel With Fur* (animal biography) and *How To Sell A Gazillion eBooks In No Time* (even if drunk, high or incarcerated), a parody of all things writing-related.

Blake is co-author of *The Eye of Heaven* and *The Solomon Curse*, with legendary author Clive Cussler. Blake's novel *King of Swords* has been translated into German by Amazon Crossing, *The Voynich Cypher* into Bulgarian, and his JET novels into Spanish, German, and Czech.

Blake writes under the moniker R.E. Blake in the NA/YA/Contemporary Romance genres. Novels include *Less Than Nothing*, *More Than Anything*, and *Best Of Everything*.

Having resided in Mexico for a dozen years, Blake enjoys his dogs, fishing, boating, tequila and writing, while battling world domination by clowns. His thoughts, such as they are, can be found at his blog: RussellBlake.com

Books by Russell Blake

Co-authored with Clive Cussler

THE EYE OF HEAVEN
THE SOLOMON CURSE

Thrillers

FATAL EXCHANGE
FATAL DECEPTION
THE GERONIMO BREACH
ZERO SUM
THE DELPHI CHRONICLE TRILOGY
THE VOYNICH CYPHER
SILVER JUSTICE
UPON A PALE HORSE
DEADLY CALM
RAMSEY'S GOLD
EMERALD BUDDHA
THE DAY AFTER NEVER – BLOOD HONOR
THE DAY AFTER NEVER – PURGATORY ROAD

The Assassin Series

KING OF SWORDS
NIGHT OF THE ASSASSIN
RETURN OF THE ASSASSIN
REVENGE OF THE ASSASSIN
BLOOD OF THE ASSASSIN
REQUIEM FOR THE ASSASSIN
RAGE OF THE ASSASSIN

The JET Series

JET
JET II – BETRAYAL
JET III – VENGEANCE
JET IV – RECKONING
JET V – LEGACY
JET VI – JUSTICE
JET VII – SANCTUARY
JET VIII – SURVIVAL
JET IX – ESCAPE
JET X – INCARCERATION
JET – OPS FILES (prequel)
JET – OPS FILES; TERROR ALERT

The BLACK Series

BLACK
BLACK IS BACK
BLACK IS THE NEW BLACK
BLACK TO REALITY
BLACK IN THE BOX

Non Fiction

AN ANGEL WITH FUR
HOW TO SELL A GAZILLION EBOOKS
(while drunk, high or incarcerated)

Printed in Great Britain
by Amazon

61235421R00153